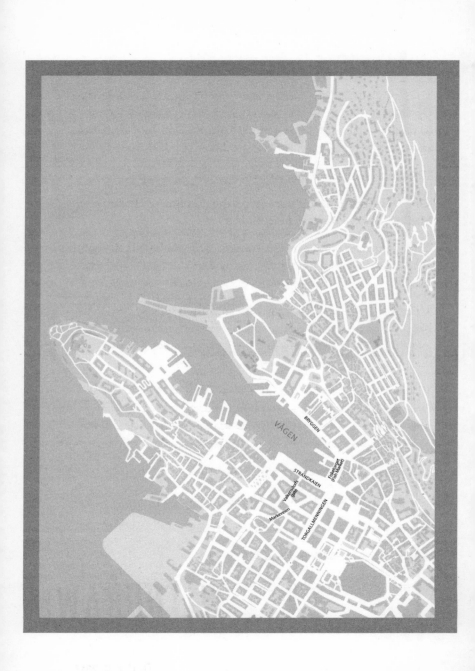

WE SHALL INHERIT THE WIND

We Shall Inherit the Wind

GUNNAR STAALESEN

Translated from the Norwegian by Don Bartlett

**ORENDA
BOOKS**

Orenda Books
16 Carson Road
West Dulwich
London SE21 8HU
www.orendabooks.co.uk

First published in Norwegian as *Vi skal arve vinden* in 2010
First published in English by Orenda Books 2015
Reprinted 2016

A catalogue record for this book is available from the British Library.

ISBN 978-1-910633-07-6

Typeset in Arno by MacGuru Ltd
Printed and bound by CPI Group (UK) Ltd, Croydon CR0 4YY

Orenda Books gratefully acknowledges the financial support of NORLA.

SALES & DISTRIBUTION

In the UK and elsewhere in Europe:
Turnaround Publisher Services
Unit 3, Olympia Trading Estate
Coburg Road, Wood Green
London N22 6TZ
www.turnaround-uk.com

In USA/Canada:
Trafalgar Square Publishing
Independent Publishers Group
814 North Franklin Street
Chicago, IL 60610
USA
www.ipgbook.com

For details of other territories, please contact info@orendabooks.co.uk

WE SHALL INHERIT THE WIND

If you go in search of Brennøy, in Gulen, on the map, I'm afraid you will be disappointed. This place and all the characters in the book are products of the author's imagination and do not exist in reality. But you won't need to look far for plans for wind turbines, not in Gulen or anywhere else …

1

They say a dying man sees life passing before his eyes. I don't know. I haven't died that many times yet. But I do know it happens if you have the misfortune to sit beside someone on their death bed.

I sat at her side in Haukeland Hospital, looking at her battered face, the needles in her arm, the probe in her nose, the tube in her mouth and the oscillating lines on the screen above her bed, which showed her heart function, blood pressure and the oxygen content of her veins, and I felt as if I were watching a stuttering amateur film of the years we had known each other, played on a somewhat antiquated projector I had never quite been able to focus. But then I was no technical whiz. I never had been.

I met Karin Bjørge for the first time in early 1971, when I was still working in social services. She was shown into my office by Elsa Drage. Drage is Norwegian for dragon, but she was the nicest one I had ever known. At that time Karin and I were both considerably younger – neither of us a day over thirty. Siren, her sister, was fourteen and it was because of her that Karin had come. She and her father had been searching for Siren for days. They had contacted the police, who had put her on the missing persons list, but as no unidentifiable body had been registered and there was nothing, initially, to suggest anything criminal had happened, they had not been able to make any promises. 'But Dad's got a bad heart,' Karin said to me, 'and my mother keeps fretting and fretting … that's why I've come to you, to find out if you can do something.'

By 'you' she meant the social services' Missing Children Department; and in fact we were able to help her. I found Siren three times in the course of the next two years. The first time I had to go to

Copenhagen, the second to Oslo. The third she settled for our very own Haugesund. On the last occasion she was so debilitated by dope and sexual abuse that she couldn't even be bothered to escape. A psychologist we used at the time, Marianne Storetvedt, did a great job on her; we got her into a young people's psychiatric clinic, and when Siren was discharged six months later, she appeared to be fine again.

Out of gratitude for my efforts, Karin invited me for coffee and cake, and as I left we gave each other a hug. Seemingly by happenstance, we turned to face each other, and for a few seconds we kissed, as lightly and tentatively as teenagers doing it for the first time. However, I was still married to Beate, and I had no idea what Karin had up her sleeve. At any rate, nothing came of this until twelve or thirteen years later, when I had taken my leave of social services, set up my own private investigator's office in Strandkaien, by the harbour, and when, once again, Siren had gone missing.

In the interim, I had been in regular contact with Karin, who was working at the National Registration Office. In a moment of exuberance she had promised me that, if I ever needed any help, all I had to do was ring, which I did. Often. Sometimes, perhaps, to excess. She had been married for a short while, but when I met her again in 1986, the marriage was over, after less than a year. She never told me what had happened, even though we stumbled into a relationship in the summer of 1987, without putting up much resistance, a relationship that had lasted until now – and was still ongoing, for as long as the doctors could keep her alive.

I leaned forward, studied the vibration under her closed eyelids, listened to her faint breathing, felt her pulse at the side of her neck. Her skin was soft and warm, as though she were merely resting. I ran a finger down her face, from her scalp to her pronounced chin and out to her cheek. Inside me, the pain and turmoil were bursting to be released.

Every year we had celebrated each other's birthday in cosy intimacy, hers on the nineteenth of March, mine on the fifteenth of October. We had each kept our own flat, but the nocturnal visits had increased over the years. We had hiked through Rondane and Jotunheimen, staying in cabins; we had driven all over the south-western coastal region of Norway; and we had spent occasional long weekends in cities such as Dublin, Paris, Berlin and Rome. In Rondane, we had conquered the rocky mountain pass known as Dørålsglupen, both from the north and the south, and, a couple of days later, eaten trout sautéed with sour cream at the Bjørnhollia tourist cabin. In Jotunheimen we had slept in bunks at the self-service Olavsbu cabin before following the Mjølke valley down to Eidsbugarden and eating a proper gourmet meal in Fondsbu. In Dublin she had taken me somewhere that looked like the place where all books went when they died – the old library at Trinity College. In Rome, we had cuddled up on a bench on Mount Janiculum and watched the sun set over the city, before slipping through the side-streets down to Trastevere and enjoying a crepuscular repast at one of the restaurants there. But above all else we had been each other's lodestar in our hometown, Bergen, the city between the seven mountains. For each other we had been somewhere to go for a hug when life became too depressing, when the National Registration Office was on the move again and the view from Strandkaien 2 was sadder than last year's snow.

After I was shot in Oslo four years ago we became closer. She had jumped on the first plane and sat at my bedside for several days, as I was now sitting at hers. Later I had often thought it had not been so much the doctors' efforts but her mental strength that had pulled me through. Had it not been for her, I might already be history. Things had come to such a pass a few weeks ago – at the back-end of summer – that I had said to her: 'What if … if one sunny day I were to ask you to marry me, what would you answer?' She had looked at me with an amused glint in her eye and said: 'Tell me, Varg. Would you be proposing now?' And I had answered: 'Maybe …' She had kissed me gently and whispered: 'Were you to do it, I would probably take you at your word …'

Now she was lying here on her death bed. And it was all my fault.

2

Barely a week before, we had driven down to a quay in Nordhordland. We had parked in the space allocated, behind the large shop, but when we got out there was no one waiting for us.

Karin looked at me in surprise. 'She said she would be here. It's twelve o'clock, isn't it?'

I nodded. 'The clock strikes twelve and there's no one to be seen. Send for Sherlock.'

She took out her mobile phone. 'I'll see if I can call her.'

While she was doing that I mooched around. The quay at Feste ran alongside Radsund, the main waterway north of Bergen for boats that were not too large. The Hurtigruten coastal cruises were further out. There was a black-and-white navigation buoy in the middle of the sound. On the other side there was a tall, dense spruce forest, something that might have been a bay or another sound, and beyond that we could glimpse some red-and-brown cabins.

Karin had got through. 'Yes, we're on the quay … Fine. We'll wait here then.' She glanced at me and rolled her eyes, then switched off the phone.

'Everything OK?'

'She'd forgotten the time. You wouldn't believe it was her husband who had gone missing.'

'Perhaps it's not the first time.'

'Well, I think it is. That's why she's asked for help.'

'You know …'

'Yes, I know you don't do matrimonial work, but this is different. Take my word for it.'

'There's so much more of you that I would rather have.'

She sort of smiled; well, it wasn't a great remark, but what else can you come up with on a chilly Monday morning in September with summer definitively on the wane and autumn beckoning on the horizon!

While we waited we nipped into the shop and bought a couple of newspapers. High in the gloom behind the cash till sat the shopkeeper, a friendly smile on his lips. He must have been wondering who we were and what our business was. This was one of those places where everyone knew everyone and a new face stuck out like a flower arrangement in a garage workshop.

The shop was quiet at this time of the day, and we were given a plastic mug of coffee each while we waited. I flicked through the newspapers. There were no world events hitting the front pages in the second week of September, 1998. Most of the coverage was given over to the Norwegian football team's defeat to Latvia at Ullevål Stadium, the first at home for seven years and thirty-one matches and a sorry start to the upcoming European campaign. The Prime Minister was still off sick, and Akira Kurosawa had died in Japan. The eighth samurai had found his permanent place in the film history firmament.

After a while we went out onto the quay. Karin checked her watch again and peered north. 'It's not that far away.'

'You've been here before, have you?'

'Yeah, yeah, several times. Ranveig and I were at school together. For a few years we worked at the National Registration Office together, before she moved on.'

'And – how long have they been married?'

'Thirteen or fourteen years, I suppose it must be now. Mons has been married before. His first wife died – round here, in fact.'

'Oh yes?'

She was about to expand on this when she was interrupted by the sound of a large, black Mercedes turning into the car park by the shop. The right-hand door opened, and a woman with short, dark hair stepped out and waved to us. Behind the wheel I made out the oval face of a man with slicked-back, steel-grey hair.

'Oh,' Karin said. 'You came by car?'

The woman with the short hair hurried over towards her. 'Yes, I ...' And the rest of what she said was lost because she gave Karin a big hug and her face was next to Karin's cheek as she finished the sentence.

The man who had driven her was getting out of the car now, too. He was around sixty, tall with broad shoulders, wearing a brown leather jacket, blue jeans and robust, dark-brown shoes.

The two women released each other and half-turned to their companions.

'You have to meet ...' Karin began.

'This is ...' said the woman I assumed was Ranveig. They both paused, looked at each other and smiled.

By then I had joined them. 'Varg,' I said, holding out my hand.

She introduced herself in a solemn voice. 'Ranveig Mæland. Thank you for coming.'

She was wearing a leather jacket too, but hers was short and narrow at the waist, and the tight jeans revealed athletic thighs and slim hips. Her face was pretty and heart-shaped, with quite a small mouth and large, dark-blue eyes. She had a single white pearl clipped to each earlobe. Beneath the lobes I noticed a vein throbbing hard, as though she were afraid of something.

'Bjørn Brekkhus,' her companion said, greeting first Karin, then me.

'Varg Veum,' I said, and added: 'Bjørn the bear and Varg the wolf. The beasts of prey are well represented then.'

He shot me a look of mild surprise, then went on: 'I'm a friend of the family.'

'I couldn't stand it out there ... on my own, after Mons ... Bjørn and Lise live here, on the mainland. Besides, Bjørn was Chief of Police in Lindås,' Ranveig hastened to add.

'Yes, but I've retired from the force now,' he said. 'Since June to be precise.'

She half-turned. 'Shall we make our way across?'

Brekkhus nodded. 'That was the idea, wasn't it? I'll just park properly.' He got back in behind the wheel and moved the car a hundred metres or so to the marked parking spaces at the northernmost end of the quay area. I followed Ranveig and Karin in the same direction. Most of the boats were inside the harbour, safely moored and already semi-equipped for winter, as far as I could see.

The two women had come to a halt in front of an immense, white, glass-fibre ocean-going boat. A broad blue speed-stripe ran along the side of the boat to its registration number and name: Golden Sun.

Ranveig looked at me. 'I gather that Karin has mentioned ... the old case as well.'

I watched her, waiting. 'You're referring to ...?'

She looked over her shoulder at me and the water. 'Mons' first wife, Lea. She disappeared out there as well.'

After her gaze returned, I said: 'Disappeared?'

'Yes.'

Brekkhus coughed at my side. 'I was responsible for the police search, and I can assure you ... we turned over every last stone.'

'But ...'

'She was never found.'

'Vanished without a trace?'

'As if borne aloft by the wind.'

'This we will have to hear more about.'

'Yes, but ...' He motioned towards the boat. 'Shall we cross the sound?'

'Yes, OK.'

He turned to Ranveig. 'Have you got the keys?'

'Yes, here they are.'

She passed the keys to Brekkhus. He led the way alongside the boat, grabbed a painter and nimbly swung himself on board. Karin and I found seats at the very back. Brekkhus started the engine and glanced at Ranveig. She released the mooring ropes, he turned the boat in an arc northwards, and we were off.

No one said a word. Ranveig took a seat at the front, beside Brekkhus, as if he needed a pilot. I glanced at Karin. The return-look she gave me was inscrutable. When I held her eyes she pursed her lips into a little kiss and smiled cautiously. The wind caught her hair and raised it from her scalp. With one hand she gathered it behind her neck and focussed her gaze on the sound, where we were heading.

3

The cabin was situated on a rocky promontory facing the fjord. It was surrounded by spruces, almost certainly planted in the 1950s by Bergen schoolchildren on a re-foresting boat trip. Now the trees stood like dark monuments to a time when not only the mountains had to be clad but every tiny scrap of island skirted by the fjord. Accordingly, spruces lined long stretches of the Vestland coast. No one had thinned the striplings, and no one had cut down the trees, except the cabin-owners who had desperately tried to clear themselves a place in the sun. It looked as if they had given up here ages ago.

The path to the cabin wound upwards from the cement quay. To the north-east lay the islands of Lygra and Lurekalven. On the larger of these, in the middle, we could make out the slate-tiled roof of the new Heathland Centre. On the other, I knew there had been a medieval farm, which had been abandoned during the Black Death and remained uninhabited. Above us hung the sky, grey and heavy with rain, and the cortege making its way up from the sea was none too cheerful, either. We walked in formation: Ranveig Mæland and Bjørn Brekkhus in front, Karin and I right behind.

The cabin was a deep red colour, almost purple, with black window frames and facia boards. It was a classic 1940s cabin, erected either just before or just after the war. A west-facing annexe had been added later, and behind, bordering the forest, there was a structure that must have been an extension of some kind, painted the same colour as the main cabin, but with only one window and a plain wooden step up to the front door.

As we mounted the step, a light went on inside.

'Ah,' I said.

Ranveig craned her head round. 'No, I'm afraid not. It comes on automatically, at random times. So that it looks as if someone is in.'

'If only everyone was so sensible,' Brekkhus said.

Ranveig produced a key and unlocked. She pushed the door open. Then gestured that we were welcome to enter.

We came into a classic cabin hall with small, woven tapestries of various dark colours, a large sea chart on one wall and a long row of hooks for an assortment of raincoats and weather-proof jackets on the other. There was no shortage of sailing footwear, walking boots and knitted socks, and in the corner facing us was a fibre-glass fishing rod, complete with line and lure, ready for use.

We followed Ranveig and Brekkhus to the end of the hall where we emerged into the cabin's main room, which had a view of the sea and a kitchenette to the right. There was nothing luxurious about the furnishings. Traditional Norwegian pine furniture dominated. The TV set in one corner was between ten and twenty years old, the portable radio on the tiny bureau even older. The walls were decorated with a mixture of landscape paintings, nature photographs and the odd collage, the latter clearly put together by children. Tucked into one corner was a cabinet, which I imagined contained drinks, and along the wall to its right a bookcase so crowded with books that they were stacked higgledy-piggledy on top of one other without any obvious system. The electric radiators under the windows made a clicking noise, but the room wasn't warm enough for us to take off our coats.

Ranveig went to the kitchenette, ran water from the tap and put a kettle on the stove. 'I'll brew us up a nice cup of coffee.'

'Or two,' I said.

Bjørn Brekkhus stood musing in the middle of the floor. He appeared uncertain what role to play, whether he should be the host, the guest or some point in between. Karin went over to Ranveig to ask whether there was anything she could do to help.

From the kitchenette Ranveig said: 'Relax. It won't take a second.'

I refrained from a witticism, despite the temptation. Besides, Brekkhus was much bigger than me. We each put a slightly under-sized chair by the pine table, which was scarred from years of use and covered with a red and green runner in the middle, on which sat a pewter candle-holder shaped like a Viking ship with a half-burnt candle inside, probably a present from such close friends that it would have been embarrassing not to display it.

I glanced up at the retired policeman. His steel-grey hair was cut in a short-back-and-sides fashion, but the combed-back fringe was long and parted over the rear part of his head to reveal his scalp. His oblong nose had a visible network of thin veins and resembled a sallow marine animal caught in a red net. His eyes were a glacial blue and his gaze was measured, as though he regarded everyone he met as potential suspects.

I snatched a sidelong glimpse at the kitchen. 'Could you tell me a bit more about what happened to … Mons Mæland's first wife?'

He puckered his lips in thought. 'There's not much more than I've already said.'

'When did it happen?'

'Early 80s, one hot August day. She used to go for a morning swim from the quay here, often on her own, but on the odd occasion she managed to entice Mons or one of the children to go with her. On this day she was alone. We found her dressing gown and a pair of slip-ons on the quay. When she didn't return, Mons began to suspect something was amiss. There were just the two of them out here, and he was dozing in bed. They had been fishing the night before. She used to make breakfast after the swim, but … as I said, on this day, she didn't return, and when he went to look for her he just found her dressing gown and shoes.'

'How old was she?'

'About forty, if I'm not mistaken.'

Karin came in and put out mugs. Ranveig poured freshly brewed coffee from a white Thermos flask. 'What are you talking about?' she asked.

Brekkhus made a vague motion with one arm.

'Lea?'

'Yes.'

'I don't understand what she has got to do with this.'

'Well, Veum was asking about her.'

I nodded. 'I was just wondering what happened.'

'The general assumption was that she drowned in a swimming accident.'

'But?'

She shrugged. 'It's no secret that she had her problems. Periods of terrible depression.'

'She was never found,' Brekkhus repeated.

'Did you know them at that point?' I asked, focussing on Ranveig.

She flushed. 'Not really. I was employed there later on. In the company.'

'Your husband's company?'

'Yes.'

'And what does it do?'

'Property, investments. Mostly property. Developing industrial complexes, housing estates, cabin sites. Lots here in Nordhordland.'

'And the name of the company is …?'

'Mæland Real Estate AS. We just call it MRE.'

There was a slight pause, as a couple of us took the first swig of hot coffee. So far we had skated around the reason for our being here. But this was no chance meeting between friends or family. Nor was the cabin up for sale and we were not being shown around.

I considered it an opportune moment to tackle the matter head-on. 'So your husband has disappeared?'

She had just lifted the mug to her lips. Now it hung in mid-air, in front of her gaping mouth. Her eyes widened a mite, and a helpless, hurt air came over her, which hadn't really been there before.

She put down the mug, splayed her fingers out on the table, as if to support herself, and said softly: 'Yes, two days ago.'

'And you haven't contacted the police yet?'

'Present company excepted …' She glanced fleetingly at Brekkhus, who was sitting with a mug in his hand and a pensive expression on his face.

'Why not?'

'I don't think … I don't know … When I rang Karin she told me about you, and what you do. I don't think Mons is … if you see what I mean. We had a … a difference of opinion. Which became a little heated. Raised voices. The upshot was he left, grabbed his coat and slammed the door, and not long afterwards I heard the boat starting up.'

I nodded towards the window. 'The one down there?'

'No. We've got an Askeladden with an outboard motor.'

Brekkhus cleared his throat to attract attention. 'It was found adrift to the south of Radsund on Sunday afternoon.'

'I see! And he disappeared …?'

'On Saturday evening,' she said.

'But …'

'But the car was gone,' Brekkhus said.

'Uhuh?'

She took over. 'His car was parked by the quay, where we met you. But now it's gone.'

'You both had a car?'

'Yes, of course,' she said in a tone that suggested she was talking to a young child. 'Even at weekends he often had to travel because of his job, and I had more than enough to do here. At any rate, during the summer.'

'All the indications are that he took it,' Brekkhus said. 'He may have moored the boat, and it worked its way loose or … well.' He shrugged.

'You've done some investigating?' I asked. 'Off your own bat?'

'I made a couple of telephone calls. That's about it.'

'Well … in that case there are a number of leads, but … Karin probably told you, I don't do, what in our branch we call matrimonials.'

'Fine, but this isn't,' Ranveig said. 'You do missing persons, don't you?'

'Yes, as far as they go. But rarely of this vintage.'

'Is he too old, do you mean?' She glowered at me.

'No, no, please let me explain. What I meant was … the missing persons I am asked to find are usually young people with serious problems. What was your problem?'

'Problem?'

'You said you'd had a row. Or a difference of opinion, as you called it. Could you tell me what it was about?'

She licked her lips. The tip of her tongue was small and pink, like a naked little animal, it poked its head out, took fright and quickly retreated. 'It was a family … matter.'

'Mhm?' I watched and waited.

'You don't need all the intimate details to find him, do you?'

'Not everything maybe, but a rough sketch would help. If you want me to find him, that is.'

'If I want …! What do you mean by that?'

'The more you can tell me, the easier it will be.'

Karin and Bjørn Brekkhus sat in silence, listening now. What Ranveig had to tell us was important. She took a mouthful of coffee and pulled a face before starting: 'Everything centres around Brennøy.'

'The island in …?'

'The municipality of Gulen. Quite a way out. About as far as you can go before you hit the sea.'

'And what has your husband got to do with Brennøy?'

'At the end of the 80s he bought a large plot there. Nothing to write home about. A few wind-blown cliffs and rocks to the north of the island. But he didn't pay much for it. An investment for the future, he said at the time.'

'That was what most people said at the time.'

'Yes, I know. The worst yuppie period. But Mons was looking further ahead.'

'By which you mean …?'

'Renewable energy. He could visualise the rocks being … the perfect place for a wind farm. The technology was being developed. In Denmark and several other countries the first wind farms were already up and running and there were several more on the drawing board. Here, there were plans for wind turbines in Northern Trøndelag and in Nordland. Mons was convinced that Vestland would follow suit, above all with a view to making money after the seabed had no more oil to offer.'

'A forest of wind turbines along the whole coast? Passengers on the Hurtigruten cruise ships have got something to look forward to.'

Her eyes flashed. 'Exactly! That's like listening to his daughter, Else. Green in every respect.'

I arched my eyebrows. 'Is that what you were arguing about?'

'You could put it like that, yes. Else was the apple of his eye, of course. She had just turned four when she lost her mother and there had been a few pretty awful experiences before that, in the bargain.'

'Really?'

'Yes. Anyway ... Mons had started to listen. Something of a sea-change, I can tell you. Generally he used to, well ...'

'Even die-hard socialists can go green in their old age.'

'Must be with mould then. Anyway, Mons was never a socialist, I can promise you that.'

'No, it doesn't sound like it, but ...'

'But, if I might be allowed to finish what I was saying ...' She adopted a sarcastic expression.

I nodded, and opened a palm.

'It was two against two. Mons and Else on one side. Kristoffer and me on the other.' She answered my question before I could ask. 'Kristoffer's his son. He's the one who will take over when Mons retires.'

'I see. But who is the largest shareholder in the company?'

'That's Mons. Still.'

'So he could do what he liked, then?'

She sent me a desperate look. 'Why do you think we disagreed?'

'Fine, but ... Was that all? And this – what shall I call it? – ecological disagreement led to Mons slamming the door and leaving? And since then no one has seen him?'

'Yes.'

'No other ... disagreements?'

'Like what?'

'Well ... most marriages are like waters littered with submerged rocks. You never know when you'll hit one.'

'We didn't have any other disagreements.'

'If you say so, I'll have to believe you.'

'Yes, you will, actually.'

'I assume you've tried to ring him? Does he carry a mobile phone on him?'

She glanced at Brekkhus. 'Yes, but there's no answer. He must have switched it off. Or else ...'

I paused for a moment to follow her eyes. 'Perhaps you also made a couple of calls regarding this matter, did you, Brekkhus?'

He cleared his throat and looked ill at ease. Stiffly, he said: 'No activity on his phone has been observed since Saturday afternoon.'

'Nothing since he disappeared, in other words?'

'That sounds serious,' Karin said.

Brekkhus shrugged. 'It might be. But – as Karin said – he might have switched it off.'

'Or he might have dropped it in the sea as he left,' she added. 'He could have thrown it into the sea for all I know. He could get into quite a temper.'

'Really? Could he be violent?'

'No, no, not so that he would hit anyone. Not at all. But he could take his temper out on ... physical things. Once when we were quarrelling he slung his mobile on the floor and stamped on it so hard it broke.'

'Expensive habits. But he didn't just go straight home, did he?'

'No. I checked that, of course. I got Kristoffer to pop up, but there was no one at home.'

'Where do you live in Bergen?'

'In Storhaugen.'

I had taken out my notebook, and she gave me the house number. Then I jotted down the home telephone number, Mons Mæland's mobile number and hers.

'And Kristoffer, where does he live?'

'In Ole Irgens vei.'

'Family?'

'Has he got any? – a wife and two children, although I can't see what that's got to do with this case.'

'It hasn't got anything to do with the case. It's just to get a picture. The daughter?'

'Else lives in Kronstad – in a student collective,' she added with a sarcastic undertone.

'And the address?'

'Goodness me! Ibsens gate. But I'd rather you didn't bother them with … this.'

'They know about it though?'

'I told you I asked Kristoffer to pop home to see if Mons was there, but, as I said, there's no need to bother them.'

I looked at her. 'Their father has gone missing, and you don't want me to bother them with this?'

'What I mean is they can't know anything anyway.'

'No? But it may turn out that … It may have been quite traumatic when they lost their mother. Else was only four years old, didn't you say?'

'Yes.' She looked at Brekkhus. 'And Kristoffer must have been, well, twelve, wasn't he?' He nodded, and she continued: 'They don't want to talk about it.'

Brekkhus coughed. 'It was a shock for them, of course. But they weren't here when it happened, fortunately.'

'Where were they then?'

'Well … in fact I can't remember, but I think Kristoffer was on a hiking trip with a friend and his family, and Else had a sleep-over at a friend's.'

'In other words, the parents had a kind of free weekend. With a catastrophic outcome.'

'Yes, that's about the long and short of it.'

I turned my attention to Ranveig again. 'How's your relationship with your step-children?'

She hesitated for a moment before answering. 'Quite … run of the mill. I'm not exactly the evil stepmother of fairy-tales, if that's what you're suggesting.'

'I'm not suggesting anything at all. I've just noted that you don't want to bother them with this disappearance …'

She sighed. 'Of course you can talk to them. I didn't mean it like
that. But they have their own lives to lead. I can't imagine they have
anything to contribute. That was what I meant.'

I nodded. 'Fine. So where do you think I should begin? Where are
the company offices?'

'In Drotningsvik. But ...'

'Perhaps you don't want me to bother them, either?'

She rolled her eyes. 'You'll see Kristoffer there anyway. What I was
thinking was ... if anything should leak out about Mons being ...
missing. It's a sensitive line of business.'

'Mine, too. Especially when I'm not given anything to work on.' I
considered the matter. 'What about Brennøy? Could he have gone
there?'

She studied my face, unsure. 'It's just a plot of land. No houses.'

'But that was what the row was about. He may have gone there to
see the place with fresh eyes. Maybe see if he agreed with you after all.
You and Kristoffer.'

'Mm ...'

'There's another question I have to ask you.'

'Right.' She gazed at me with apprehension, and I could feel a chill
in her eyes.

'Have you any cause to believe ... Is it possible that there might be
someone else?'

She heaved a deep sigh. 'If there had been, well, fine – almost. That at
least would have been an explanation. Somewhere to start looking. But
no, I'm afraid I have to disappoint you, Varg. I have no cause to believe
any such thing.'

'Disappoint? I don't take that kind of case, so ...'

A sudden silence descended over the gathering. I let my gaze wander
from Ranveig Mæland to Bjørn Brekkhus – both had equally glum
faces – and on to Karin, who also looked resigned.

As if to rid me of any last doubts, Ranveig said: 'Of course you'll be
paid for your work. I can transfer the money as soon as I'm home. Just
give me your account number and a figure.'

She jotted them down without any indication of an impending nervous breakdown. Then looked around. 'Everyone got what they need, coffee-wise?'

'Yes, thanks,' came the motley chorus from around the table.

'I'll just rinse the cups. Then we can go.'

'I can help you,' Karin said.

I caught Brekkhus's eye. 'Could we go outside for a moment?'

'Dying for a fag?' he said with an amused glint.

'I don't smoke. But there was something I ...'

He nodded and got up, and we went out together. Ranveig watched us leave. She looked as if she would have liked to join us. What did I know? Perhaps she was dying for a fag herself?

4

It had begun to rain. The sea mist lay low over the countryside, and the island of Lygra had vanished in the grey haze. The heavy, vertical rain hit the ground with immense force. We stood in the porch to stay dry. Beneath us the boat bobbed up and down by the quay like a gluttonous gull weighed down with belly fat.

Brekkhus glanced at me expectantly.

'Didn't look like Ranveig placed much importance on what happened to Mæland's first wife, Lea, did it.'

'No.'

'Could you fill me in with a few more details?'

He rocked his head from side to side. 'There's not a lot more than I've already said, and … well, I can't see how it can have any bearing on this case.'

'I'll be the one to judge that.'

'I've said that sentence many times myself.'

'So you know how necessary it is. Well …'

His eyes wandered down to the boat, the quay and the small inlet. 'As I said … They found her dressing gown and shoes down there. None of the boats was missing. Everything pointed to a drowning accident.'

'But Ranveig mentioned something about bad bouts of depression.'

'Yes. She'd had what doctors call post-natal depression. Both times.'

'How serious was it?'

'After the last round she was admitted to hospital – for a lengthy period.'

'I see. So suicide wasn't so unlikely …'

'No, it wasn't, which only underlined the gravity of the situation.'

'But the body wasn't found.'

'No, but the currents round here can be pretty dramatic.'

'Yes, I know. But most bodies float to the surface at some point, don't they?'

'Of course. Over the years that followed we had reason to go back to her file on several occasions. In fact, the very next month, but the body we found was that of a much younger woman and there was no birthmark.'

'Birthmark?'

'Yes.' He automatically touched the small of his back. 'Lea Mæland apparently had a birthmark just here. Star-shaped we were told. I'd never seen it personally.'

'And of course after a while it would be useless as a distinguishing mark.'

'That goes without saying. Bodies that have been in the sea for more than a month … pretty drastic things happen to them and they're often eaten.'

'And still people call crab a delicacy.'

'Yes, but then we don't eat the crab's stomach, do we.'

'No, thank bloody Christ for that, as Martin Luther would say.'

He looked at me in surprise, a common reaction to townies' attempts at humour around these parts.

'Was Mons Mæland taken in for questioning during this case?'

'We had to question him as a matter of form, but as Mons and I knew each other, someone else at the station had to take responsibility for the investigative side of the case.'

'And the conclusion was … ?'

'No grounds for suspicion. He'd been fishing in the Lure fjord the night before and came home late. By then Lea had already gone to bed.'

'No marital differences at the time?'

'Not as far as we could gather, no.'

'How well did you know each other, you and Mons?'

'We'd met a few times when we were young, but it wasn't until later … We became friends when we started taking our holidays here. I live over there.' He pointed across the sound towards Lygra.

I was about to say something else when the door behind us opened and Karin came out. 'Why are you standing out here?'

'We're waiting for Noah,' I said.

She looked anxiously up at the heavens. 'Yes, looks like the sluice gates have opened.'

'And there's no sign they're going to be closed any time soon.'

Ranveig appeared behind her. 'I was wondering if you wanted to see the annexe, Varg.'

I glanced towards the corner of the house. 'Yes, why not? Any special reason?'

'That's where he has his office when we come here.'

'OK, let's take a peek,' I said, stepping into the rain and pulling my jacket over my head as I dashed towards the small annexe we had seen from the sea. The others followed, both Ranveig and Karin having the foresight to carry an umbrella, Brekkhus the mettle to set off bareheaded, with water streaming down his neck. Within seconds the rain had flattened his hair, so much so that it looked painted on.

Ranveig was there first with the bunch of keys, she quickly found the right one and let us in. We ran inside shaking the water off us like stray dogs sheltering from a cloudburst.

She switched on the light and we looked about us. The annexe consisted of one room. A high table had been placed in front of the window. On it there were piles of paper, documents, writing implements and a stack of floppy discs. Along one wall there was a bunk bed, and in the corner an old-fashioned washstand in front of a small mirror. On a slim bureau there was a kettle, some mugs, a jar of instant coffee and a couple of packets of tea: English breakfast in one, green tea with lemon in the other.

'No computer?' I asked.

'He uses a laptop … there.' She pointed to the empty space between the piles of paper.

'But he's evidently taken it with him?'

She nodded. Brekkhus sent me an eloquent look.

'Is there anything as advanced as an internet connection out here?'

'No, of course not. But it wouldn't surprise me if there was one day.'

'So it was more like a portable typewriter, was it?'

'Yes, I suppose so. But he could bring a whole heap of papers with him and sit working on them until he took them back home – or to the office – when the weekend was over.'

I went over to the desk and placed a hand on one pile. I looked at Ranveig. 'May I …?'

'By all means!' She extended a hand.

I flicked through the top sheets of both piles. They were mostly job-related documents, which didn't mean a lot to me. There were several property projects, among them a summer cabin to the north of Øygården and a major industrial venture in Gulen. The latter appeared to be connected with renewable energy: wind or wave power. I noticed one signature seemed to keep popping up. The name was Jarle Glosvik.

The document on top of the pile to the right was a letter adorned with a dynamic, blue logo, a windblown N merging with a P, furnished with the explanatory subtext, Norcraft Power. In the letter, which was addressed to Mæland Real Estate AS, attn. Mons Mæland, the signatory, Erik Utne, confirmed that the planned survey of Brennøy would take place as arranged on the ninth of September at twelve thirty. The company would be represented by a delegation consisting of four people, led by Utne himself.

'He's going to Brennøy on Wednesday,' I said, holding up the sheet.

Ranveig took it and read. Then she nodded. 'Let's hope he gets there, eh?'

'Yes … do you mean we should let the matter rest until then?'

'No, I don't mean that. But …' She searched Brekkhus's face, as if hoping for support from him.

'What Ranveig means to say is that Mons probably should be at that meeting. If he isn't, the whole deal could go down the plug hole.'

'So if Mons doesn't turn up …'

She met my eyes again. 'Talk to Kristoffer,' she said in a low voice.

'There's a lot to suggest that I should,' I said. 'Can I take this with me?'

She nodded.

I found nothing else of immediate interest on his provisional desk. I was given permission to open the drawers of the slim bureau as well, but all I found was a small collection of envelopes of various formats, several floppy disks with labels describing the contents, all of a work nature. Going though each of them would take time and, judging by their appearance, be of doubtful significance. In the bottom drawer I found something which gave me a stab of longing for my own office: half a bottle of aquavit, half full. But it wasn't my favourite brand. This was Danish and had to be drunk chilled.

We left everything as it was. I cast a final glance around before leaving. On the wall there was a solitary landscape painting of the kind you inherit from parents with a simple taste in art. I had a couple myself, of Sunnfjord, where my father grew up, neither exactly masterpieces.

'They used this place as living quarters while the cabin was being built, I suppose. Just before the war, I think it was,' said Brekkhus.

'His parents?'

'No, no. Mons and Lea bought this when Kristoffer was small. Early 70s it must have been.'

'I see.'

Then we left. The rain had let up. The light haze lay like a silk blanket over the countryside. High above us we glimpsed a white orb, the sun, like a beating heart, , still not strong enough to burst through.

While Ranveig locked the cabin I stood slightly apart with Brekkhus. 'Tell me: What do you personally make of this disappearance?'

'Personally?'

'Yes, as a good friend. Do you think something has happened to him?'

Neither Ranveig nor Karin was within earshot. Nonetheless, he lowered his voice. 'If you ask me, I think he'll turn up again. My guess is he went underground – if I can put it like that – to avoid the unpleasant confrontation there might well be on Brennøy at this survey on Wednesday. Or ...'

'Yes?'

'Well … probably to avoid any improper attempts at persuasion.'

'Are you thinking bribes?'

'For example. But it's impossible to know, of course. Only time will tell.'

'And the mills of time grind slowly. As in Lea's case.'

'Well, the case was declared closed after a few years.'

'She was declared dead?'

'Yes.'

He had no more to add. Ten minutes later we were on board the boat and heading back. Brekkhus steered us safely into Feste, where a boat was moored at the quay taking on diesel, with the assistance of the helpful grocer, who checked us over one last time as we got into our cars. He was probably wondering what we were up to on the island. After all, not a lot happened in this area of Nordhordland on Monday mornings in September.

Before we went our separate ways, I said to Ranveig: 'Could you ring Kristoffer and warn him I'll be calling?'

'Will do,' she answered with a brief smile. 'Good luck, Varg. I hope you find him before …'

'Before what?'

'Before the meeting on Wednesday.'

I nodded and smiled encouragingly, but even before I had got into the car the smile was gone and my mind was already churning. Or *before it's too late*, I said to myself.

'God knows how I'm going to find him with so little to go on,' I said to Karin.

As we negotiated the narrow, winding road to Seim and then took the main road from Mongstad south to Bergen, I barely listened to what she said.

Before we had reached the roundabout at Knarvik my mobile rang. I gave it to Karin to answer. After a few words she looked at me. 'It's Ranveig. Kristoffer's expecting you at half-past three. Is that OK?'

I looked at the clock in the car. It read 14.10. 'So long as there are no unforeseen hold-ups … Tell her I'll be there.'

She confirmed the arrangement, chatted for a while and then rang off.

As we drove onto Nordhordland Bridge the sun was beginning to break through the cloud. Stout beams of white sunshine fell diagonally across Byfjord, the contours of a colossal construction, erected to hold in place the safest source of energy known to man, provided that it kept burning.

I dropped Karin in Fløenbakken, after kissing her lightly on the lips and arranging a late dinner, then I drove on to Ytre Laksevåg and my first real engagement of the case so far.

5

The main office of Mæland Real Estate AS was on the outskirts of the new industrial estate at Janaflaten, due south of Sotra Bridge. The estate was still being built, and the signposting left something to be desired. The massive, grey concrete building was divided between various companies, and an in-depth study of the information board in the empty collective vestibule was required to establish where the office was.

The staircase had corner windows from floor to ceiling and a magnificent view of the main road from the south, and the islands and sea beyond. The grey clouds from earlier in the day were being swept away by a strong northerly wind, and in the distance there was a clear line of blue sky, like a silken membrane on the horizon. It promised improved weather in the days to come. But you could never be completely sure. Behind the sky the clouds are always grey, as we say in our part of the country.

After a few abortive jaunts I finally found my way to the sign proclaiming in big letters that I had arrived at Mæland Real Estate AS. I opened the heavy, blue door to the offices, where I was met by a smiling young lady with large glasses, fair hair, a grey-flecked black jacket and white blouse. She was sitting at a minimalistic desk and looked as though she had spent the whole of her life waiting for me to come through the door.

'I have an appointment with Kristoffer Mæland. The name's Veum.'

She smiled brightly. 'I have that down here,' she said, nodding to the computer, which, along with the keyboard, filled the majority of her desk. 'Kristoffer's expecting you.' From the use of the Christian name I inferred that this was a young, dynamic atmosphere.

'Sorry,' I said, putting on an apologetic face and consulting my watch. 'I had some difficulty finding the way here.'

'Everyone does,' she said lightly and with a consoling smile. 'It'll all be sorted by spring.'

'Not before?'

'Well, everything comes to him who ...'

'... laughs longest.'

She seemed to find this droll and made a clucking sound, then showed me into the brightly lit corridor, to a glass cage with a view, containing a desk of much more generous proportions than her own and a suite of sofas where a young man was flicking through a file. When he saw us he put down the file, got up and nodded.

The secretary opened his door and said: 'This is Varg Veum.'

'Thank you very much,' I said, passing her on my way in. She smelt of lily of the valley, which never failed to attract me, even though I knew how poisonous they were. Then she closed the door behind me and I greeted Kristoffer Mæland.

Since I had neither met his mother nor his father it was impossible to say whether he resembled either of them. He was roughly my height and had fair, curly hair cut close to the scalp. His face was broad, his smile measured, and his eyes were blue. His clothes were both practical and elegant: a dark jacket, blue jeans and a white shirt open at the neck.

He pointed to a chair and sat down opposite me, across a massive piece of glass. 'Ranveig said I had to talk to you.'

'Did you have to be persuaded?'

He sent me a chill look. 'My father's gone off for a few days. No reason to make a big drama out of this.'

'Has it happened before?'

He shrugged. 'I don't have a complete overview of what goes on in their marriage.'

'But there is friction?'

'No more than in any marriage, I assume.'

When he didn't follow up, I said: 'You don't have a close relationship with Ranveig, do you.'

'She's not my mother. Let me put it like that.'

'But there were disagreements between them?'

He gesticulated. 'Not as far as I know, as I said. Bit of door-slamming. That's not unusual in most homes.'

'But he didn't say anything to you? About going away, I mean.'

'No, no, he didn't.' After some reflection he added: 'You have to understand: Dad's considering pulling out of the company. And leaving everything to me.'

'To you alone?'

'Yes, and the other staff, of course.'

'But what about your sister?'

'Else? She has her shares and can keep them, but she's still young and has never had any interest in what we do.'

'What does she do?'

'She's a student.' And then he added, 'History of Art,' in a tone that made it sound rather suspect.

'So what's the company's main activity?'

'Property and project management, basically. We're not primarily after profit, but we try to add value and be forward-thinking.'

This was something he had learned off by heart. But I wasn't there to buy anything, and the projects I had in mind were not of the value-adding and forward-thinking variety. Mine were more of the keeping-my-head-above-water kind.

'That's why you're investing so heavily in wind power?'

He regarded me with respect. 'So you've heard about it?'

'Ranveig told me.'

'Right. Yes. In co-operation with a company called Norcraft Power we're planning a wind farm at the edge of Gulen, on an island called Brennøy.'

'Yes, I'm aware of that. You're going there to do a survey on Wednesday, I understand.'

'Did she tell you that, too?' He looked almost impressed.

'No, we found a letter addressed to your father confirming the arrangement.'

'Yes, he's been involved in – how shall I put it? – the practical side of things: he knows Brennøy well, you see.'

'I see?'

'Yes. My father's mother is from Brennøy, and they used to spend their holidays with the family there. That was how he got to hear about the property. An old boy put it on the market – he died straight afterwards, in the late 80s – and Dad made an offer.'

'And this survey with Norcraft Power, was he going to attend it on his own?'

'No, the idea was that we would both ... but ...'

'Yes?'

'Well, I was thinking. He might just have gone out there in advance.'

'Without telling you?'

'No, that does sound strange.'

'He's not answering his mobile if he has. And Ranveig said you don't have a house there.'

'No, that's right. But there's always Naustvik.'

'Which is ...?'

'Somewhere to stay. After the bridge was built to the island things have livened up, and for those keen on adventure holidays they've got the ocean straight ahead. German tourists are especially crazy for that. I know he's spent the night there.'

'Great. I'll check that out. Have you any other ideas?'

'Ideas about what?'

'About where he might be.'

'No, that's ...'

'He's probably got his laptop with him. You haven't heard from him?'

'Not since the weekend. My understanding was they'd had a row on Saturday. Anyway, even if he's got his laptop with him he still needs a connection somewhere.'

'Don't you get worried if you don't hear from him for a few days?'

He looked away. 'Worried? We ... Even though we work together we ... We're a bit of an unusual family, Veum. My sister and I, we lost our mother when we were children.'

'Yes, so I've heard.'

'Although Mum had her problems and there were difficult periods in our lives, it was as if a wall had collapsed in our house. One of the load-bearing ones. And the way it happened … I don't know …' He looked at me and shook his head.

'Yes, I know what happened.'

He nodded. 'One day she was there. The next she was gone. We didn't even have time to say goodbye. I was on a walking trip with a classmate and his parents. It came as such a shock when I was told. I couldn't believe it.'

'And your sister?'

'She understood even less, of course. She was so small. Just four years old.' He stared into the middle distance. Then he seemed to pull himself together, straighten up and carry on: 'So when this … when Ranveig turned up, only a short time afterwards … we've never had any kind of relationship with her. Nothing real.'

'A short time afterwards, you say. How short?'

'I don't remember. But that was how it felt.'

'But Ranveig was also employed here, wasn't she?'

'Yes, she was. She had the job Elisabeth – you met her – has now.' He nodded towards reception. 'But then she stopped. She hasn't worked here for as long as I've been involved.'

'But she's interested in the business, I understand.'

He shrugged. 'If it's making a profit, she's making money from it.'

There was a silence. 'So no other ideas apart from this Naustvik – on Brennøy?'

'If he's not at home or at the cabin, that's where I would look first.'

'You wouldn't like to ring him?'

His face went a little pink. 'No, I wouldn't, Veum. If Dad's decided to go underground for a few days then that's his business. I don't want to drag him out unless he wants to appear.'

'Hm. Tell me now, you wouldn't have a photo of him, would you?'

'Yes. I'm sure I have one here somewhere.' He got up and went over to a shelf, ran a finger down the pile and returned with a brochure in his hand. 'We made this a couple of years ago, but he hasn't changed much since.'

'Thank you very much.' I took the brochure, opened it and found a photo, taken at a desk in front of a panoramic window. The countryside through it suggested it was a different office from the one we were in now. Mons Mæland was sitting at a desk with Kristoffer beside him, bent over a brochure, but both were looking up at the photographer and smiling as though someone coming in was a pleasant break from an otherwise busy day. Kristoffer hadn't changed much since the day the picture was taken, either. Mæland had a long, rectangular face with a prominent jaw and blond, slightly greying hair, brushed back off his high forehead.

I looked up. 'This was taken here? In your father's office?'

He nodded.

'Could I see it?'

He didn't seem particularly enthusiastic, but did reluctantly get up. 'Follow me.'

I walked out of the office after him and we continued down the corridor. He opened the door to an office which was identical to the one we had left, except that there was no sofa suite. I recognised the desk from the photograph. It was big and heavy and belonged to a far more classical office set-up than this. The surface was so shiny you could see your face in it, and there were no piles of paper waiting for Mons Mæland here.

I glanced around the room. The shelves were full of files, books and folders. On a separate table stood a desktop computer, switched off. On the glass wall opposite the desk a large photo was suspended from the ceiling by wire. It showed a windblown coastal landscape with the foaming surf breaking over the rocks and the waves towering like cliffs in the grey sea beyond.

'That's Brennøy,' Kristoffer said from behind me.

'Looks pretty windy.'

'The perfect place for a wind farm, if you ask me.'

I turned to him. 'But you father didn't agree.'

'Didn't agree!' His face was crimson. 'He was one hundred per cent in favour at the planning stage.'

'So why did he change his mind?'

'It was that bastard Ole who sank his claws into him. Ole Rørdal.'

'Ole Rørdal? The conservationist?'

'Please don't call him that, whatever you do. A troublemaker, that's what he is. A conservationist who says no to wind power? I mean to say – what rubbish!'

'The technology is a little controversial, isn't it?'

'Not among sensible people!'

'So you didn't consider your father sensible, either?'

He lowered his voice. 'Not as far as this matter is concerned. And Rørdal has roots there himself.'

'On Brennøy?'

'Yes. Or on Byrknesøy, next to it. He's been against this project from day one. And don't ask me why.'

'I'll have to ask him myself then, I suppose.'

'Be my guest!' Kristoffer said, with a resigned expression. 'But that won't stop us. I can guarantee you that.'

'Your father threatening to pull out – was that connected with the family row?'

'Partly, yes. But … He's getting on now.'

I raised my eyebrows. 'Fifty-five? He's younger than me.'

'So?'

'Well, we've both got a few years left in us, I reckon.'

Kristoffer smiled wryly. 'Our line of work may be a bit harder than yours, Veum. People get ground down. Dad has certainly shown signs of fatigue recently.'

'I see. In what way?'

'Well, as I said: shifting viewpoints, having difficulty making up his mind, general dissatisfaction … the way I see him anyway. Yes, it's time he considered giving up.'

'Could that be the reason he's disappeared? That he's simply sitting somewhere and reflecting on things?'

'Let's hope so.' He glanced at his watch. 'I'm afraid I'll have to terminate this conversation here. I have other duties to attend to.'

'I understand. I'm sure we'll see each other again.'

'Oh, yes?'

'On Brennøy, for example.'

'Well, time will tell. I'm hardly going to be visiting you.'

Then, in a sense, he did the opposite. He came towards me and accompanied me all the way out, as if to make sure I left the premises. Elisabeth had gone home, or wherever it is women like her go. At any rate, she was no longer there.

'Good luck, Veum.'

'Thank you,' I said, although I had drawn something of a blank with him. But I had a new name on my pad: Ole Rørdal. And I had to ring Naustvik on Brennøy to enquire whether they had a room free for Tuesday night. And whether anyone had seen Mons Mæland over there.

6

How so many people who worked all day for the same admirable purpose – to create a better global environment – could end up in their own camp, beneath their own flag, with impassable territorial lines, often led by colourful figureheads, was one of life's mysteries.

Bergen had Kurt Oddekalv, who in the early 90s broke away from Friends of the Earth Norway to found Green Warriors of Norway. With its central office in Oslo there was another environmental organisation called Bellona, which had an equally high-profile leader. Among the other stand-out protagonists in this struggle were Future-in-our-Hands, World Wide Fund Norway and Greenpeace Norway.

In the Bergen region, Ole Rørdal from Gulen had been a vociferous spokesman against wind power in recent years, a theme that had caused groups to splinter off from various movements. Arguments pro and contra were not exactly in short supply. Fears for the exposed coast, local plant and animal life, threatened bird species and the consequences for the countryside of building wind farms along the whole coastline from Lindsnes to the North Cape were issues that were emphasised time and time again. An interview Ole Rørdal gave to *Bergens Tidende* in June 1997 was often quoted from: 'The day they decide to build a wind farm in the north of Oslo, on the island of Tjøme and along the Gjendineggen ridge is the day I will consider taking the discussion of wind farms seriously as well.'

No one had gone that far yet. Which was why, as far as I had heard, Ole Rørdal took such an entrenched position. His two-year-old organisation, *Naturvernere mot Vindkraft*, NmV, Conservationists against Wind Power, was still at the recruitment stage, and no other major figures had appeared on the scene, as yet. Nor were they necessary.

I rang Enquiries and was told NmV's office was in Lille Øvregate, the town's oldest street and a worthy conservation phenomenon in itself. Speaking to Rørdal was not such a simple matter.

I had barely introduced myself when an abrupt Bergen voice stopped me in my tracks. 'What's this about?'

'Ole Rørdal?'

'What's this about, I said!'

'I'm working for Mons Mæland's family. For his wife.'

'C'mon on! I'm very busy.'

'He's disappeared. I need to have a word with you.'

'With me! Why?'

'It'll take too long over the phone. Can I come and see you?'

'I haven't ...'

I interrupted him. 'It won't take long.'

He growled: 'Well, well, alright. If you come in thirty to forty minutes, I'll be ready for you.' I heard someone speaking in the background, but Rørdal interrupted him too and repeated in a louder voice: 'In forty minutes!' Then he rang off.

I found a parking spot in Øvre Korskirkeallmenning and strolled down to Kong Oscars gate, bought a paper and occupied a free table in one of the street's newest cafés, a former grocery store, where they served coffee in big cups with great hunks of bread, in an atmosphere that was vaguely reminiscent of an Amsterdam coffee shop, but without the smell of dried grass and the rhythmically swaying heads of the town's ruminating cows. Half an hour later I folded up the newspaper, found my way to Lille Øvregate and a white, eighteenth-century timber house with a hairdressing salon on the ground floor and NmV on the first.

I had no sooner walked through the front entrance when a door upstairs flew open with a crash. A compact, stocky little man burst out onto the landing, wearing something akin to a uniform: camouflage combat fatigues with a wide selection of pockets. He had close-cropped ginger hair and was yelling back in the direction of the room he had just left.

'I'm telling you, Ole. We do it on Wednesday. If not, you'll only live to regret it! You know what I'm going to do. I won't hesitate.'

He paused for a moment to listen to the grunted reply from inside. Then he slammed the door hard, turned on his heel and set off down the stairs at a speed that suggested it was almost closing time and all the exits were being locked.

I stepped aside to let him pass, but he stopped in front of me, glared and barked: 'And who the hell are you?'

'Who's asking?'

'Are you going up there?' He jerked his head to indicate where he meant. His eyes glinted with suspicion. 'Have you come from Norcraft?'

'Eh? I've just come from Vågen Deli, along the street. Sorry, I didn't catch … What was your name?'

Then the door upstairs opened, and a stout man came out onto the landing. I recognised him at once from photos in the papers. It was Ole Rørdal.

'Veum? Come on up.'

The man standing before me said: 'Veum?'

I grinned: 'Varg Veum.'

He didn't appear to believe me, but he wouldn't have been the first. I left him with the surprised expression still on his face, and started up the stairs at a slightly more leisurely pace than he had come down. Before I reached the top, I heard the door downstairs slam with a resounding bang. Clearly grand exits were this man's forte. His fragmented goodbyes crashed to the ground like shattering china.

For centuries, the complexion and diminutive stature of Vestlanders has fuelled rumours of a distant past when shipwrecked Spaniards swam ashore and found a local welcome committee waiting for them. In which they immediately implanted their seed. More recent research has concluded that there weren't enough wrecks for them to have left such significant genetic traces. In fact, it was more likely that the tribes who settled here during the Migration Period (400–600 AD) brought these features with them, after travelling from the south of

Europe through the Germanic forests and over the ice all the way to the country known as Nordvegen – the road north.

Ole Rørdal looked well equipped to withstand a similar migration himself. He was powerfully built, broad chested, and his gait betrayed the fact that he had spent a lot of time at sea since childhood. In a way it was as if someone had put his head on upside down. An impressive, black beard grew from his chin, but his head was shaved so closely that there was only a dark shadow of hair. If he had put a helmet on, he could have got a job as an extra in any Hollywood Viking movie. This impression was reinforced by a suede shirt, a brown leather waistcoat and grey-brown trousers with large, external pockets. He had black military boots on his feet, which left no room for doubt – he would be ready to fight his corner whenever and wherever the wind turbine issue was raised.

'You'd better come in,' he said, although he didn't sound like he meant it.

I jerked my head in the direction I had come from. 'And who was that powder keg?'

'Stein Swineson,' he said irritably, 'Or Svenson, as he's actually called. He's our deputy leader.'

'You didn't seem to be quite on the same wavelength?'

He gave a dismissive wave of his hand. 'A disagreement about strategy. There's a lot at stake. It's important to choose the right … approach. But I don't suppose that's what you came here to discuss?'

'No, I'm here to talk about Mons Mæland.'

'What's happened?'

'No one knows yet. He's disappeared.'

His mouth dropped, but he clearly didn't have anything to say on the matter. I followed him into the room and looked around. This organisation was conspicuously disorganised; it was like stepping into a beehive. Big posters from international green agencies hung on the walls, some of them with stunning images of threatened rain forests, wild waterfalls and drifting icebergs. In one of them, a wind turbine loomed like a monstrous edifice above two intrepid cyclists – the Don

Quixote and Sancho Panza of our day. Rudimentary bookshelves heaved with stacks of paper, brochures, case files and various pieces of office equipment. An over-worked hard drive, printer, scanner, three computer monitors with freestanding keyboards and an old-fashioned fax machine whirred in what seemed to be the technology corner. A long, untreated wooden table stood in the middle of the room, surrounded by folding canvas chairs; it looked Norwegian and handmade, and definitely hadn't come from any rain forest.

Ole Rørdal motioned towards a coffee machine using an unnecessarily wasteful amount of electricity on a little kitchen worktop. 'Coffee, Veum? 100 percent organic.'

'As long as there aren't any coffee beetles in it.'

He looked offended, as idealists do whenever anyone cracks a joke, but he nodded, walked over to the counter, rinsed two fired-clay mugs – doubtless organic too – poured the coffee and came back to the table.

I sat on one of the chairs. It was rather rickety and not particularly comfortable. Mind you, the people here weren't the type to sit around – the sooner you were out in the field the better. 'While I was investigating a case, the row over the planned Brennøy wind farm blew up.'

'Oh, yes?'

'I'm told you're from around there.'

'Not from Brennøy, if that's what you mean. But I come from one of the neighbouring islands, Byrknesøy. You don't get much closer to primal Norwegian terrain than that. Viking ships sailed past there once, on their way from Nidaros to Bergen or vice versa.'

'And now you've got tankers instead.'

His face darkened. 'And polluting tourist boats. The shipping authorities don't seem to care much about the environment, when you see what they dump in our waters. Same goes for the utterly ridiculous plans they have for these so-called wind farms of theirs. Far away from people and livestock and with cables running through some of the most beautiful countryside in Norway. There's not even that much of a benefit to the environment. No, I'll say again what I've said all along: when they're willing to set up turbines in Nordmarka, on Tjøme or the plateau here in Bergen I'll allow myself to be drawn into a debate about them.'

My voice cracked: 'On the plateau?'

'Yup,' he said, with a provocative glare. 'Are the mountains that much more important than the district of Gulen or the island of Smøla? And what do you think people in Ålesund would say if they set up a wind farm on Aksla?'

'Well, but …'

'We're challenging God's own creation. "And God saw everything that he had made, and, behold, it was very good," as it says in the scriptures.'

I held up my palms in surrender. 'OK, Rørdal …'

'Call me Ole, everyone does.'

'Ole. I didn't come here to argue the toss about wind farms, one way or the other. This is about Mons Mæland …'

'I know, but what I still don't know is why you're talking to me about it.'

'I had a meeting with his son, Kristoffer. He said that you'd got him – his father, that is – to change his mind about the wind farm.'

He grinned. 'You don't say? Imagine that.'

'It's true, then?'

'Well, we had a good long chat about it a while back, and I dare say our dear friend Mons Mæland had a lot to think about afterwards. I heard he went back to his company and tried to get them to change their plans. But it's no secret that his proposal didn't go down well. We know all about that.'

'All?'

'Yeah, well, things got a bit fraught in any case. You know their property company, Mæland Real Estate, is only one little cog in the machine?'

'Oh yes? Who else is involved then?'

'Too numerous to mention. The Norwegian state amongst others.'

'People so influential that they might conceivably put pressure on … other interested parties?'

His eyes narrowed. 'What are you getting at now?'

'I know, for example, that they're working with a company called Norcraft Power, which will be responsible for the construction work.'

'If there is any, yes.'

'Are you expecting a visit from Norcraft?'

His eyes flashed. 'Me … ? Why do you ask?'

'Stein Svenson asked me if I was from Norcraft when we were downstairs.'

'That bloody Stein Swineson is a muppet! Would you spread rumours about everyone in the organisation just because we couldn't agree on a strategy? I'll make him eat his words.' He paused. 'My father's a preacher,' he said abruptly, as if that explained everything. 'Lars Rørdal. Farmer and preacher. He's delivered impassioned sermons against Mammon and the idol worship that is modern capitalism. "And again I say unto you, it is easier for a camel to pass through the eye of a needle than for a rich man to enter into the kingdom of God." And I subscribe to everything he says.'

'So the rumours are unfounded?'

'What rumours? It's just something Svenson's said without a thought in his head! Do you want me to spell it out for you?'

'That won't be necessary. But this is still, quite literally, tilting at windmills, isn't it?'

'Fighting for the environment?'

'Yes.'

He turned and pointed at the poster of the two cyclists and the wind turbine. 'That's what it feels like sometimes. But on the other hand … should we just lie down and let ourselves be walked over?' He brought a fist crashing down on the table. The two mugs jumped. 'No, we'll fight to the last drop of our blood. If necessary we'll chain ourselves to the rocks out there and make Brennøy another Alta controversy – the Sámi didn't just sit back and let them flood that village.'

'But … even between environmentalists there are differences of opinion on this, aren't there?'

A quiver ran through him as if he was trying to restrain himself. He looked depressed for a moment. 'To cut a long story short, Veum ... some of the so-called environmental agencies have their headquarters in Oslo. Too close to the politicians and the money. I'll say no more. Wind turbines in Nordmarka etc.' He dismissed it with a wave of his hand.

'You'll be present for the survey on Wednesday, I hear.'

He smiled grimly. 'We will. No doubt about that.'

'But Mons Mæland might not make it.'

He grew serious. 'If you're ... If Mons Mæland's disappeared, I see two possible explanations.' He took a deep breath and continued. 'He's either gone underground voluntarily, or someone's offered him something he can't refuse.'

'His family have no idea what's happened to him.'

'Worst-case scenario ...'

'Yes?'

'They've killed him.'

'Seriously? Do you honestly think they'd go that far?'

He leaned across the table. 'You have no idea what they're capable of. They're ruthless when someone's in their way.'

'Who do you mean? Norcraft?'

'Or others.'

'Others? Who?'

'I have no more to say, Veum.' He stood up. 'I've got bigger fish to fry. If something's happened to Mons Mæland, I can't help you. Sorry.'

I stood up, too. 'Svenson said something about some action planned for Wednesday. Is that what you've been arguing about?'

He shrugged.

'What's the plan?'

'You think I'd tell an outsider? My lips have seven seals.'

'Won't those seals break on Judgement Day?'

'This is not Judgement Day, Veum.'

'Maybe not, but what about Wednesday?'

His eyes glinted. Then he indicated that the audience was over. To emphasise his point, he walked to the door.

'Chow!' he said, grinning as I left. 'That's Italian. Means time for some grub.'

He shut the door behind me as I mumbled: 'I've heard that one before.'

Out on the street I looked left and right. No one was waiting to buttonhole me about my investigation or whatever else might occur to them. I needed a beer, but for the time being I would have to make do with the bottle of water I had in my car.

7

When I reached my car I still had ten minutes left on my parking ticket. I used the opportunity to ring Ranveig Mæland to ask whether she had heard anything from her husband. She hadn't. 'I'm seriously concerned,' she said.

'I've spoken to Kristoffer. He didn't know anything, either. Have you been in touch with Else?'

'Yes, she rang. Kristoffer had told her what was going on. That Mons was missing.'

'And what did she say?'

Ranveig hesitated. 'She's not easy to draw out, but she was as surprised as everyone else.'

'She hadn't heard from him, either?'

'No.'

'Perhaps I ought to have a chat with her myself.'

'Why?'

'There might be things she doesn't like talking to her stepmother about.'

'Such as?'

'Well, you disagreed about the wind farm, for example.'

'For goodness' sake! She's only a child.'

I rewound. 'Nineteen or twenty, isn't she?'

'Yes.'

'I wouldn't describe her as a child any more.'

'Oh really! You can describe her as you like, of course. So long as you get a result.'

'OK. Since we have no other substantial clues to follow, I'll go to Brennøy tomorrow. Have you ever been there?'

'Brennøy? No, never.'

'So you're not going this time, either?'

'For the survey you mean?'

'That's one possibility.'

'You go. I'll hold the fort back here in case he gets in touch.'

'Don't forget to tell me if he does.'

'Naturally. I wasn't going to pay your fee for a moment longer than necessary.'

'Fitting epitaph for my gravestone. But for the time being … see you.'

I rang off. After considering what she had said for a moment I called Directory Enquiries and asked for Else Mæland's telephone number. She had only a mobile number, they said, and asked if they should put me through. 'No, thank you,' I replied, but I noted the number and tapped it into my mobile.

Then I rang Enquiries again, and it didn't take them long to find the number of Naustvik Hotel & Harbour on Brennøy, either. I dialled the number and a woman answered. When I asked whether she had a room free for Tuesday, she burst into laughter. 'One? You can have the whole lot if you like.' Then she backtracked. 'No, I was joking. Several of the other rooms are taken.'

'I only need one.'

She jotted down my name and asked if I was interested in having dinner. 'It's perfectly OK to cook in the cabins, but many guests like to order a meal.'

'Thank you. I think I'll join the latter.'

'We look forward to seeing you tomorrow then, *herr* Veum.'

'Just a quick question. Do you know someone called Mons Mæland?'

There was a tiny, barely perceptible pause. 'Yes?' Now she didn't sound quite so friendly. 'What would you like to know?'

'Have you seen him recently?'

'No, I haven't.'

'When was the last time you saw him?'

'Tell me, what is this about?'

'The thing is, he's disappeared.'

'Disappeared? Mons?'

'Yes.'

'But that's terrible. He's supposed to … There's supposed to be some sort of survey here on Wednesday. They've booked a conference room with me, for afterwards.'

'Exactly.'

'I don't understand, but at any rate he's not here, as I said.'

'Well, we can talk more when I'm there. Tomorrow.'

'Yes …' She hesitated, and I had the feeling she was about to discover that the hotel was booked up after all. I concluded the conversation and rang off before she had a chance.

I stuffed my mobile into my side pocket, pulled away from the kerb and headed for Årstad. At Haukeland Hospital I turned onto the Kronstad road and found a place to park down a side street, then continued to Ibsens gate on foot.

Else Mæland's flat was in a block with an entrance directly onto the street, which was probably one of the busiest in Bergen. The cars were so close it would have been useful to wear a gas mask, and the queue moved so slowly that Mr and Mrs Snail on a Sunday outing would have been able to keep up. The result was filthy grey deposits around the green front door, and the handle of the door felt sticky as I pressed it down and pushed. In the dark hallway I found her name along with four others all on one post box, two men and two women apart from her.

I took the stairs. On the first floor I found the same names on a scrap of cardboard beside the door handle. I buzzed and waited. Then the door opened and a long-haired young man in a T-shirt, jogging pants and trainers examined my face inquisitively. 'Yes?'

'Else Mæland … is she in?'

He turned and shouted into the flat. 'Else! Visitor!'

He stood in the doorway staring at me without much interest as we waited. Then I heard the patter of bare feet behind him. 'Who is it?'

He shrugged and made room for her.

I summoned a friendly smile and said: 'Varg Veum. I'm trying to find your father. Have you got a moment?'

Her face changed. Then she nodded with a grave air. 'Yes, Ranveig said. Come in.'

The young man stepped aside and let me pass. I followed her into a long corridor reeking of a potent herb I couldn't quite place. From one of the rooms I heard loud music with a heavy bass and when she ushered me into hers the music came through the wall so loudly we might just as well have been sitting in the same room.

'I live here,' Else said, with a wary smile. She looked younger than I had expected. Her hair was smooth and fair, none of her brother's curls, and she had it gathered in a ponytail. She was dressed simply: blue jeans and a red T-shirt. Her face was even, quite narrow, and her eyes were the same light blue as her brother's, vaguely reminiscent of gun-smoke.

The room was spartan: a sofa bed in one corner, a couple of chairs round a little table in the opposite corner. There were built-in cup-boards, and on the walls there were large posters of the same kind I had seen at Ole Rørdal's: beautiful pictures of nature, encouraging you to fight for the environment with Gaia – an ecology organisation – which was written in big, blue letters on one of them.

Through one window in the room I could see the tops of the trees, which were still green. Once again I was reminded that, even in heavily trafficked areas, there were hidden idylls, in this case on the side of the house that didn't face the street.

'Grab a chair,' she said, and I chose the one that looked the more comfortable of the two she had: a battered, reddish-brown armchair. She sat on the edge of her sofa bed and looked at me expectantly.

'I hope I'm not disturbing you.'

'No worries,' she said. 'We're going to eat soon, but it's not my turn to cook today, so …'

'You're all students, are you?'

She nodded.

'As I said, I've been commissioned to investigate your father's disap-pearance. You haven't heard from him, either, I understand?'

'No.' She eyed me with concern. 'Not a word since Saturday, it must be. He rang from his cabin then.'

'To tell you something?'

'No, to wish me a good weekend. We chatted a little.'

'Nothing came up to suggest he had any travel plans?'

'Not at all. Now, after Kristoffer rang, I've been trying to call him, but I just get the standard voicemail answer on his mobile.'

'How is … Are you frequently in touch with each other?'

'Mostly on the phone. You know what it's like … Everyone's busy. I have my own life. Kristoffer has a wife and small children, plus more and more responsibility at MRE. Ranveig and us … I suppose you've heard what happened to our real mother?'

'Yes, I have.'

'When Mummy drowned I was only four. Kristoffer was twelve. When she and Dad … Ranveig, I mean … When they decided to get married we were a couple of years older, but for some reason we never had a very close relationship with her. I always thought about … Mummy.' She stared into the middle distance, and her face puckered in sadness. 'That had been hard enough, from what Kristoffer told me.'

'Yes, he mentioned that to me as well. Do you remember any of it?'

She stroked an invisible strand of hair from her forehead, played with her ear lobe and looked past me. 'No, I must have repressed it. But what I will say is that Ranveig never managed to fill her shoes. Not even she could do that. And now – now we're adults. It's very rare that we eat with them. For Christmas and Easter maybe, and if Dad has an important birthday. We never go to the cabin. I'm uncomfortable there after *that* happened. It was several years before Dad started going there again. With Ranveig.'

'And your father: What's your relationship like with him?'

She tossed one shoulder. 'We never really thought …'

I waited. In the end I said: 'Thought what?'

'Well … that he would get married so quickly. To her.'

'Yes, but he was still a relatively young man.'

'They knew each other before Mummy disappeared as well.'

'You can remember that?'

'No, not me. I was four, as I told you. But Kristoffer told me.'

'Ah, do you mean …? Are you suggesting that they had a relationship even then?'

'No, but things go through your head.' She tossed her shoulder in the same quirky way, and I was beginning to understand more and more about why family meals in the Mæland household were few and far between.

'The sole clue I have so far is Brennøy.'

'Right.'

'Have you ever been there?'

'Not for many years, but I'm tempted to go.'

'Oh, yes?'

'Because of the wind farm that's planned.'

'You're against it, I gather. So is your father.'

'As of quite recently, yes.'

'Quite recently?'

'In the last month or so. Are you hard of hearing or what?' She glowered at me as if to show how hopeless she thought I was. After a brief pause she added: 'We got him on our side anyway.'

'We?'

'I got him on our side! For Christ's sake!'

'But Kristoffer and Ranveig, they hold the opposing view.'

'Kristoffer just wants to earn money, and she … She has her mind on profit as well. The more money Dad has, the more for her. They've been on quite a few luxury trips in recent years while … Dad never went to places like that when he and Mummy … Fishing in Lure Fjord, that was his idea of happiness.'

'This change of heart of your father's …'

'He was definitely on the cusp the last time we spoke to him.'

'Someone must have a good reason to keep him away from the survey on Wednesday, in other words.'

Her eyes widened. 'You don't mean …'

I shrugged. 'Norcraft Power, others with vested interests in the project, what do I know?'

'I can't believe that. After all, this is Norway.'

'The sunny side of life where it's all fun and laughter and liquid gold from the North Sea?'

She swallowed. 'Well …'

I leaned forward again. 'It was my understanding, from your brother, that you've got shares in the company.'

She looked a trifle embarrassed. 'Yes, but they're just something I inherited. I'm not in the slightest bit interested in them.'

'Nevertheless, if you and your father stuck together you'd be the majority shareholders, wouldn't you?'

'Yes …' She seemed unsure. 'We probably would be. But as I said, that's not something I go around thinking about.'

'Nonetheless. You and your father could put a stop to the sale to Norcraft, if it came to a vote. You could bring all the speculation about the wind farm to an abrupt halt.'

'Yes, I suppose we could …'

'Have you talked about it?'

'No. I think Dad was counting on persuading Kristoffer – in a peaceful manner, if you understand what I mean.'

'And now, now that he's gone?'

Her lips quivered. 'Yes, if he … if he's gone for good his estate would have to be distributed and his shares re-allocated. How that would end I have no idea. It's not exactly the sort of thing that keeps me awake at night.'

'No – what is then?'

'What?' She looked at me, confused. 'Erm … other things.' She moved her gaze to the poster on the wall above me. 'How the earth's going to fare, for example.'

'Gaia?'

'Yes?' Now she looked aggrieved. 'If only a few more people thought the way we do, then …'

'Then everything in the garden would be lovely and green?'

'Anything else you'd like to talk about? If not I ...' she snapped, making for the door. Then she turned to me again.

I got up as well. 'No, I don't think there is, for today.' I gave her my card. 'Here you are. If you hear from your father, or if you remember something that might be significant, then don't hesitate to contact me.'

She glanced at the card. 'Alright.'

She accompanied me to the apartment door. The smell of food was stronger now. From the kitchen I heard voices, a high-pitched woman's voice and a darker bass. Their laughter mingled like a musical piece they were rehearsing.

Else Mæland closed the door as soon as I was in the corridor, as though afraid I would turn back on the threshold and ask another unpleasant question. I trudged down the stairs and out.

While I was waiting for the green man at the zebra crossing further up the street, I wondered what Ibsen had done for Bergen to have this street named after him. However, when the street was named it was probably a great deal more idyllic up here, with grass to the south, where FC Brann would soon site its football ground, scattered houses up towards Kronstad and horses and carts on the road to and from the farms in Fridalen and Landås. Now the traffic crept past in one long, slow stream, like an endless cortege on its way to burying someone, whoever the dead person was this time.

8

Fløenbakken had a free parking area, which was primarily used by hospital employees who found the fee for designated places in the car park below Haukeland Hospital, a couple of stone-throws away, too expensive. At this time of day shifts were changing and I found a free spot not far from the block of flats where Karin lived.

As I was going to the islands the next day she had decided to cook *'sidl og pote'*: salami and potatoes, complemented with sour cream, beetroot and sliced leeks. I didn't object at all, especially as she had opened a beer and put a bottle of Simers on the table beside her best aquavit glasses.

'Are we celebrating something?' I asked cautiously.

'Nothing special,' she said with a smile.

After we had eaten she made some coffee in the kitchen. When it was on the table she poured herself a liqueur and a brandy for me. Once again I asked, with no little trepidation, if there was some special date I had forgotten: 'Are you sure we aren't celebrating something?'

She sat close to me, turned her face to me, leaned forward and kissed me on the mouth. 'Have you forgotten what you asked me? Two weeks ago?'

'You're thinking about …?' Gradually the gravity of the situation dawned on me.

'Yes. You haven't changed your mind, have you?'

'You mean that you, that we …?'

She kissed me again, held her head back a little way, looked me in the eye and said: 'The answer's yes anyway.'

'Well, I'm …' I put my arms around her, hugged her tight and felt my heart beating unnaturally and a kind of breathlessness seize me. 'Does that mean we have to start planning for something?'

She smiled warmly. 'Yes, we probably do. But we'll wait until you're back.'

'I'm very happy now, Karin.'

'Me, too. I was when you asked.' Suddenly she turned serious. 'I love you, Varg. A lot. Now you be careful when you go wherever it is you're going.'

'Even more now. You can bet on that.'

'Do you believe in premonitions?'

'Not much. What is it?'

'Well, ever since this morning, out at Mons and Ranveig's cabin, I've had an unpleasant sense that something was going to happen.'

'Something's always going to happen,' I said flippantly. 'How well do you actually know Ranveig?'

'What can I say? We've never been close, intimate friends, but as I told you, we were in the same class at secondary school. At Tanks *gymnas*. Then we lost contact for a few years. She stopped when she married Mons, but afterwards we still met. Not that often, but for a couple of walks in the mountains, usually when Mons was on his travels or busy. The occasional glass of wine or lunch in town. I still didn't really know her though. It was as if she always maintained a façade. Found it difficult to open up. And actually that suited me just fine. It meant I could do the same.'

'When did they get married?'

'Mmm .... I would guess 1984. By then they would have been together for more than a year already. '

'So he didn't grieve for very long.'

'No, he didn't.'

'She has expensive habits, her stepdaughter said. Costly trips abroad, that kind of thing.'

'Maybe. She has a sort of shell around her. I don't know if you noticed as well. Attractive, well-dressed, articulate. Impeccable down to the last detail. No scratches on her nail varnish, as far as I know.'

'But no children.'

'No.' She gave a wry smile. 'Neither have I, Varg.'

I arched my eyebrows. 'It's too late now, isn't it?'

'Yes ...'

'Else was so small when it happened, but both she and Kristoffer felt that Ranveig came into their lives too quickly after their mother was gone. One could be tempted to think something was going on before the mother disappeared.'

'If so, she never said anything to me.'

'Did you know her at that time?'

'Yes, we were colleagues, but then she stopped work.'

'Why did she stop?'

'There was a job going at his company and, well, he could offer a higher salary than the state could. I didn't like it. It smacked too much of ... erm ... nepotism. That's the right word, isn't it?'

'But you still met her?'

'Sporadically, as I said.'

'This Bjørn Brekkhus, has she ever mentioned his name?'

'Never. Do you think that ... ?' She didn't complete the sentence.

'In my line of work we tend to believe the worst of most people, so why not?'

'But in that case they wouldn't have shown their cards so openly – or called in the likes of you, would they?'

I smirked. 'What do you mean? The likes of me?'

She laughed. 'You know what I mean.'

'I'm sure you're right. It's unlikely.'

'What do you think has really happened to Mons?'

'I can tell you one thing. It's rare for someone to vanish without a trace in this day and age. We leave all manner of electronic trails after us. We only have to pass a road toll, ring someone from a mobile or swipe a card at a till. Big Brother sees you.'

'In other words ...'

'If you haven't left an electronic trail – no card use, no computer activity, nothing at all – then there's a strong chance you're dead.'

'But then it would be a police matter.'

'Of course. As soon as there's a body. Until then ... well, I've got rent to pay too.'

This time she kissed me with a little more passion. Her mouth tasted of coffee and liqueur. 'You ...'

'Yes?'

She smiled at me brightly. 'You know the old fisherman's custom, don't you? What they did before they set out to sea?'

'Are you referring to the belief that the act of sexual communion the night before departure foretokened a good catch?'

She assumed an expression to imply that her mind was on something quite different, but the way she snuggled up to me told me the opposite. 'Or two,' she whispered in my ear as we made our way to the bedroom.

There we made love as passionately as if it were the first time and with such vigour that her solid bed creaked ominously. Afterwards we lay chatting until we took up her suggestion and did it again, but this time with an almost mournful tenderness, as though we would never see each other again. As though I would never return with the big catch, but would remain out there, somewhere at the bottom of the sea, beneath the dark waves and the wind that blew and blew and never abated.

9

The fifteen minutes or so the ferry trip from Leirvåg to Skipavik took was just enough to buy and knock back a cup of bitter black coffee of the classic Norwegian ferry genus plus a sad-looking Vestland flatbread spiced with cinnamon and wrapped in plastic.

From the quay at Skipavik the journey was through rolling countryside with tiny patches of green, isolated houses and mountain formations scoured clean by the wind, over the three bridges that had brought the westernmost islands together for the last ten years, and north to Byrknesøy to the very last bridge, as far out to the sea as it was possible to go. In a couple of places I was stumped as to which road I should take and had to get out the map. In another I was distracted by a large, white-tailed eagle peacefully hovering above the road before it was roused out of its reverie by an aggressive gull and both disappeared westwards to the sea.

The bridge over Brennøy Sound was so new that the scars in the rock by the bridge abutment were still visible. It wasn't a high bridge; if it had been there was a good chance you would be blown away by the wind when it was at its worst. All the buildings on the island were collected around the old quay south of the bridge. There weren't many houses to speak of: a couple of smallholdings, a chapel, what looked like an abandoned fish hall on the quay, some cabins and summer houses of more recent origin. South of the quay was a little marina and a row of six conspicuously large fishermen's cabins painted in a classic combination: red, yellow and white.

A spruce forest had been planted around the oldest buildings. To the north of the island the terrain rose to the sky, naked and unpopulated, though not much higher than eighty metres above sea level.

What they wanted with a bridge out here was best known to the Sogn and Fjordane Highways Department. It was possible they had been far-sighted enough to visualise the current plans for the wind farm or some modern industry, unless it was the age-old collaboration between politicians and businessmen that had given the Brennøyers a bridge they had happily survived without for all the years they had lived there.

The road from the bridge down to the community had recently been tarmacked. As I approached the quay I turned towards the fishermen's cabins, where a sign informed me that this was where Naustvik Hotel & Harbour had their premises. There were two cars parked outside: a ten-year-old, unwashed, red Opel Kadett and a white VW of even older vintage.

The light drizzle dampened my forehead as I got out of the car and looked around. There was no sign of life, but I assumed that every single person who happened to be on the island had observed my approach a long time ago. As I made my way down to the fishermen's cabins I had my assumption confirmed. The door of the first house opened and a robust woman with remarkably beautiful features appeared in the doorway.

She was wearing practical clothes: a checked flannel shirt and baggy work pants stuffed into a pair of boots, not that the masculine clothing could camouflage her natural radiance. Her dark brown hair was tied into a plait, which hung over one shoulder.

'Veum?' she said, and I recognised the voice from the telephone the previous day.

'Correct,' I said, proffering my hand.

She gave me a firm handshake. 'Kristine Rørdal. I run this place.'

'Oh, yes. Are you related to Ole Rørdal?'

'Do you know Ole? He's my son.'

'Your son? You must have been young when you had him.'

She tossed her head back and pouted. 'Not that young … but thank you anyway. I'm expecting him here some time today. This evening, he said.'

'For the big survey tomorrow?'

'Of course. But come in and we'll get you registered.'

I followed her into the white cabin. It turned out to contain a little reception area with a wardrobe and toilets, a mezzanine floor where there were sofas and a main room with several long roughly hewn tables and a view of the sound through a high window. Behind a small glass desk there were a bowl of waffles, covered in cling film, and a variety of jams in jars, and the smell of coffee wafted over from the machine on the counter by the wall.

Kristine Rørdal took a seat behind the reception desk and pulled out a guest book. 'Name and address, please.' When she had entered my details, she asked: 'It was only one night, wasn't it?'

'For the time being, yes.'

'Breakfast from seven, and you wanted dinner in the evening, didn't you?'

'Yes, please. What's on the menu?'

'Fresh fish in a white sauce.'

'Sounds good.'

She turned to the board behind her, took one of the keys hanging there and gave it to me. It was number six. 'It's the second cabin you come to.'

'Thank you.' I looked around.

'Would you like a cup of coffee?'

'Yes, please. And the waffles look very good.'

'Coming up. Just find yourself a table.' She slipped behind the desk and got everything ready.

'It seemed very quiet here. When I arrived.'

'The calm before the storm, eh?' She flashed a smile. 'A Tuesday morning in September. You know what it's like. Holidaymakers have long since decamped. The boat people have as good as packed up for the season. The locals who aren't on the North Sea have jobs inland, in Sløvåg or Mongstad.'

'No one fishes any more?'

'A few do.' She came round the desk with the cup of coffee, a little jug of cream and some sugar cubes on a tray. 'How many waffles?'

'Two'll do me. Blueberry jam on one, brown cheese on the other.'

She beamed. 'I like a man with a good appetite.'

I met her eyes. 'You're not from these parts, I can hear.'

'No, no. I'm from Bergen. We spent our summer holidays here when I was small, and later I met the man I would marry, as you do.'

'So perhaps you know Mons Mæland from that time?'

'Oh, yes. They had a cabin just down from us. Now I'd better ...'

She turned round and went towards the reception desk.

When she returned with the waffles, I said: 'Your son's involved in the campaign against the wind turbines. How do people feel about that?'

The smile vanished. 'Well, they don't like it, as you can imagine. There's talk about quite a few jobs being created – and it's a handy income for the local council.'

I nodded towards the big window. 'And big, beautiful electricity-producing towers right along the coastline ... '

'Our family is split down the middle.'

'Not just yours, from what I understand.'

'Personally, I think it's a good idea. It's good for local trade. But my husband says it's a crime against creation, and you already know what my son thinks. You're against it, I take it.'

I shrugged. 'As with most things, there are compelling arguments for and against. But I definitely don't believe the tourist industry – which you might be part of – will benefit from it. And there won't be that many construction workers here either, at least not when the wind farm is up and running.'

'Oh, they'll always need to do maintenance and repair work. And they'll need surveillance people, but what do I know?' She pulled out a chair and sat down at my table. 'When you rang yesterday you said that Mons ... that he'd disappeared.'

'Yes, that was why I asked when you last saw him.'

'He was definitely here a week or two ago. How long has he been missing?'

'Since Saturday.'

'Several days then! And you haven't heard anything?'

I shook my head. 'Not a sign of life. No mobile activity, no card use, in short, nothing.'

'Sounds scary.'

'Tell me about him.'

'About Mons?' Her eyes became distant, and the corners of her broad mouth drooped. 'What can I say? I've known him since we were children, as I told you. In fact, we're roughly the same age.'

She gave me just enough time to raise my eyebrows to emphasise my previous surprise and smiled quickly. I folded the waffle with brown cheese in the middle and took a bite, without releasing her gaze.

'Well, he might be a year or two older, but he was here every single summer, with his parents. When we were children we were as thick as thieves – with all the other children too. The population multiplied during the summer, and for us kids this was paradise. Later, when we were in our teens, we went dancing together. To Byrknes by boat. Sometimes all the way to Eivindvik.'

'Dancing was allowed then?'

'Not in all circles, of course.'

'What about your husband?'

'Lars? Do you know him?'

'Ole mentioned his name.'

Her lips parted. 'He went dancing too … in those days.'

'But you met him again later, as an adult?'

'Mons?'

I nodded.

'Yes. Now and then. My mother was from Byrknesøy, so while we she was alive he came over regularly. After she was gone visits were rare because he bought a property on the north of the island. In recent years he's been here quite often, since the grand project was launched. Planners, investors and others. They always stayed here when they needed accommodation. And he had conferences and seminars here as well.'

'Then I can see why you're a fan of the project.'

'And I'm not the only one! Most of the locals share my viewpoint. The Deputy Chairman on the council often came here with him.'

'I see. And what's his name?'

'Jarle Glosvik. He's from Byrknesøy, across the sound from here.'

'Jarle Glosvik?' I recognised the name from the documents I had leafed through at Mons Mæland's. 'He's got vested interests as well, hasn't he?'

'He's got property on the island, but it's mostly wasteland, if you ask me.'

'And where can I meet him?'

'You'll have to go to the council offices in Eivindvik. If he's not working. He runs a construction company on the side.'

'And he's in *favour* of the wind farm, I suppose?'

'One of the most energetic in the campaign.'

'Not your husband though?'

'No,' she said drily. 'Not Lars.'

'How many guests can you accommodate here actually?'

'You'll see when you get there. There are beds for eight in each cabin, shared between four bedrooms. We can also put in extra beds. So we have forty beds and room for twenty more. But it's the marina that does us proud in the summer.'

'So when Mons was here – a week or two ago – he stayed here?'

'He always stays here.'

'I see.'

'There are no alternatives.'

'No, I can see that. But tell me: In recent times, did he seem different? As if something was bothering him?'

'Now you say it; it did strike me that he was a bit more tight-lipped than usual. I never thought there might be something bothering him though.' Then she stared straight at me again. 'But I've let my tongue carry me away here. Who are you actually, and why all these questions?'

'I'm a private investigator.'

'Private … ?' She gaped at me in disbelief. 'A sort of detective?'

I grinned. 'Yes.'

'And you're searching for Mons?'

'You could put it as simply as that, yes.'

She opened her palms. 'Well, I'm afraid there's not much to see here.'

'So it seems, but … What did he usually do when he was here?'

'I've already told you. Surveys, conferences, on-site inspections.'

'He didn't visit anyone?'

She smirked and tossed her head in the way she did. 'He had to make do with Lars and me. Social life on Brennøy is somewhat limited out of season.' She pulled her chair away from the table. 'Now I have to get back to what I should be doing.'

'Which is?'

'Accounts, paperwork. You have no idea how much red tape there is – even for such a small business as this.'

'Oh, I'm afraid I do. One final question. Have you met his wife?'

'Only Lea. I knew her, of course, before she went missing. Well, I assume you know she drowned in the sea many years ago.'

'I know about it, yes. She was never found.'

'No, but that's not so unusual. Those of us who live by the sea know that. The sea gives and the sea takes, but not always with a righteous hand.' She made this sound like a quote from the Bible – or maybe the Havamål, an old Norse poem. 'I've never met his second wife. She never came with him.'

'So in other words …'

'I've got to work now, Veum. If there's anything else of a practical nature, you can find me here.' She pointed to the mezzanine. 'In my office.'

'Thank you very much. I'm going to walk over to where they've planned the wind farm. Is it hard to find?'

She shook her head. 'Put your finger in the air and walk north. Through the copse north of the chapel. Take the path by the small red house on your left. Soon you'll be out on open ground and bare rock. You'll see the cross in the distance.'

'The cross?'

'Yes, the cross,' she said, shrugging and leaving me with the dregs of my coffee and the as yet uneaten waffle with blueberry jam. She didn't ask if I wanted any more. I finished the meal, got up, took my bag and left.

Outside, it had stopped raining. But the wind was picking up.

10

The neighbouring cabin with the bedrooms was furnished differently from the first. Instead of a reception area the whole of the ground floor was a communal room that could be quickly turned into a meeting room. A broad staircase led up to the mezzanine, where there were two west-facing rooms and two facing east. I unlocked the door to mine and entered a light, rectangular room with a slanting ceiling, a bed broad enough for two people and a small, practical en-suite with a toilet, sink and shower. The window faced the sound.

I put down my bag, took out my toiletries and put them in the bathroom. Then I changed into light walking boots with a good tread and grabbed an anorak and a camera as I left.

It was still just as quiet outside. There were several boats moored to the pontoons in the marina. They were of various sizes, from small dinghies with outboard motors and polished rowing boats from Os, to swanky island powerboats, the kind that could be seen moored at Bryggen, in Bergen, in high season.

I looked down at the abandoned building by the sea. I had forgotten to ask Kristine Rørdal about it, but it still looked like a fish hall whose owners had shifted their business to Poland, Portugal or somewhere with cheap labour. On Brennøy they hadn't left so much as a fading company name. The walls were white, but the paint was peeling off, and the grey concrete was visible underneath, stained green. The windows were black. The brown door appeared to be locked and bolted.

I set off towards the chapel. It was in better condition. The walls had been painted relatively recently, white as well. Inside the tall windows, lights were lit, and I stopped by the information board at the entrance, protected by glass against the wind and rain. There were invitations to regular meetings every Wednesday and Sunday evening, and morning meetings at the Missionary House, one of which was taking place at this very minute, if I felt a need to knit mittens in support of the missionaries in Africa.

A poster caught my attention. The title was: WEDNESDAY MEETING. Beneath it was a quotation from the Bible: '*He that troubleth his own house shall inherit the wind: and the fool shall be servant to the wise of heart. (Proverbs 11:29)* And after it: *Hear LARS RØRDAL speak on Wednesday evening at 7.00. A warm welcome to you in the name of God.*'

I didn't bother with the Missionary House, left the chapel and found the path leading through the wood north of the village. The last building before the copse was a little red house with white curtains. As I glanced in its direction I noticed a movement behind one of the window panes. I caught a brief glimpse of a pale woman's face before the curtain was drawn, as if Evil in person were passing.

I crossed through a classic tree plantation of tall, dark-green spruces, most of them far taller than Christmas-tree height. The lowest branches were dry and brown, and there was a soft covering of needles on the ground.

Then I emerged into open country. A quartz moonscape – furrowed, weather-bitten above the water – rose to the north of Brennøy. The path disappeared. Now it was a question of following the natural grooves in the terrain. Occasionally I came across narrow patches of grass in crevices, where the path reappeared in part. The wind off the sea grabbed hold of me, ruffled my hair and swept it across my face, wantonly caressing me, panting like a paramour, immense, invisible to all.

After five minutes I saw the cross. It towered aloft on one of the outermost crags. At first sight it resembled a mock-up of a wind turbine. But as I came gradually nearer there was no doubt. Like a local Golgotha it rose up, silhouetted against the sea, on the north of the island, a *mene, mene, tekel, upharsin* to wind-turbine supporters or whatever the meaning was supposed to be. When I was close it stood like a gigantic gravestone, cemented to a concrete base and so solidly constructed that it was intended to withstand even the fiercest blasts of wind. But there was nothing to explain why it was there and what it was supposed to symbolise. In its silent way it still gave me an indefinable sense of unease, a warning that something was about to happen.

I scanned the surroundings. This was Norway's westernmost limit. To the north I glimpsed the mountain formations in Ytre Sula and Lihesten further down the Sognefjord. This was windblown terrain where the sea broke against the rocks with regularity and only very seldom came to rest. You could hardly go any further.

Suddenly I felt very small. This landscape had been here since the dawn of time, covered with ice for long periods, only trodden underfoot by man for a fraction of a historical second. The sea had been there for even longer, solidified into ice for thousands of years, rolling to its own rhythm for just as long, with a pulse that was too slow for us to perceive and a global circulation we barely caught a shadowy glimpse of during our short sojourn on earth.

For understandable reasons there were no houses or quays here on the exposed rocks. A few wild sheep might have survived on the heather and other vegetation. For any other creatures survival prospects were poor. So, from that point of view, there was nothing to stand in the way of building a wind farm here.

When I turned back again I saw that I was about to have company. A tall man dressed in dark clothes, snow-white hair fluttering in the wind, was on his way towards me. In the rough-hewn countryside the man heading in my direction with long, determined strides was so stylised and unreal he could have been a figure from a Norse family saga.

From the very first glance there was something prophet-like and Old Testament about him. So it didn't come as much of a surprise when he came to a halt in front of me, ran a hand through his hair, fixed me with a stern look and said in a deep, sonorous voice: 'I'm Lars Rørdal. And who, if I might ask, are you?'

'Varg Veum.'

A twitch traversed his face, somewhere between a smile and a grimace. 'Did I hear you aright? A wolf in a sanctuary?'

I smiled back. 'And you? A voice crying in the wilderness?'

He looked at me gravely. 'You could say that.' His gaze moved to the cross that towered up behind us.

'You're Ole's father, I assume.'

He nodded. 'I cannot deny it.'

'I met your wife too when I rented a room at Naustvik.'

'Ole's a grand boy. No one can say otherwise.' He gave me the opportunity, but I didn't take it, and he continued: 'What are you doing here?'

'Looking around.'

He peered at me sceptically. 'Right. Do you represent a company?'

'A company? No. Just myself. But I have a job.'

'And that is …?'

'You know Mons Mæland, don't you?'

He opened and closed his mouth twice before answering. 'Yes. Do you represent him?'

'I can't say that, either. I work for his wife.'

'I'm afraid I don't understand.'

'Have you seen him recently?'

'Mons? He was here … a week ago, two weeks maybe. I don't remember exactly. I just saw him briefly. Asked him how he was.'

'And what did he answer?'

'He'd been better, he said. I asked him if he wanted to talk about it. You might already know, but I'm a … preacher. I'm used to people confiding in me. But he didn't. No, he said. Not now.'

'Did you touch on …?' I looked around me. '… what's going to happen here?'

His face hardened. 'What's going to happen? Or what some people want to happen?'

'The wind farm.'

'Yes, I knew what you were hinting at. Yes, we did talk about it. He'd had a change of heart, he said, and it wasn't popular, I gathered. Not even among closest family.'

'No, so I understand. There was definitely a difference of opinion.'

'Yes. The daughter's on our side, but the lad … that's what I call him … Kristoffer. He's stubborn. And he's got financial muscle behind him.'

'By which you mean?'

'Norcraft Power.' He pronounced the English words the Norwegian way, with deep contempt. 'But they've forgotten one thing. This land is the work of Our Lord. He's given it to us, but not so that we let it rot as we're doing at the moment. It's an abomination in God's eyes, and He will strike back with a vengeance. Pestilence, destruction, storms, flames and other catastrophes will smite us all if we don't change course and learn to live according to God's word.'

He glowered at me as if expecting me to protest. I held my tongue as I had learned to do when confronted by people with vaguely fundamentalist views. It was usually a waste of energy trying to discuss with them. When I said nothing, he nodded and moved his gaze again to the cross.

'Did you erect this?' I ventured.

'I did, with some brethren. As a warning to the faithless.'

'But you weren't planning to crucify anyone here?'

He strode over to me. 'Do not mock! The earth itself is being crucified, and Domesday is near, believe me. Only the Lord's mercy can save us!'

'My understanding is that Mons Mæland was a frequent visitor here.'

'Of course. He had no other reason to come out here. He owns the land, but you probably know that. Him and his company.'

'Yes ... Did you get his permission to erect this?'

'Did they ask God for permission to build wind turbines here?'

'I doubt an application on high constituted part of the legal proceedings.'

He scowled at me. 'Do not mock, I said! You should show the Lord our God respect, man. I've told you once!'

'My apologies, but now Mons Mæland and the others own this property.'

'And how do you think they got their hands on it?'

'I have no idea.'

'They cheated an old man out of it. He was barely conscious at the hospital in Eivindvik. Per Nordbø, his name was, and he died straight afterwards, in 1988. An old bachelor with no heirs.'

'But the purchase must have been approved by the council, at least?'

'And what is the council in the greater scheme of things?' he almost spat. 'Has it been sent by God?'

I reflected for a few seconds before answering. 'No, strictly speaking, it hasn't.' After a little pause I added: 'But, in other words, you're putting God above the council and following his commands rather than theirs.'

'You can certainly say that.'

I found it hard to stop myself. 'Legal proceedings are a bit quicker up there perhaps.'

He shot me a furious glare. To show what he thought he put his hand in one jacket pocket and pulled out a small, well-thumbed Bible bound in black leather with a gold cross on the front. He held it out, in front of my face, as if urging me back whence I had come. 'Everything's written here, Veum, from the very first day on earth. I need no other laws.'

'OK. I'd like to get back to Mons Mæland if you don't mind. Did you meet him when he came here?'

'Now and then. Far from every time. We didn't have much to talk about.'

'But when you were young ... I heard you went dancing together. You and him and ... your wife.'

His face developed a tic. 'That was then. Did Kristine tell you this?'

'I asked her about Mons.'

He sent me a stony look. 'Alright. I saw the light the year I turned twenty. Before that I took part in worthless activities, but I'm on the straight and narrow now.'

'Do you and your wife run the business together?'

'It's a family business, yes, but Kristine runs it. I don't deal with things like that.'

'No, I can imagine. Are you intending to be present at what's going to happen here tomorrow, the survey of the area?'

'Of that you can be sure, yes. They won't be leaving here without hearing the Lord's word!'

It was good the Lord had his representative here then, I thought. But I didn't say anything. Instead I asked him if I could take a few pictures of him in front of the cross. Strangely enough, he had no objections. He posed with an expression as if he were the Master Builder at a topping-out ceremony, ready to celebrate with all his employees. But there was only him and me.

Afterwards I took a few pictures of the countryside. The light was falling from a new angle now, and the contours were changing character as they always did on the margins of the mainland, with the constant roar of the sea in eternal motion, unchanging it seemed. But if there was something life had taught me it was precisely the opposite: nothing of what the Lord God, or whoever it might be, had created was unchanging.

We walked back together. At the chapel we parted company. He went in, perhaps to say a little prayer for the Missionary House. I went down to the quay and the fishermen's cabins. As I passed by I noticed a black Audi A4 with a Bergen number had parked beside my car, a grey Toyota Corolla.

A big cabin cruiser was mooring at the quay. In the cockpit I glimpsed the face of Ole Rørdal. On the deck, with the mooring rope in his hands, stood Stein Svenson. As I approached I even recognised one of the passengers. The young woman standing next to Ole Rørdal was Else Mæland.

11

As soon as the boat was secure she jumped ashore in a hesitant, slightly awkward manner. She stretched her legs and looked sulkily in my direction.

I ambled over to her. 'So you came after all?'

She tossed her head back. 'As you can see.'

'I wasn't aware you knew … them.' I motioned towards Svenson and Rørdal.

'Weren't you?'

Stein Svenson scowled suspiciously at us. Ole Rørdal was fiddling with something in the cockpit, but he too was following events on the quay.

'You came to see me about my father.'

'I did.'

'Is there anything new?'

'No, I'm afraid not. Unless Ranveig's heard something. Have you spoken to her?'

'Not since our conversation, no.' She looked around as though searching for an avenue of escape.

Svenson was wearing the same militaristic uniform as the day before. Now he came over to us. 'What's this about?' he asked with an aggressive stare at me.

'Mons Mæland,' I said.

His eyes narrowed. 'Haven't we met you before?'

'*En passant*, outside the office in Lille Øvregate. You were on your way out; I was on my way in. Yesterday afternoon.'

'You're from Norcraft, aren't you.'

'No, I'm not. You asked me the same question yesterday.'

'TWO then?'

'Two what … ?'

'T W O. Trans World Ocean.' He articulated it in capitals, as though he considered me too dim to understand. 'An international shipping company with Norwegian roots. Registered in the Bahamas, in case you were wondering.'

'Oh, them,' I said airily.

'Them, yes!' He glared at me. Else looked as if she would rather be anywhere else. Ole Rørdal was still observing us from a safe distance.

'I've come across them before. Several times. The first time so far back that you were hardly out of kindergarten. At that time they were called Helle Shipping, and Hagbart Helle was the big boss.'

'Then you do know who we're talking about. Capitalists of the worst kind. They sail ships that should have been scrapped several decades ago to Mongstad and back without a thought of the catastrophes that would ensue if one went aground in the already polluted waters around Austrheim and Fedje. That is, they know well enough; they just don't care. All they're concerned about is how much profit they can squeeze from transporting crude oil from Norway to the rest of the bloody industrial countries.'

'The last time I had any dealings with them it was to do with transporting toxic waste and people smuggling, so you won't find me in their fan club, either. But what has that got to do with this?'

'So you don't know?'

'No.'

'They're the owners of Norcraft. At least they're the majority shareholders. In other words, we're not dealing with little boys.'

'No, I can see that.'

Svenson had calmed down now. 'So what are you doing here actually?'

'Strictly speaking, that's none of your business. Else can tell you, if she feels like it. But the wind farm, you might say, is a sidetrack for me.'

He turned to her, unsure of himself now.

She said: 'We can talk about it later. Right now we've got more important things to think about.'

He hesitated for a moment. Then he nodded. 'OK, of course we have!'

As if at a signal they turned towards the boat.

'More important?' I said in a low voice.

She craned her head round and sent me a dirty look: 'Yes!'

'OK,' I mumbled, watching them until they were on board again and moving towards Ole, who was clearly waiting for a report on our brief exchange of opinions on the windblown quayside.

I strolled back to the fishermen's cabins. As I rounded the bend Kristine Rørdal came out in a worn leather jacket over the same blue trousers she had been wearing earlier in the day. In my view, she didn't look at all like a preacher's wife should. The wind caught her chestnut-brown hair, and she flicked her head to free her eyes.

She stopped for a moment. 'Find it?'

'Yes, thanks. And I met your husband there.'

'Lars? Yes, he often goes there – to consult the Lord, as he says,' she said without a trace of irony in her voice.

'And you?'

'Sometimes I accompany him. When things are quiet here. And they often are.'

'And whom do you consult?'

She sent me a cool look. 'I'm keeping that to myself.' Then she walked on. 'I'm off to see Ole.'

I nodded towards the black Audi. 'More guests?'

'Yes. Anyone would think it was peak season.'

For a moment I wondered whether to pop my head into the reception-cum-café to see if anyone was there, but I dropped the idea. Instead I went up to my room to make some telephone calls, the first to Ranveig Mæland.

She sounded anxious. 'Anything new?'

'No, I'm afraid not. Nor with you, I can hear.'

'Nothing. Not a peep from anyone. Not even from the children.'

'Else's here, and Kristoffer's probably coming tomorrow.'

'Else?'

'With Ole Rørdal, amongst others.'

'To demonstrate?'

'Looks that way.'

'Goodness me! It's got that far.'

'Yes.'

'And you …'

'I'll stay here in case Mons shows up. He might have needed space to think. And he was lying low for strategic reasons.'

'Strategic? With respect to … ?'

'Well, I was thinking of what's going to happen tomorrow. The survey. The meeting afterwards. What were you thinking of?'

'Well, he could have told me, couldn't he?'

'That wouldn't have been unnatural.'

'So, we're as far as we were before.'

'No further anyway.'

'Well … Keep going, Varg. If we're lucky he'll turn up tomorrow. If he doesn't I don't know what I'll do.'

'If he doesn't, my advice would be to go to the police. Then they'll have to organise a search. I can't do that.'

'Yes, I understand. But thank you for everything you've done.'

'Not much to thank me for, if I say so myself …'

We said our goodbyes and I rang off.

Karin had just arrived home when I phoned her. Her voice was bright and cheerful. 'Hi! How's it going?'

'Nice place. We should think about coming here for a weekend ourselves when all this is over. If the food's good, that is. I haven't checked that out yet. Only the waffles.'

'And Mons?'

'Nothing, unfortunately. I've just spoken to Ranveig. Nothing new here, nothing new there.'

'What do you reckon then?'

'I don't have a good feeling. I doubt a man like Mons Mæland could have kept his hands off his phone for several days, however underground he was supposed to be for business reasons.'

'Business … what do you mean?'

'I mean that with the opponents he's got over this issue, if he really has had a change of heart about the wind farm, then he could have decided to lie low so as not to be exposed to inappropriate pressures.'

'And by that you mean … ?'

'Everything from financial incentives … to other methods.'

'That sounds serious.'

'This is no bloody Sunday School outing, that's for sure. Even if he does seem to have God on his side.'

'God?'

'I told her about Lars Rørdal and the huge cross, and she replied: 'My goodness, Varg. You're in the African bush. Make sure you don't get converted while you're there.'

'Bit more's required for that, I'm afraid.'

'OK …'

I finished by promising to keep her posted on any new developments, and we rang off. I went to the window and stood gazing across Brennøy Sound to the land beyond. The closest islands were smooth and hilly as though it was still only a short time since the great ice sheets scoured their way past. Further away, the mountains rose like breakers in the sea, towards Masfjorden and the Stølsheimen mountain plateau, and in the north I had the Gulen transmitter on top of Brosviksåta as the clearest landmark, visible all the way from Bergen if you stood on the right peaks.

Down on the quay I saw Kristine Rørdal in conversation with her son. Else and Stein Svenson were on the sidelines, slightly apart from them, and the black Audi kept watch on them all, like a panther ready to spring, a hitherto unknown danger.

12

There were far fewer people in the dining room than I had anticipated. My dinner was served in solitary majesty next to the panoramic window overlooking the sound. Kristine Rørdal had changed into a flowery dress, small red-and-white blooms on a black background, an outfit that revealed many more of her generous curves than the one she had been wearing earlier in the day.

Without my asking, I was given a small hors d'oeuvre: parboiled potato slices with capelin roe, sour cream and herbs. When she enquired whether I wanted anything to drink with my food I allowed myself to be tempted by half a bottle of red wine.

'So you serve alcohol?' I asked when she brought me a glass and poured.

'After six.'

'What does your husband say to that?'

'I run the business.'

'See no evil, hear no evil, speak no evil?'

She flashed a smile. 'The figures are there for all to see. Had it not been for the summer season, then …'

Her figure was there for all to see as well as she plied to and fro between the kitchen and the table. The fish dish she brought brimmed over with delicacies: at least three kinds of fish, shrimps, mussels, herbs, vegetables and a sauce that tasted out of this world.

'And where are all the other guests?'

'There aren't so many. Ole and his group are making their own food. They've moved into one of the cabins.'

'And the owner of the black Audi?'

'He'd eaten in Bergen, he said.'

'And his name is … ?'

She looked at me in surprise. 'I couldn't possibly pass on that information.'

'No?'

'No. We have certain principles.'

'Yeah, well, principles are there to be broken.'

'Not mine,' she said, slightly flushed, then retreated into the kitchen area.

I concentrated on the fish. After a while she returned and asked whether I liked the meal.

'It's the best fish casserole I've had for a long time.'

'Thank you …'

'So Ole and his crowd are ready for the fray tomorrow?'

'Yes, I suppose they are.' She sighed. 'It ought to be a good cause that everyone could agree on.'

'The wind farm?'

'Yes, that's the type of energy we all want. Instead of all the CO_2 we're spewing out into the atmosphere every single day.'

'Mm, I agree. But in a country with such a long coastline as ours, wouldn't it be better to invest in wave power?'

'They've tried that.'

'It was a half-hearted effort in Øygarden, and it wasn't properly thought through. But I hope they're still working on new versions. If you want my opinion, I'd prefer to invest in wave rather than wind power. In this I'm actually on your son's side. And your husband's, for that matter, although for different reasons.'

'Well, I take more of a regional politics stand here. It's important that things happen outside the big towns.'

'Yes, of course …'

She left me long enough to finish my meal in peace and quiet. Then she re-appeared. 'Coffee?'

'Yes, please.'

'Anything with it?'

'What have you got?'

'The selection isn't immense, but the usuals: Cognac, liqueur …'

'I have to admit you really push the boat out in chapel land.'

'Seminar participants expect it.'

'And Mammon wants his cut. Isn't that so?'

'From us all, doesn't he. You must get paid for what you do as well?'

'Yes, just about.'

She chuckled in a disarming way. 'OK, what's it to be?'

'You don't have any aquavit, do you?'

'Only Løiten Linje.'

'Then I'll have that, please.'

When she returned with the coffee and aquavit, I asked: 'And your husband … Doesn't he have dinner?'

'Not here. We live over there.' She nodded towards Byrknesøy. 'I eat afterwards. Alone.'

'That sounds sad.'

'That's the way it is. When there are guests I have to sleep here.'

'Where?'

'I've got a room upstairs.' She indicated the mezzanine. 'Safety regulations.'

'Even if there's only one guest?'

She nodded.

'Such as Mons Mæland, for example?'

This time her face went scarlet. 'What on earth are you talking about? I sincerely hope you're not suggesting that … that …' She searched for words.

'No, no, no, I didn't mean it like that. I just meant …' I beat a hasty retreat. 'What I said … a single guest.'

Her cheeks still red, she subjected me to a cool stare. 'Those are the rules.' Then she turned on her heel and left.

I slowly drank my coffee and ordered another aquavit. After the second glass I thanked her and went back to my room. She wished me a measured 'good night' from behind the reception desk. I spent the rest of the evening in front of the television screen and over a novel of the uncomplicated kind. Two unexplained murders and a detective who drank. Home from home.

I slept dreamlessly until I woke with a start. Something had roused me, but I didn't know what. A sound, something.

I looked around. It took me a second or two to remember where I was. Then I whipped the duvet aside and swung my feet out. The floor was cold underfoot. I looked at the door. No one. I turned my gaze to the window, which I had left open before I went to bed.

Now I could hear it. Loud voices, which soon afterwards were lowered.

I walked to the window, leaned over and looked out. It was dark outside. I couldn't see anyone. I read the time under the TV set: 02.30.

I opened the window latch a bit further and leaned out. On the quay I glimpsed two people gesticulating furiously. They were Ole Rørdal and Stein Svenson. Then a third person appeared. Else Mæland. She strode between them, as if to pacify them, successfully it seemed. They continued to discuss, but with less arm-waving, and after a while the two fighting cocks disengaged. Else stayed with Ole while Stein made for the boat, grabbed the railing at the side and swung himself on board. Then he pointed peremptorily to the fishermen's cabins and afterwards to the cockpit. His body language was unmistakeable: *Go to bed and I'll stay here.*

I quickly moved away from the window and stood back while Else and Ole walked by underneath in heated conversation. As they passed Ole's voice penetrated the night: 'We're not terrorists for Christ's sake!' Then the voices faded. I leaned forward and watched them for as long as I could.

When they had gone I stood for a while gazing at the quay and the moored boat. All of a sudden I noticed a movement in the narrow passage between two of the fishermen's cabins. I leaned forward a bit further. Now I could see him clearly. He was a big, powerfully built man. It was hard to make out his facial features in the darkness, but there was no doubt he had his eye on the boat, as though expecting something to happen.

We both stood like that for close on ten minutes, me set back from the window, expectant, him in silhouette, like a wax doll, with the white boat in the background. Then he slowly slid back into the passage. Immediately afterwards I heard the low creak of a door being quietly closed. Only then did I come away from the window.

Nevertheless it was more like twenty minutes before I crawled back into bed. I wasn't able to sleep anyway, not until it began to lighten in the east, over the mountains in Masfjorden, and then it was much too late. The night shrank to nothing, and I dragged myself up in the morning, as hesitantly as a tardy butterfly, unprepared for September, the month when summer is definitively over and implacable autumn awaits on the horizon.

13

There were only two of us for breakfast, and we sat on opposite sides of the room, as silent as the wallpaper. I had nodded to the well-built man sitting at a table next to reception when I entered. He had nodded back, but said nothing.

Kristine Rørdal had set out a simple breakfast buffet, but still had to replenish it with a couple of extra fried eggs for me after the other guest had taken all of those in the tray. He was in the process of demolishing an impressive spread: a pile of bread, eggs, bacon and bean stew plus two or three big glasses of milk, a couple of cups of coffee and a sliced grapefruit. But then, judging by his size, he must have weighed around a hundred kilos, which were well distributed over the fit-looking body; he had broad shoulders, supple thighs and two hands no one would want to be on the receiving end of, not even to shake politely.

As for me, I stayed constant to my regular four slices of bread and partook of some herring in tomato sauce, pepper mackerel, ham and marmalade, as well as the two fried eggs Kristine brought to my table and served personally to ensure they didn't also disappear down the primordial void. She was wearing the same dress as the previous evening, but looked freshly showered and sprightly, as if she'd had a good night's sleep, all alone in her bed.

'When are you expecting the main influx?' I asked.

'They've reserved a conference room from two o'clock, so I suppose they'll do the on-site survey first.'

'Ole and the others … they couldn't even be tempted by breakfast?'

She didn't answer, just gently shook her head and returned whence she had come.

The other guest sat at his table eating, immense and self-assured.

His gaze was turned inward, almost meditative, and there was a tiny smile playing around his lips, as if what he saw inside his skull was all bright lights and laughter. I allowed the occasional glance to stray in his direction. I was fairly certain he was the man I had observed from my window last night. If I had seen him more clearly it is unlikely I would have been left in any doubt, for his appearance was quite striking. There were two pronounced clefts in his large face: one in the middle of his chin and one between his eyebrows. His hair was cropped short, dark blond, and he was dressed like a Secret Service man, in a dark-grey, made-to-measure suit with a jacket full enough to conceal a weapon in a shoulder holster. His clothing was not very well chosen if he was here to take part in the survey. However, the black, ankle-high military boots with sturdy soles were more suitable for such activities.

He didn't hang around nursing the last cup of coffee. As soon as he had finished breakfast, he demonstratively pushed away his plate, heaved himself up, gave a brief nod and left the room at a controlled tempo, quick and efficient, without a word of thanks to Kristine. I met her eyes across the desk and we were both thinking the same, it seemed.

'Nice chap,' I said.

'Not one of the chattiest,' she answered.

'What was his name again, did you say?'

She sent me an indulgent smile, shook her head and returned to what she was doing.

I sat over my cup of coffee and said no more. A short time afterwards she brought me the latest edition of *Bergens Tidende* and showed me the front page.

Fight over Turbines in Gulen, one of the headlines read. The opening paragraph explained that demonstrations were expected during the planned inspection of Brennøy in Gulen today, and the newspaper quoted both Deputy Chairman Jarle Glosvik of Gulen District Council and Ole Rørdal of NmV, who made diametrically opposed statements, which came as no surprise to me, or indeed anyone else, I supposed.

I said nothing to Kristine about what I had heard during the night, but did ask gently whether it was her impression that Stein Svenson and her son were not entirely of one mind, either. She shrugged.

I finished reading the newspaper. Before going back to my room I strolled down to the harbour. Another boat had arrived early that morning, a medium-sized fishing smack with fifteen to twenty young people on board, colourfully dressed with hair of varying lengths and hues, some men with beards, an entourage undoubtedly destined to join NmV and Ole Rørdal in the fight against the wind farm. Ole was already in full flow explaining the situation to them. He pointed northwards and gesticulated in a way that left no one in any doubt. Else Mæland was among the others, easy to spot in her red anorak. I couldn't see Stein Svenson anywhere.

I spent the next couple of hours in my room. This wasn't one of my best days as a private investigator. Finally, at twelve, something started to happen. The demonstrators had already gathered on the quay. They had produced posters and banners from nowhere and were ready to meet the assembled world press with their opinions on the matter. *Renewable energy? Not at any price! NO to power lines across the country! Preserve the coastal landscape! Wind power is a loss-maker, both economically and ecologically!* were some of the slogans.

Ole Rørdal held a portable PA system over one shoulder and stood with a microphone in one hand. Else Mæland shifted around restlessly, her eyes alternately jumping from her watch to the bridge over Byrknesøy Sound. Stein Svenson was still nowhere to be seen. At one point I saw Ole call Else over. He asked her about something, but she splayed her hands to signal she didn't know. He pointed to the bridge, but she shook her head.

If nothing else, we were lucky with the weather: intermittent cloud with the odd patch of sun over the greyish-blue water, and the temperature had risen since the previous day. Just a few sudden gusts of wind spoiled the picture, as if the weather gods hadn't quite made up their minds about when to usher in the next blast.

The official participants of the survey arrived in a mini-procession, judging by the assembled column from the ferry in Skipavik. At the front was a big, grey Toyota Rav4, behind it a black Mercedes, a VW minibus, a white Ford Mondeo and bringing up the rear a Volvo 850 estate, white with a red speed stripe and POLITI in large, dark-blue letters on both sides. As if in a rehearsed formation, they all turned into the car park beside the vehicles already parked there, among them my Corolla, the black Audi and the battered Opel Kadett from the day before. It was a collection of cars that would have had a second-hand car salesman rubbing his hands with undisguised glee. Personally, I was more interested in who got out of them.

For a moment or two it was hard to grasp what was happening. I recognised a casually dressed Kristoffer Mæland as he stepped out of the mid-size Toyota SUV. He strode around the vehicle to where an elegant woman in leisure attire had effortlessly swung her legs out onto the ground. They exchanged a few words, and with swift professional ease she took stock of the situation.

The four doors of the black Mercedes opened and out popped four youthful men with clean-shaven faces, and also in new leisurewear, as if this were an après-ski gathering they had been invited to and not an inspection of the exposed westernmost Vestland coast. I guessed that this was the Norcraft delegation with Erik Utne at the head.

There was something more congenial about the big blue Puffa jacket and brown trousers of the man getting out of the minibus with a couple of other people kitted out in practical clothing. I recognised him as the Jarle Glosvik from the newspaper article I had read that morning. I thought I also recognised the tall, sparsely haired man getting out of the white Mondeo. It was Johannes Bringeland, a business lawyer from the middle stratum of Bergen society.

Glosvik looked around and then nodded quickly in my direction before turning to his travelling companions. For a moment I wondered whether he had nodded to me, but when I took a discreet peek to the side I saw the immense guy from the breakfast room had also come outside and was leaning against the wall by the entrance to reception. Right, OK, and I made a mental note. Jarle Glosvik and What's-His-Face.

Two uniformed officers stepped out of the police car. They quickly took their bearings and then focussed their attention on the demonstrators by the two boats in the harbour. Like a delayed rear-guard, five minutes after the others, the sole press representatives made an appearance, a female journalist and a male photographer in an unwashed white Mazda, which, according to the logo on the door, belonged to a local Nordhordland newspaper, *Strilen*.

After spotting me, Kristoffer crossed the square. 'Veum ... any news on my father?'

'I'm afraid not, no. If he doesn't turn up here, I've recommended your ... that is, Ranveig ... should go to the police.'

With a serious expression, he said: 'I don't understand why she hasn't already done that.'

'I imagine she was also hoping he would turn up.'

He scanned the crowd. He pressed his lips together when he read the text of the demonstrators' banner and saw his sister on the quay. But he made no comment.

The woman with whom he arrived came over to us, accompanied by the four young men. Kristoffer Mæland said perfunctorily: 'This is Veum. He's making some investigations for us regarding my father's disappearance. I think I told you about it.'

The woman held out her hand. 'Stine Sagvåg. District Manager of TWO.' She was around forty, had a narrow face and short, auburn hair with grey streaks, unless it was vice versa. 'We're all concerned about Mæland. Is there any news?' She looked me in the eye.

'Not yet, I'm afraid.'

There was a resigned set to her face and she twisted to the side as if disappointed that yet another person had not done their job. Then I was introduced to Erik Utne and his three henchmen, all with the same polished appearance I had noticed when they stepped out of the car. They reminded me of estate agents, the smoothest variety, so anonymous that it was hard to tell them apart, however high up in the pecking order they were.

Jarle Glosvik joined us. He introduced his retinue as representatives of two of the coalition parties on the local council, before suddenly turning to Bringeland and asking: 'And who are you?'

Bringeland nodded to me. I already knew him. 'Johannes Bringeland, of the law firm Bringeland & Kleve. I represent Stein Svenson.'

'What?' barked Jarle Glosvik. 'In what capacity if I might ask?'

'On behalf of the family.'

'Which family?' Kristoffer Mæland asked.

Johannes Bringeland lapped up all the attention for a second or two. Then he gave a formal cough. 'Stein Svenson's paternal grandfather was related to Per Nordbø, from whom, in 1988, Mæland Real Estate, in the person of Mons Mæland, bought the land in the north of Brennøy. We will launch a legal investigation into all the circumstances surrounding such sale.'

The Deputy Chairman's face reddened. 'Related to! How close was the relationship?'

'They were cousins.'

'And why didn't you take this up earlier?' Glosvik demanded.

'It has not been relevant hitherto,' Bringeland said with the natural arrogance he shared with so many of his professional brethren.

'Not relevant!'

'It's only now that we have become aware of the realities of the matter.'

'And who is this Stein Svenson if I might be so bold?'

It was a good question, and even Johannes Bringeland lost his composure when he looked around and was unable to see his client anywhere.

Kristoffer Mæland shouted over to what he assumed was the enemy camp: 'Else! Is Stein Svenson over there?'

General unrest broke out, and everyone looked around nervously until the answer came back: 'We haven't seen him today. We don't know where he is!'

'Another disappearance?' Kristoffer muttered, looking at me.

'He was here yesterday – last night,' I said, then it struck me that there was another person missing: the Lord's very own trumpet-blowing angel from the entrance to the fjord, Lars Rørdal.

I peered over at the hotel. The man from breakfast had gravitated closer to us without anyone noticing him. Behind him Kristine Rørdal had emerged from reception. She was standing with a concerned expression in her eyes, scanning the gathering.

Stine Sagvåg checked her watch impatiently. 'Well, what are we waiting for? We're already behind schedule. It's twelve thirty-five.'

Kristoffer Mæland raised his hand. 'I'll show you the way. Follow me.'

From the demonstrators came loud boos, and the photographer from *Strilen* already had his camera out. The two police officers took up a position between us and the demonstrators, and gestured to them to keep their distance.

'There's such a thing as freedom of speech in this country!' shouted one of the youths.

'You can speak as much as you like, provided you follow our instructions,' said one of the officers, a tall man with fair hair and red cheeks. 'You follow us and keep to the rear. Can we agree on that?'

Ole Rørdal went to the front of his battle ranks. 'Yes, we agree to that. But that's all we'll agree to.'

Then the crowd moved off. Kristoffer Mæland led the way towards the chapel, and we others followed. Erik Utne and his colleagues joined Stine Sagvåg. Next came Jarle Glosvik and the two from the local council. I ended up alongside Johannes Bringeland.

'What brings you here, Veum?' he asked, brimming with curiosity.

'I'm on a job.'

'You, too?'

'Yes, but … it concerns Mons Mæland. He's gone missing.'

'I see! And you, as it were, have to find him?'

'That's what I've been asked to do, anyway.'

'But why the hell don't they contact the police?' As he didn't receive a response, he added, with a little chuckle: 'Bad conscience perhaps?'

I arched an eyebrow.

'Yes, as I said down there … the purchase of the property was highly dubious. Per Nordbø wasn't *compos mentis* when he signed the contract.'

'Mm … I suppose there were witnesses?'

'Yes, yes, of course. The Chief of Police in Lindås was one of them.'

'The Chief of Police in … And his name was … ?'

'Brekkhus, at that time. And there was a nurse in the ward where he was. Gunvor Matre. I'll have to speak to both of them.'

'I've met Brekkhus.'

'Yes? Trustworthy type, is he?'

'Well, I would like to think so.'

We passed the chapel, and I cast a glance at the small, red house on the opposite side of the path. Today none of the curtains stirred and no one was peering out. Then we were on our way into the woods.

I strained forward to see. This was a singular collection of people, the sort you would generally expect to meet in far more urban sur-roundings than here by a fjord. I turned round and looked back. The man from breakfast was at the rear of our group. He didn't meet my gaze; he was staring intently ahead as if to ensure nothing unexpected would happen. Who on earth was he, and what was he doing here?

Right behind him came the two police officers, and behind them a wagging tail of demonstrators with banners and posters flapping in the wind. The little photographer from *Strilen*, with the blue cap and worn, brown leather jacket was running back and forth down both flanks, snapping away furiously. I noticed that the man behind us averted his face whenever the camera came close.

The female journalist had, for the time being, attached herself to the local politicians and, judging by her face, I surmised she was asking a lot of questions to which she was not getting satisfactory answers. Jarle Glosvik turned his back on her several times and looked behind him as though searching for someone to take over, but it was doubtful Gulen had a budget for a press officer, and he was adept at avoiding the eyes of the man from breakfast, a bit too adept in my view.

We had now reached open countryside again and our advance came to a sudden halt. In front of us we could hear loud, inarticulate shouts and a dark-clad figure with white hair was running at full tilt towards us over the smooth rocks, screaming something or other we couldn't decipher. It was Lars Rørdal.

I stepped out of the procession and had made my way to the front of the column by the time Rørdal stopped in front of Kristoffer Mæland, Stine Sagvåg and Erik Utne. His face was distorted into a terrified grimace, and his eyes wandered from one to the other until they stopped at Kristoffer Mæland.

'Blasphemy! It's the devil's work,' he groaned. 'They've hung him on the cross! He's been crucified, like God's only begotten son ... Crucified!'

Then he rolled his eyes and collapsed on the ground in front of us. Erik Utne and one of his companions jumped forward to help him up as Kristoffer Mæland turned to the rest of us and asked in a tone of disbelief: 'What did he say? Crucified?'

Before anyone had time to reflect I was on my way over the rocks to the towering cross. Behind me I heard someone shout, but I took no notice. A couple of times I almost fell, but managed to steady myself and when I raised my eyes I saw that he was right. There was a man hanging from the cross with his arms stretched out like a reincarnation of Jesus of Nazareth.

I jogged the last part at a slower pace, as though to postpone the inevitable. Behind me I could hear heavy footfalls. I glanced over my shoulder. One of the two police officers and Kristoffer Mæland were following me.

We arrived at the cross at about the same time, but had to walk round to see who it was. He had been tied to the horizontal bar, fully clothed. His head hung forward, his face deathly pale, a blue tongue protruding from his mouth, like an overfed scavenger caught in the act. The vacant eyes told us unequivocally that he was dead.

But it was not Stein Svenson, as I had at first anticipated.

'Oh, God!' Kristoffer Mæland said with feeling, before turning away and stooping to retch.

'Do you know him?' the officer asked softly.

I met his eyes and nodded. 'Not personally, but I know who it is.'

I recognised him from the photo in the brochure I had been given. It was Mons Mæland.

14

There was mayhem for a while. The two police officers struggled to prevent the rest of the crowd from surging forward, and had to resort to shouting to enforce order.

'We'll have to cordon off the area,' yelled the smaller, darker-haired and less flushed of the two.

I stood beside Kristoffer Mæland, as if to offer a form of tentative consolation, but without contributing much of any value.

The taller of the two officers came over to me. 'That includes you.'

I nodded reluctantly and edged slowly across the closest rocks to the little plateau where the band of business people and demonstrators had become a gathering of shocked individuals and were now mingling freely. Lars Rørdal had got to his feet again. He stood in the background, pale and grubby, with his son, who didn't look that lively either. The only person who seemed unmoved was the man from breakfast. He towered over the others, his stony face staring intently at the cross, as though making sure he didn't miss any of what was going on.

Jarle Glosvik was at the front with Erik Utne. 'What's happened? Who is it?' he asked when I joined them.

'Impossible to say,' I answered.

I searched for Else Mæland and spotted her with some of the young demonstrators. Pallid, she met my eyes. I took a few steps towards her and beckoned. An expression of foreboding crossed her face. She walked unsteadily towards me. When she was in front of me she looked me in the eye without speaking.

I spoke in a low voice. 'I'm sorry, Else, but ... it's your father.'

Her face turned ashen. Then the tears flowed, and an inarticulate gasp escaped her mouth. She moved closer to me, and automatically I wrapped her in my arms and held her tight.

Now Ole Rørdal was ploughing a channel through the crowd. On reaching me, he made as if he wanted to take responsibility for her, but I held her close to me. She was trembling against my chest, and from deep in her body came a painful sob, a harbinger of the storm that was to erupt.

Ole placed a hand on her shoulder and eyed me stiffly. His black beard quivered. 'My father told me it's… Mæland.'

I nodded. 'And where the hell's Stein Svenson?'

He pinched his lips together, then answered: 'You don't mean to say that … that Stein …?'

'I overheard your quarrel last night, Ole. You and him. "We're not terrorists for Christ's sake," you said.' He opened his mouth in protest, but I carried on: 'Was that what you were arguing about? Were these the means that Stein Svenson wanted to use?'

He seemed to be in shock. 'Are you crazy, Veum? What nonsense are you talking? That would be … That's murder, for Pete's sake! We don't get involved with that. We're a professional organisation employing the means a democratic society allows us to. And surely you don't think …?' His gaze passed from me to Else with a tenderness that had not been present before. She had quietened down in my arms, as though listening to what we were saying.

I whispered: 'So where is he then? Stein Svenson?'

He gesticulated wildly. 'How should I know? We fell out. That was all. He's probably gone home under his own steam.' He patted his inside pocket. 'I can try and call him.' Then he stopped himself. 'Afterwards.'

The taller of the two police officers spoke up. 'Listen up everyone. My name is Karl Sætenes. My colleague here, Constable Haus, will keep watch here. The rest of us are going back to Naustvik. We've already been in touch with the Chief of Police, and he's summoned reinforcements from Bergen Police Station. No one may leave the island before the detectives arrive.'

Erik Utne instantly protested. 'What! But we've got return tickets to Oslo. The plane goes at …'

The policeman interrupted him. 'No one's leaving this island, I said!' and added in a less domineering tone: 'They're coming as fast as they can.'

Else broke away from me and burst out: 'I want to see him!'

The policeman studied her unsympathetically. 'I'm afraid that's not ...'

'It's her father!' I said.

He looked at me. 'But this is a crime scene. I can't let ...'

'Look, I'm an investigator myself. Private, I'll admit, but ... if I accompany her there, she can see him and hopefully avoid nightmares and trauma later on. It would be impossible to disturb the crime scene any more than it already has been. Your colleague's there anyway. And he's keeping an eye on it.'

'Well ...' Then he gave in. 'Well, alright. But just you two,' he said and sent Ole Rørdal a dirty look.

With my hand on her back I steered her gently to the cross. 'It's not a pretty sight, Else,' I warned her.

'I want to see him. I have to!'

Her brother had straightened up and was standing there with Constable Haus. He looked pale and shaken and kept wiping the corners of his mouth with a folded handkerchief. When he saw his sister coming, his eyes moistened. 'Else,' he sighed. 'You shouldn't ...'

'Yes, I should!' she riposted, stepped forward, turned up her face and stared at her deceased father. Suddenly I felt a cold breath from the sea, as if it, too, was sighing at the grievous sight.

It struck me that there was something theatrical and artificial about the whole situation, like a stylised tableau in a church during Easter festivities. But there was only one Mary at the foot of the cross, and her name was Else.

Thank goodness he hadn't been nailed to the cross, and I was fairly sure that he had died before he was hung up. He was tied to the transverse beam with a long rope that was fastened round each wrist and then pulled down behind the cross and round his ankles to make his pose as Christ-like as possible.

I looked at Else. She was staring up at him with an expression of shock and disbelief on her face. Her lips moved mutely, in intense, quiet prayer and tears ran unchecked from both eyes. Her fists opened and closed several times before she turned abruptly, to the side, and whispered under her breath: 'Now I've seen him. But it's only a shell. That's not how he was. He's gone. For ever.'

'Else … come on!' Kristoffer came over, put his arms around her shoulders and pulled her to him.

They remained like that for some minutes. I glanced at Haus. We didn't have much to say to each other, either. In the end, Haus coughed. 'I think the others are on their way back now. Perhaps you should follow them.'

I nodded. 'Yes …' I looked at the two of them. 'Are you ready to go? Kristoffer? Else?'

They turned to face me, both of them, as if they had forgotten who I was and what I was doing there. Then they visibly pulled themselves together. They took a final glance at their father, both with a strange, childlike shyness in their eyes, as though embarrassed about an adult. Then they took a few faltering steps away from the eerie place with the towering cross, as though they found it hard to walk. I let them go ahead, and followed afterwards.

15

When we reached Naustvik the others had gathered in the café in the first cabin. The atmosphere was tense and angry. Many of the business people were already in touch with the outside world via their mobiles. Erik Utne had opened a laptop.

Constable Sætenes was doing his best to keep a lid on the situation. 'Listen up! It's important that no one passes on any information about what has happened here until the detectives from Bergen arrive. It's especially important that the media are not informed!'

'We're already here,' mumbled the *Strilen* journalist. 'My name's Anita Brekke, and this is Pål Anderson.' She pointed to the photographer.

'Yes, but you may be called in as witnesses,' Sætenes said. 'You'll have to wait until the detectives come before you report back.'

'We'll see about that,' said Anita Brekke, looking less than convinced.

'I'll hold you responsible!' Sætenes warned with a stern glare.

'Fine by me,' she responded through clenched teeth.

Kristine Rørdal held the fort at reception with an expression of horror and incredulity. Her husband sat on a chair behind her slumped over with his face in his hands. In his lap he held the same well-thumbed Bible he had shown me the day before, as though vainly searching for a word of consolation.

Else and Kristoffer mooched restlessly around reception.

I went over to them. 'I suppose we'd better let Ranveig know. Would either of you like to … ?'

Else stared blankly ahead of her, without reacting.

Kristoffer squirmed. 'Do you think you could … In a way it was your job. To find him.'

I sighed. 'Yes, but not like that. Perhaps I should ring someone I know who is a good friend of hers? I think it's important she should be given the news in an appropriate way.'

Kristoffer seemed grateful. 'That would be great, Veum. Please do that!' Then he turned away as though there was nothing more to say on the matter.

I looked at Else. 'Agreed?'

She nodded. 'Sure.'

I moved to one side and found a corner of space for myself. Then I rang Karin.

'Varg! Any news?'

'Yes, I'm afraid there is. I … He turned up. But he's dead.' I gave her a brief summary of what had happened.

'Crucified! Can that be right?'

'Yes, or tied to a cross anyway. But the message is obvious. No doubt about that.'

'Has Ranveig been informed?'

'No, that's why I was ringing you.'

I explained to her how Else and Kristoffer had reacted, and that they would be very grateful if someone else could give the news of Mons' death to Ranveig.

She took the request with composure. 'Of course. I'll go up to hers straightaway. I would guess she's at home.'

'Thanks. I'll keep you posted on what's going on out here.'

'But … It's murder, I assume, isn't it?'

'Definitely. It would be a spectacular way to commit suicide, but this is undoubtedly the very opposite. We're all being detained here until the police come.'

We hung up, I put my mobile phone in my pocket and looked around. Two groups had formed here as well: the young demonstrators in one corner of the room and those who had been going to participate in the survey in the other. At one table I saw Jarle Glosvik and the big man from breakfast in hushed conversation. Glosvik looked strained. The other man's eyes constantly swept around the room like a search-light beam.

Beside me, Kristoffer said: 'What a mess. God knows what's going to happen now.'

Stine Sagvåg came over to us, accompanied by a policeman. 'Can you confirm this, Kristoffer? It appears one of the leaders of the demo has disappeared. I'm trying to persuade Constable Sætenes here to get a search under way immediately.'

Sætenes' eyes flitted around and he looked very uncomfortable. 'I'm loathe to do anything until the team of detectives is here.'

Stine Sagvåg gave him a taste of her temperament. 'Yes, but there are ferry terminals he has to pass through. He must be arrested at once!'

'No one knows as yet whether he has anything to do with this.'

'In which case, it's important to have that confirmed or not.'

'He had a big row with Ole Rørdal last night,' I said. 'Perhaps we should subject *him* to closer scrutiny?'

Sætenes began to look a little desperate, but he turned round, found Ole Rørdal and called to him: 'Rørdal, could you come over here, please?'

Rørdal did as bidden, with a sullen expression. 'What's this about?'

'Did you do what we spoke about?' I asked.

He scowled at me. 'Do what?'

'Try and ring Stein Svenson?'

He nodded, put his hand in his pocket and demonstratively held the phone in front of him, as though it had its own story to tell. 'I tried. But he didn't answer.'

'Really?' I said impatiently. 'Was it the usual voicemail or was it switched off?'

After a pause he said: 'No, it was just the voicemail.'

I looked at Sætenes. 'Have you got the technology to trace a mobile phone?'

'Yes, we certainly have. But we have to wait …'

'Yes, yes, I know that. Until the detectives have arrived. Have you checked on board the boat?' I looked from Sætenes to Rørdal and back again.

Sætenes looked at Rørdal. 'Have you?'

'Have we? We've got other things on our bloody minds. If you ask me, Stein's already moping at home in Bergen. We disagreed about something yesterday, and he decided to go home.'

'And you're sure of that?' I said.

'He's certainly not here! Can *you* see him anywhere?'

'Shall we go down to the boat and check it over?'

'Fine by me!' he said, but he showed with all possible clarity that it would be a waste of time.

I looked at Sætenes.

'I'll come with you,' he said.

Before we left he cast a worried glance around as though expecting all hell to break loose if he wasn't there to keep the peace between the various factions. Ole Rørdal shook his head in desperation to underline the fact that he disclaimed all responsibility for whatever might happen.

We walked down to the quay. Rørdal put a foot on the boat to bring it closer to the shore so that we could step on board. Then he followed us, produced a key, opened the door to the cabin under the cockpit, stepped aside and bowed as a sign for us to enter.

We did as instructed. There weren't many places to hide. Two berths at the front of the bow, or three, depending on how well you knew each other, and a slim possibility of lying on the sofa bench down one side. The other was a kitchen worktop. We opened the cupboards at the bottom and top, but you would have had to be of a very compact build to get in there.

We soon emerged to face Ole Rørdal, who couldn't restrain himself. 'Anything? Did you find him?'

I pointed to the fishing boat. 'What about that?'

'What about it?' Rørdal snapped. 'It didn't get here until early this morning ...'

'So?'

He didn't answer.

'By which time Svenson had disappeared. Is that what you mean?'

We looked at him.

'When did you first miss him?'

'I don't miss him in the slightest, I can tell you that for nothing. He was gone when we woke up today. That's how it was. Long before the fishing boat docked.'

I looked around. My gaze fell on the abandoned fish hall or whatever it had been. Then I jumped back onto the quay and walked towards it.

'Veum?' Sætenes said. 'Where are you going?'

I continued walking. Something had told me it was not as it had been the day before. There was something about the door, the angle of the handle …

Before I tried to see if it was open I took out a handkerchief, placed it over the handle and pressed. The door was stuck in the frame, which had swollen after many years of inactivity, but there was no resistance. It wasn't locked.

I pushed it and slowly entered. Inside, there was one large room, empty except for some fixed workbenches under the windows along the opposite wall.

I looked down. There were clear tracks in the dust on the floor. Someone had been here recently. The tracks of something that had been dragged across the floor to a door at the very back of the room were unmistakeable.

Behind me, Sætenes had come in through the door. 'Found anything?'

'Come here.'

I opened the door at the back. It led into what had once been a changing room or something similar. There were metal lockers with keys dangling along the wall to the left and there was a low bench along the other.

On the floor in front of us, gagged and bound hand and foot with a noose around his neck, making it impossible for him to move, lay Stein Svenson.

I bent down and loosened the gag around his mouth. His eyes rolled around. A violent fit of coughing burst from his chest, and convulsions racked through his body. For a moment it appeared he was going to die in front of our very eyes.

I grabbed him and lifted his head off the floor.

'Stein!'

An ominous rattle came from his larynx.

'Svenson! Can you hear me?'

Sætenes had unfolded a penknife. 'Let me …' He quickly sawed through the thick ropes binding Svenson, and together we helped him to his feet.

Svenson opened his eyes and blurrily surveyed his surroundings. He gulped down air deep into his lungs. Half-conscious, he attempted a step forward.

'Careful you don't fall …'

'What the … !' I turned round. In the doorway behind us stood Ole Rørdal with a sombre expression on his face. When I met his gaze he threw out his arms. 'What on earth has happened?'

'Svenson's been gagged. Literally. But fortunately not for ever.'

Rørdal's face reddened. 'Do you need any more evidence now to show what the opposition get up to? The next time lives could be lost!'

I was about to say something, but was interrupted by a noise outside. We knew exactly what it was. The thwack-thwack of a helicopter approaching.

'Veum!' Sætenes said behind me. 'Give me a hand here.'

Together we supported Svenson across the floor and out of the building. Ole Rørdal walked in a curious state of apathy beside us. As we came to the quay we saw a helicopter hovering in the air above us. After making sure the landing area was safe the pilot waved his hand to tell us to keep well clear.

The helicopter's landing was as gentle as a caress, as precise as a pinprick. The rotor blades slowed and finally came to a rest, the engine was switched off, a side door was slid open and out jumped six officers from Bergen Police Station with Divisional Commander Jakob E. Hamre at the forefront.

The first person Hamre clapped his eyes on was me. He threw his arms in the air. 'Veum! You here as well? Will we never get any peace?'

'Not for the time being anyway,' I mumbled, so low that only those close by could hear.

16

I looked at Stein Svenson. 'What happened? How the hell did you end up in there?'

He looked at me, confused. 'I have no idea. I didn't even know where I was. Everything was black.' He rubbed the back of his head.

'Were you attacked?'

'The detectives will deal with this!' said Sætenes, beside me.

Hamre came over to us. His eyebrows were raised and he addressed Sætenes. 'Is he at it already?'

'Er … who?' Sætenes answered.

Hamre nodded towards me. 'Veum. He's on the repeat offenders list in Bergen.'

'Repeat offender? What do you mean! He told me he was a private investigator.'

'Yeah, yeah,' Hamre said genially. 'They give themselves so many names.' Curious, he examined Svenson. 'What happened to this fellow?'

'Apparently he doesn't even know himself,' Sætenes said.

'No?' Hamre's attention shifted. 'But we have more dramatic events to consider, don't we?'

'Yes. A murder.'

'A kind of crucifixion we've been informed.'

Sætenes nodded. 'Yes, that's correct. I'll bring you up to date with …'

'I can fill in,' I said.

'I don't doubt it,' Hamre said, but beckoned me to join them. 'Come on. Let's find somewhere to sit down.'

I nodded to the other police officers who had arrived by helicopter. Hamre had brought with him three of his best – newly promoted Inspector Bjarne Solheim with his colleagues Annemette Bergesen and

Atle Helleve – and two Crime Scene officers, Pedersen and Kvamme.

The sound of the helicopter had brought most people in the cabins to the windows or outside. We all walked towards them. Jarle Glosvik and the well-built man were still outside. Before entering, Hamre discreetly glanced at the muscular man, stopped and commented under his breath to me: 'What the hell's he doing here?'

'The beefcake? Do you know him?'

'Not personally, but we know who he is.'

'And that is …?'

'His name's Trond Tangenes. Comes from round Oslo. He's what people in refined circles call a debt collector. In the police we have another name. Has a background as a bodyguard in Norway, Africa and the Middle East.'

I nodded slowly. 'He has some kind of connection with Jarle Glosvik, the Deputy Chairman of Gulen District Council. The guy beside him.'

Hamre looked at me with his stony face. 'Interesting. Any more to report?'

'We can do it inside.'

'Oh, really, Veum? A formal briefing?'

In the large room, Hamre took charge. 'I'm Chief Superintendent Hamre and I'm responsible for investigating what has happened here. Now we just need to get a quick overview of the situation. Thereafter we will allocate tasks and get the show on the road.' With raised palms, he rejected the first questions from the gathering. 'Everyone will get their chance, one by one. Have a cup of coffee while you're waiting. We'll soon be ready.'

He turned to grey-faced Kristine Rørdal, who was at the reception desk. 'Is there a room where we can be private?'

She pointed to the stairs. 'We've got an office up there.'

Hamre nodded. 'Veum, Sætenes, Solheim, Annemette: come with me. You two, as well.' He indicated Pedersen and Kvamme. 'Atle: take charge of the situation here. Try to get some sense of who's who and allocate them to officers accordingly.' Finally, he focussed on Svenson. 'Can anyone take care of this gentleman?'

Two of the young girls from the demonstrators' group put up their hands. 'We can see what we can do.'

'Right. Excellent. But he mustn't talk to anyone before he talks to us,' he said, sending them a stern glance. 'Not about what has happened at any rate,' he added in a gentler voice after he saw their frightened reaction.

I noticed Ole Rørdal make for Else to explain what had gone on. For most of the others, Stein Svenson was an unknown quantity. Stine Sagvåg stood with a pensive furrow between her eyebrows. Erik Utne and his companions looked impatient and restless. Jarle Glosvik was chatting with his allies from the Council, and Trond Tangenes was keeping an eye on proceedings with never-resting eyes, conspicuously alert compared with his large body.

Johannes Bringeland came over to us. 'I'm Svenson's solicitor.'

'Does he need one already?' Hamre commented acidly. He made for the stairs to the mezzanine. 'Veum … the briefing. It's more populated here than in Bangladesh on a festival day. I can hardly see the sun for locals.'

Bringeland remained downstairs with a miffed expression on his face. Then he turned and said something to Kristine, so low it was impossible to hear.

As soon as we were installed in the office I started talking. Hamre listened attentively. Now and then he asked a question, and he made some notes in a little book he was holding in his hand. At the end he said: 'A crucifixion. Well, I'm damned. It's the first time in a long and dubious career. But I suppose it had to happen at some time. After all, the other side burns churches. But I note there've been huge disagreements about the planned wind farm here. The deceased Mons Mæland was on the developers' side, but he may have been about to change his mind.'

'He did change his mind,' I interrupted.

'We'd like to have that confirmed by those directly involved, Veum. But this gives us two groups of suspects. On the one hand, we have those who are against the developers and might be considered likely to manifest their opposition in such a drastic way as this. Or perhaps they thought by taking Mæland's life they would defer the decision – and in fact they have definitely achieved that. And on the other, those who were behind the wind farm and were making plans, but who were less than pleased that Mæland had had a change of heart and could therefore put a spoke in their wheel. But it's rare for Norwegian businesses to go to such extremes.'

'TWO sails under a foreign flag now and can no longer be regarded as Norwegian, strictly speaking,' I said.

'TWO?'

'Trans World Ocean, represented by Stine Sagvåg down there.' I pointed to the main room.

Hamre made a note of this before going on. 'What about these demonstrators? You say you heard some of them discussing actions one referred to as terror …'

'Well, he said: "We're not terrorists!" And the person these objections were addressed to was Stein Svenson, whom we found gagged and bound, very professionally I might add, just a short time ago. What I forgot to say by the way was this: I'm not the only one who heard this exchange of views. Trond Tangenes did, too.'

'You mean that the person who attacked Svenson and put him out of circulation for a while could have been Tangenes?'

'It's a possibility, yes.'

'But the terrorist action was carried out.'

'If that was what they had been talking about, yes. I doubt it though. Mæland's own daughter is one of the demonstrators. She would never have given her consent to something like that, not even as a proposal, that's obvious. And she was present at the row. There were just the three of them: Svenson, Ole Rørdal and her.'

'Plus you two eavesdroppers,' Hamre said, before turning his attention to his colleagues. 'Kvamme and Pedersen: you get off to the crime scene. There's an ambulance on the way to take the deceased to the Pathology Unit. We'll make a start on the interviews downstairs. It could be a long, drawn-out affair. We should probably requisition one of the cabins so that we can have separate conversations; stop any ear-wigging. If anyone's of interest we'll take them to Bergen. Questions?'

None of them appeared to have any. Sætenes was visibly relieved that the responsibility was out of his hands.

'And me?' I said.

Hamre surveyed me from under heavy eyelids. 'You? You can go home. My understanding was your task was to find Mons Mæland. Now he's appeared without any help from you, so we'll take over from here.'

'Have you contacted his wife?'

Hamre looked at Annemette Bergsen, who said: 'No, not yet.'

'I have a girlfriend who knows her well. She said she could do it.'

'Have you got a girlfriend, Veum?' Hamre asked.

I ignored him. 'They're old friends. It's OK if I visit her as well, I take it?'

'Yes, you should write a report though. About the successful outcome, I mean.'

The other policemen had stood up and were itching to get started. Hamre slowly rose to his feet. 'If we need anything else from you, Veum, we'll be in touch. Don't ring us, we'll ... so to speak.'

We went back downstairs. Pedersen and Kvamme were given directions to the crime scene by Sætenes. Helleve appeared with a list of all those present, divided up into several groups over many sheets of paper torn from his pad. Hamre allocated tasks, and they began to take people aside. I noticed that Hamre went over to Trond Tangenes. That was a conversation I would have loved to hear. So far, I hadn't heard him utter a word.

I joined Svenson, who was sitting on a chair surrounded by a group of young demonstrators and Bringeland, his solicitor. 'How's it going?'

Bringeland nodded. 'He's recovering. This just shows how important this case is, Veum.'

'Yes, have either of you got a theory about who could be behind this?'

'We interpret it as a warning. If you take this case any further, etc. ...'

'And who could have carried out the attack?'

Bringeland glanced across the room at Trond Tangenes. 'We can all see whom the opposition have on their team.'

'You know Tangenes, too, do you?'

'He was involved in a case I took on some years ago. I don't know if you've noticed the person he's been in conversation with?'

'Jarle Glosvik.'

Bringeland nodded pointedly. 'Exactly. And that man not only has political interests in the development, but commercial ones too.'

'A company?'

'For example.'

I turned to Svenson. 'And you still don't remember anything?'

Gingerly, he shook his head.

'You have no idea who hit you?'

'No ...'

'How did it happen?'

'Don't remember diddly. The last thing I did was clamber on board the boat.'

'He's very shaken up,' Bringeland said. 'But a doctor's supposed to be on the way.'

I watched Svenson. His eyes flickered, but that wasn't so strange. He was probably dizzy as well. 'I may contact you again.'

Bringeland wasn't pleased. 'For what reason, might I ask?'

'Well, I just have this congenital tendency, Bringeland. I'm so damned inquisitive, and when things like this happen in my immediate vicinity I have to find out why.'

'Leave that to his solicitor, Veum.'

'Is that cheaper? For him, I mean.'

He smiled patronisingly. 'So ... what happens now?'

'All of you will be questioned by the police, every single one of you. As for me, I'm heading home.'

'Oh? Aren't you going to be questioned?'

'I've already told the Boy Scouts everything I know. And they've got my telephone number.'

I said goodbye and left. After going to fetch the little baggage I had, I returned to reception, flashed my bank card and said to Kristine: 'I've been told to check out.'

She nodded lethargically and wrote out the bill. After I had paid she whispered: 'This is the worst thing I've ever experienced. And Mons, of all people. I sincerely hope you find out who did it …'

I cast a final glance at all the people there. In one corner of the room sat her husband talking to Atle Helleve. In another, Bjarne Solheim was talking to her son, and Annemette Bergesen was on her way upstairs to the mezzanine floor with Erik Utne. Jarle Glosvik was pacing to and fro by the window with the view of Byrknesøy. The others sat in impatient clusters, waiting for their turn. I couldn't see Hamre or Tangenes anywhere.

I thanked her for the stay. She put on a sad smile in return.

As I was leaving, Stine Sagvåg caught up with me. 'Veum?'

'Yes?'

'I'd like to have a word with you.'

'Now?'

'No, not here. Where can I get hold of you?'

I put my hand in my inside pocket, tugged out my wallet and gave her one of my business cards. 'You'll find me here, at one of these numbers. The surest option is my mobile.'

She took a quick peek at the card. 'You'll be hearing from me.'

'Look forward to it,' I said, wondering what this word would be about.

I walked out to my car and drove over all the bridges back to Skipavik, where the ferry was arriving and I was able to drive straight on. From the deck I stood taking in the beautiful view: the industrial plant at Sløvåg to the north and the oil refinery at Mongstad to the south of the fjord. It struck me that one wind power plant would hardly change the landscape. The plant in Sløvåg would never win first prize in any beauty contest, and Mongstad lay like a dark, industrial excrescence on the original coastline. From the tall chimney the flame inside burnt like a sign of impending doom for anyone who approached. If it went out there really would be trouble afoot.

Above all this, the greyish-yellow September sky shrank in the afternoon light. It looked as though it had eaten something it couldn't stomach. Soon it would be sick over all of us.

17

Darkness had begun to fall when I arrived back in Bergen. I parked on Skansen and rang Karin on her mobile.

'Hiya, Varg.' She didn't say any more. In the background I could hear classical piano music.

'How did it go? Did you talk to Ranveig?'

'I'm here now.'

'How's she taking it?'

I heard Ranveig Mæland's voice in the background. Karin said: 'Just a moment …' I heard them talking. Then Karin was back again. 'I've promised to sleep here tonight. But she's asking if you could pop up. She'd like to hear everything from the horse's mouth, as she put it.'

'Yes, I was going to suggest that …'

'We're making something simple to eat, and we've made enough for you in case you should turn up.'

'Great. I'll drop my bag off and be with you in about half an hour.'

We hung up. I nipped down to Telthussmauet, emptied the post box, dropped my bag off and flicked quickly through what the postman had delivered: window envelopes, advertising and a postcard from my son and daughter-in-law, which had taken one and a half weeks to arrive from Milan. Thomas was lecturing on Norwegian literature at the university department for Nordic languages, while Mari was attending a course on Italian Renaissance painting. It would be hard to be any further from my reality. Half an hour after my arrival I was on my way to Storhaugen.

The part of town east of Årstadveien lay like an enclave between Lake Svartediket, Mount Ulriken and Mount Fløyen. From Storhaugen you could see into Isdalen Valley over the solid concrete dam constructed in 1954, which concealed the town's main reservoir for drinking water. In Lappen and Stemmeveien most of the houses were either detached or terraced, many of them built by Hansa Brewery to accommodate their employees. The big housing estate from the early 1920s was a very special construction. The original social dividing lines were still visible. Down below the dam lived the workers and officials; up at Storhaugen, the upper class, most in detached houses with views on all sides. In today's society the border was more fluid, but there was still a hint of insouciant arrogance about the grand houses that covered the heights, with the little lake the locals still called the 'Duck Pond', an idyllic centre both in winter, when ice formed and you could skate on it, and in summer, when the tadpoles romped beneath the surface, hidden from the urban noise and commotion.

I parked my car in Lappen and walked up the last stretch. Mons Mæland's house faced the west with a view of Bergen from the sitting-room windows and almost certainly of Isdalen Valley from the attic, but I had never been up there. I rang the bell, and it was Karin who answered. She held the door open, and when I was inside, she gave me a quick hug.

'How's it going?' I whispered.

'She's pretty upset, naturally. In shock, of course.'

'Have you contacted a doctor?'

'She doesn't want one.'

Obviously quite at home, she opened the wardrobe and fished out a clothes hanger. I hung up my jacket and followed her into the well-kept hall with white panelling, a large, old-fashioned mirror in a gilt frame and a selection of historical prints of old Bergen in plain, dark-brown frames.

We entered the sitting room, it too in a stylistically consistent white, where there was a big, speckled-grey sofa suite set around a black coffee table in the middle, a shelving system with books, a little radio and a stereo along one wall and a large escritoire against the wall facing. Through a spacious opening, the sliding doors partly drawn, I glimpsed a dining room with polished furniture. The paintings on the walls were few in number, but select, a very big landscape painting and a more impressionistic picture dated the early 1960s and signed by an artist whose signature would never adorn any of the pictures on my walls, let alone a cheque in my office.

The music on the stereo was of the same genre as when I phoned Karin less than an hour before: Chopin, Brahms, Schubert … I was no expert, but it sounded wonderful.

Ranveig Mæland got up from the sofa when I went in. It was as though her heart-shaped face had cracked. She looked wan and drawn, her narrow mouth was pursed like a raisin, and her dark-blue eyes were large and shiny. Her short-cropped hair emphasised the shape of her skull, and she resembled an image of death as she walked towards me, limply shook my hand and said in a faint voice: 'Thank you for coming'.

'It was the least I could do,' I said.

There were three cups of coffee and a silver pot on the table.

'Karin's made some coffee. We'll have something to eat later. But first I must hear how they found him.'

I glanced at Karin. 'I don't know what you've told Ranveig.'

She swallowed. 'Only that Mons was found dead under dramatic circumstances on Brennøy.'

I nodded. 'Shall we sit down?'

We sat around the low table, Karin poured coffee for me and refilled the other two cups. Ranveig looked at me with her strikingly large eyes, and I had a sense of what Mons Mæland had fallen for when he was alive. They were eyes to drown in.

'I'm afraid I wasn't of much help.'

Her voice was low, almost apathetic. 'But it was you who found him?'

'I was present when he was found, yes, but several people were, and the man who brought the crime to light was Lars Rørdal.'

'Lars?'

'Ole Rørdal's father, who was at the forefront of those campaigning against the wind farm on Brennøy.'

'Yes, I know about them.'

'Well, the most dramatic aspect … I don't know how to formulate this, but … We were all on our way to the planned survey. Kristoffer and Else were there, too. Representatives of the companies involved. Local politicians. Demonstrators. At least twenty to thirty people in all. But then Lars Rørdal ran towards us and told us what he had seen … Mons was hanging from a cross, if you understand what I mean. Like a kind of … crucifixion.'

She stared at me in stunned disbelief. 'Crucified?'

'Yes, but not with nails or anything like that. Only tied,' I hastened to add. As though that made any difference actually. 'I would imagine he'd died before the perpetrator performed this … stunt, or whatever it was.'

'But who would … ? What could the motive be for such an act?'

'Well, the most likely explanation is that it must have something to do with this wind farm business. An extreme demonstration – an act of terrorism some would call it – against what was planned. But that seems rather un-Norwegian. We stopped using nithing poles to curse our enemies many centuries ago. Since then, by and large, we've kept to more Parliamentarian approaches here.'

'Nithing poles … ?'

'Yes, this had that kind of appearance. A pole erected to curse all those who were planning the big wind farm. It was hardly a coincidence that this happened on the same day as the inspection.'

'But …' Profoundly puzzled, she searched my face. 'He disappeared on a Saturday. And today's Wednesday. What was he doing in the meantime?'

'Good question. But you didn't give me a lot of clues to go on. I spoke to Kristoffer and Else, and also Ole Rørdal. Then I went to Brennøy, hoping he would turn up there.'

'And he did.'

'Yes, although …' I raised my hands as if to say: not in the state we had hoped. Then I added: 'Now this is a police matter, of course, and I'm fairly sure they will get to the bottom of it.'

'Do you think so?' She appeared doubtful.

'At any rate, they have quite different resources at their disposal from those I have. So there's not a lot more to say, other than that the assignment is concluded.'

The spectre still haunted her eyes. 'No, I suppose there isn't.'

Karin, beside her, coughed. 'Perhaps we should go and eat? The soup's ready.'

We stood up and went into the dining room, where the table was already set with elegant mats and deep dishes. There were slices of French bread in a basket and knobs of butter on small plates. Ranveig and I sat down while Karin went to the kitchen and entered through a side-door, holding a substantial steaming tureen. It smelled strongly of beef and diced vegetables: carrot, swede, celeriac and leek. I could feel it had been a long time since breakfast.

We ate in silence.

'You haven't heard from either Else or Kristoffer yet, I understand?'

Ranveig looked up from her plate. 'No, and I can't say I'm exactly looking forward to hearing from them, either.'

'No?'

She looked past me this time. 'I'll probably be blamed for this, too.'

'This, too?'

'Yes. Surely you don't believe there could be anyone else to blame for their mother disappearing that time? They were able to forgive their father after a while, when they became older. But they've never been able to stand me. Mons and I got together after the mother's death far too quickly, they said.'

'But you said yourself that you knew each other ... before Lea disappeared.'

'Yes, so?' For the first time she showed a bit of temperament. 'That was precisely why he came to me – for comfort. Someone he already knew well.'

'Mm.' I nodded and took a few more spoonfuls. 'But tell me: You had to divide the estate, did you?'

'Yes, we had to when we got married. The whole of their mother's inheritance had to be transferred to the children, but with Mons as the guardian until they came of age. Everything, cash and property.'

'He had to sell up, too, did he?'

'Lea and he had a very good life insurance policy covering both of them.'

'How good?'

'I don't remember. Million and a half, two, maybe three …'

'Wow.'

'You mustn't forget he was running a large company, with a lot of employees. They had a lot of responsibility – people to look after.'

'Nevertheless, did she have anything to do with the company?'

'No, but if anything had happened to Mons, all the responsibility would have fallen on Lea until Kristoffer was old enough.'

'So you could say – and please don't take this amiss – he made money from Lea's death?'

She sent him an icy stare. 'It meant he had to go several rounds with the insurance company, but in the end they came to an agreement on certain terms and conditions.'

'And they were?'

'Well, purely hypothetically, if it turned out that Lea wasn't dead …'

'… then the insurance pay-out would have to be returned?'

'Yes, that doesn't so unreasonable, does it?'

'No, no, no. Not at all.'

Another silence punctuated the conversation. I was scraping the bottom of my dish, but said no when Karin offered me more soup from the tureen. Ranveig pushed her dish to the side after the first helping.

'Now of course there will be another parcelling up of the estate,' she sighed. 'I can't say I'm looking forward to that.'

'Do you think it might be tricky?'

'Yes. Now Kristoffer's at the heart of the company and probably regards the majority of the projects they're dealing with as his personal property. Else has a major shareholding in the company as well, even though she's young; and of course, I'm entitled to my part of the shares Mons was sitting on.'

'Fifty per cent, I've been told.'

'And we're barely on speaking terms ...' She sat looking into the middle distance, more worried now than grieving, as far as I could judge.

'That wasn't the impression you gave me earlier.'

'No, maybe not. However, that's the way it is.'

When the meal was over we went back into the sitting room.

'More coffee?' Ranveig asked.

'Just a drop, please.'

She looked at Karin, who squeezed a cup from the silver pot. 'I don't know how hot it is,' she said.

'I'm sure it's fine,' I said. 'One more thing, Ranveig ...'

'Yes?'

'Out of curiosity.' Karin rolled her eyes. 'I'm afraid, that's how I am.' When she didn't object I continued: 'You and Mons got married in 1984, is that right?'

'Yes ...'

'And he bought the property on Brennøy in 1988, I've found out. Do you remember the circumstances surrounding the purchase?'

She looked at me, puzzled. 'The circumstances? No, honestly, I don't. He never talked about that kind of thing at home. But I do remember he went to examine the property and that later he went to ... Eivindvik, it must have been – to get the contract signed.'

'Bjørn Brekkhus, who at that time was Chief of Police in Lindås, was one of the two people who witnessed the signing ...'

'Was he? That's not so strange. Mons and he had known each other since boyhood.'

'The other witness was a nurse at the institution where the seller was admitted. Her name was Gunvor Matte. Does that name mean anything to you?'

'Not at all. What's roused your curiosity?'

I reflected. 'Well, since now you'll become a co-owner of the property on Brennøy I can inform you that the sale in 1988 will be contested and that the matter, as far as I can judge, will end up in court.'

She was still puzzled. 'And?'

'Stein Svenson, who's one of the campaigners against the wind farm, is related – distantly – to Per Nordbø, who sold the land. He died shortly after the sale, by the way, and Stein Svenson's solicitor, the not entirely unknown *herr* Bringeland, will claim that he was not of sound mind when the contract was signed.'

'Well!' She sighed with exasperation. 'There you have a sample of what I can expect in the weeks to come. Is it any wonder I'm desperate?'

'I appreciate the loss of your husband has driven you to despair, yes.'

Karin sent me an admonitory glare, but Ranveig didn't seem to have registered what I had said.

'Well …' She took a sip of her coffee and put the cup down with a determined air. 'You'd better send me your invoice, Varg. I'm afraid I won't be writing to thank you for a satisfactorily completed job.'

'No,' I said quietly. 'I can understand that.' I got up. 'Should, however, there be anything I can do, you know where to find me.'

'Yes, thank you …'

'Good luck.'

'Thank you.'

Karin followed me out. After I had put on my coat I leaned towards her and whispered: 'There's something she's not telling us.'

Karin raised her eyebrows. 'Really?'

'Are you sleeping here tonight?'

'Yes, she asked me if I would.'

'If she's in the right mood, see if you can get her to open up.'

She looked at me disapprovingly. 'If she does, don't rely on me passing anything on to you.'

'OK, OK … but there is something.'

'What?'

'Don't know, I can't quite put my finger on it. Well …' I glanced towards the sitting room and grinned. 'Enjoy yourself.' I leaned over and lightly kissed her on the mouth.

She smiled and stroked my cheek. 'And you? What are you going to do?'

'Drive home.'

But I didn't. As I got into my car, my mobile phone rang. It was Stine Sagvåg, and she got straight down to brass tacks. 'Veum? I told you I'd like a word. Is this a good time?'

'It is. Where can I find you?'

'In the bar one floor above your office. I saw your sign down below when I arrived.'

I chuckled. 'Give me fifteen minutes and I'll be there.'

I had to find a parking spot first. Somewhere to leave my car overnight. If I was being invited to a bar there was a distinct possibility I would be there for a while.

18

She was sitting at a table by the window facing Vågen. When she saw me she nodded, as if to say, yes, you've come to the right place.

I nodded to the owner, a jovial guy with smooth, dark hair, a pear-shaped face, white shirt and bright-red braces. 'The usual?' he asked.

I glanced over at Stine Sagvåg. She had a green drink in a cocktail glass. I definitely didn't want anything like that. 'Yes, please,' I said.

I went over to her table. She had changed into an evening outfit: a short, black skirt with a tightly fitted top in black shot with gold, which revealed that there wasn't a gram too much on her body, except where it counted most. Her muscular but slim upper arms testified to the regular use of weights. When she got up to greet me her handshake was firm and resolute, and her beautiful smile came as if cut out of a glossy fashion magazine that retailed at more money than I had in my account. 'What can I offer you, Veum?'

'I've ordered, thank you.'

Her face was lean, her red hair with grey streaks fashionably dishevelled, and she radiated a strength that made me think of a female marathon runner crossing the finishing line with consummate ease.

The bartender came over with a round tray in one hand, placed a glass of dark-brown Hansa and a small glass of Simers Taffel aquavit on the table in front of me, said 'Enjoy' and retired discreetly with an amused smile. The bar was quite new, a couple of years old, and had raised the standard of the hotel on the fourth and fifth floors by several notches. It was located by the hotel reception area, and the view of the fish market and adjacent splendours did not diminish the attraction. The owner was a pleasant man who liked to chat with his customers, but he knew when to withdraw if the situation required.

On a Wednesday evening in September the place wasn't exactly jam-packed, but we weren't the only customers, either. There was a middle-aged couple sitting at one table, a group of three, well-dressed young ladies at another, two of them with immense cigars in their mouths, and from the side room I heard loud laughter coming from a party of men out on the town to celebrate something, most probably being out on the town.

Stine Sagvåg raised her glass and looked at me invitingly. '*Skål* ...'

I chose the dram, *skål*-ed her, sipped the aquavit and felt the taste of caraway ripple reassuringly through my body. '*Skål.*'

From a small handbag she took a gold case, opened it and held it out for me. 'Cigarette, Veum?'

'No, thank you. I don't smoke.'

She arched her eyebrows with a questioning expression.

'Yes, yes, of course. Don't mind me.'

She nodded thanks, plucked out a cigarette, placed it between her lips and waited for as many seconds as it took her to realise that I didn't walk around with matches on me, either. Then she took out a lighter and lit the cigarette herself. She inhaled the smoke deep into her lungs, and the image of her as a marathon runner slipped.

'You may be wondering why I've invited you here.'

'Yes, I cannot deny that.'

She turned her face to the side and considerately blew the smoke in that direction. 'What happened on the island was absolutely terrible.'

'We can all agree on that. You were questioned by the police as well, were you?'

She nodded. 'Yes, of course. But what could I tell them? Erik Utne of Norcraft deals with Mæland Real Estate.'

'So why were you at the survey?'

She smiled indulgently. 'TWO, whom I represent, has substantial property interests in Norcraft. We're obviously interested in following up our investments, also at close quarters. Especially when a fairly controversial venture such as a wind farm in virtually untouched nature is concerned.'

'There's a beating heart for the environment in TWO as well?'

'A controversial investment can soon become a poor investment. Our owners' main concern is a foreseeable profit.'

'Surprise, surprise! But you had met Mons Mæland, hadn't you?'

'Only peripherally, eighteen months ago, when we seriously began to get interested in this case.'

'In fact, I've come across TWO before.'

'Yes, I know.'

'You've checked up on me, I imagine.'

'I always check up on people I rendez-vous with.'

'A rendez-vous? Is that what this is?'

She smiled enigmatically.

'Did you speak to Halvorsen or Kristoffersen?'

'I didn't speak to anyone, Veum. I found you in our archives.'

'Wow! You don't have a copy of my file, do you?'

'It wasn't that thick,' she said, demonstratively flaring her nostrils.

'Thick enough,' I said, taking a sip of beer.

She waited until I had put the glass down. 'We have an assignment for you, in fact.'

'Oh, yes? Tell me more.'

'You probably heard what Johannes Bringeland said on the island. The claims he made about the sale of the property – in 1988, I think it must have been.'

'Yes. His client Stein Svenson was given a bit of rough treatment on Brennøy. Professional job.'

She waited for me to follow up.

'I don't know if you noticed one of the others at the survey. A certain Trond Tangenes ...'

'Yes?'

'You didn't hire him, did you?'

'Trond Tangenes? I don't recognise the name. In what capacity, might I ask?'

'I see.' I shrugged. 'He has a background as a debt collector, bodyguard, that kind of thing. Have persuasive manner, will travel. If you know what I mean.'

She raised one hand. 'If you're trying to imply that we would have anything to do with that kind of activity I can definitively reject it. At TWO we do not take recourse to such methods.'

'No?'

'No.'

For a while there was an invisible arc of tension between us that could have caught fire at any moment. Then I put a damper on the atmosphere. 'I saw him talking to Jarle Glosvik, the district council man, most of the time.'

'Then ask him!'

'I will do if the opportunity presents itself. But back to … What is it you want me to do?'

'Yes. When the murder … When whatever happened to Mons Mæland has been cleared up we want to get cracking with the project as soon as is advisable.'

'You literally want the wind in your sails.'

'Yes. Can we count on you?'

I took another sip of the aquavit. 'If I understand you correctly, you're asking me to investigate what happened in 1988 when the land on Brennøy was transferred from one Per Nordbø to Mons Mæland with the Chief of Police in Lindås as one of the witnesses. That's all?'

'In brief outline.'

'Perhaps not the greatest intellectual challenge I've had, but we all have to live.' I nodded. 'I can try. Do you know how Svenson is?'

'No idea. A doctor arrived, and they went into a different room. The rest of us were discharged once the police had finished with us.'

'Who did you talk to?'

'Solheim, I think he was called.' She pursed her lips. 'Sweet guy.'

I took note. I would have to remember to tell him the next time we met.

'You're very sweet, too, Veum …'

Or maybe not.

The bartender was at their table again. 'Everything alright?' By which, I now knew, he meant: 'Anything else to drink?'

Her glass was empty. 'Yes, please,' she said. 'One more of the same.'
I drained my beer. 'I'll keep you company. Two more of the same.'
'My treat,' she said.

'Can you write it off against my assignment?'

'That sort of thing.'

'What is it you're drinking? Broccoli juice?'

'Grasshopper. Pleasant taste of peppermint, if you have a taste for it.'

I leaned back in my chair. 'And what is an attractive girl like you doing at the top of TWO?'

'Attractive girls do what they want after a while. Didn't you know that?'

'In directors' offices, too?'

'I've got a degree and a business school diploma.'

'Not just attractive but clever with it?'

Her tongue came out and ran along her top teeth. 'Very clever,' she said as the new round from the bar arrived.

'But you're not from Bergen ...'

'You have a keen ear, Veum. You can hear the difference between Bergen and Trondheim, in other words.'

'Refined version.'

'Trondheim Posh, as it's called. Though it's never been a problem so far.'

'TWO isn't exactly well known for its environmental credentials ...'

Her eyebrows shot up and she stubbed out her cigarette in the ashtray. 'Are we back to business? No, not historically maybe. But that doesn't mean we don't have the potential to improve. Wouldn't you agree?'

'Absolutely. And is that what you're doing now? Wind power and other renewables?'

'We want to become an environmental beacon, Varg. May I call you that?'

'Of course. A beacon with maximum profit?'

She leaned forward, spreading a fragrance that was discreet and cool. She was like a perfumed glacier. 'That's where the future lies. At the cutting edge of technological development. Take Toyota, for example. They brought out the first hybrid car, and I'll guarantee you that in ten to fifteen years' time at least fifty per cent of all cars off the conveyor belts will have environmental features.'

'And you want to be part of this?'

'Not car manufacturing, but in our specialities: shipping, energy, and I'm not just thinking of oil, I'm thinking wind, wave …' She extended an arm in a circle above us. 'The sun … We want to be there, Varg, and leading from the front.'

'With all your money? And the profit …'

She smiled. 'That, too. All our prognoses point in the same direction. The environment is tomorrow's investment objective number one. Have you ever seen a wind farm?'

'In Denmark, yes. But only in passing.'

She looked up. 'It's a very attractive sight, I can tell you. The big blades rotating slowly in a rhythmical, almost dancing, fashion. Tall, white against the horizon. And the sure knowledge that this produces energy without leaving behind it the slightest form of pollution.'

'But there are those who maintain that wind turbines are not that environmentally friendly after all. They make a lot of noise, among other things. And they have the potential to cause harm to bird species.'

'Yes, and we should take that seriously. Everyone should have their say. But not in the way that … well, you know. I don't know if you caught the item on the TV news?'

'No, I was … busy.'

'This morning it was front-page news in all the papers. The authorities are going to demand an immediate explanation.'

I chuckled. 'Hamre's going to be doing overtime …'

'You're old friends?'

'I know most of them in the force, unfortunately.'

She looked at me from the corner of her eye. 'I haven't met that many private detectives before.'

'No? We're pretty normal people, so long as you don't cross swords with us.'

'Are you handy with your sword, Varg?'

I nodded in acknowledgement. 'Touché, Stine.'

She leaned even closer. 'Can I invite you to a nightcap one floor up?'

'Are you staying here?'

'Mm.'

It was tempting, of course. On the other hand ... 'Shame you've hired me.'

'What do you mean?'

'One of my hopelessly old-fashioned principles. I never get too familiar with my employer. Besides, I'm as good as married.'

She leaned back in the chair with a slightly odd expression on her face. 'You don't know what you're missing.'

'Another time perhaps.'

She smiled sourly. We were alone in the bar now. The others had gone. The owner was standing behind the bar polishing a glass with such energy he must have thought it would turn to gold if he rubbed hard enough.

'Anyway, I was only inviting you for a nightcap.'

I nodded, with a wry little smile.

Again she opened her handbag. From an inside pocket she pulled out another little gold case, the size of a business card, and indeed that was what she took out, placed on the table and pushed in my direction. 'Here you have all my phone numbers.'

'If I should change my mind?'

'When you hand in your report.'

I clocked the card. 'You're based in Oslo, I see.'

'Our division HQ is there, yes.'

'As close as possible to power.'

'No, no. Then we would have been in Brussels. Or New York.'

I sighed. 'But not in Eivindvik.'

'No, not there.'

She still looked a little put out. Attractive girls do what they want, she had told me, but they don't always get what they want, however attractive they are. She beckoned to the bartender and paid with one of her cards. We walked back to reception, where she shook my hand and wished me luck with the assignment.

She sent me a final, lingering look. Then she went upstairs to her room on the fifth. I walked all the way downstairs; I didn't even pop into the office to check my post. I postponed everything to the following day and strolled home, fairly satisfied with the day's results. But she had got me wondering, it couldn't be denied. Clever girl that she was.

Once at home, I poured myself another Simers Taffel to console myself. Gradually a new image was forming on my retina. The image of Mons Mæland on a cross facing the sea with the wind as the only witness. I thought of the quotation from the Bible that had hung on the wall outside the chapel: *He that troubleth his own house shall inherit the wind: and the fool shall be servant to the wise of heart.* Mons Mæland had inherited the wind, there was no doubt about that. Who was foolish and who was wise was still a moot point. I felt quite well qualified for both myself, and I was pretty sure which category Stine Sagvåg had put me in, lying in her bed in Strandveien, alone with her dreams – of profit or whatever it was people like her dreamed about when it was night and they were alone and had no one to be clever with.

19

On Thursday morning I rang Karin to hear how she had got on. She was on the bus and answered that the night had passed without any difficulties and suggested we talk later.

While eating my breakfast, I wondered how I should go about my new assignment. Going to the council building in Eivindvik and hoping the fish would bite at the Housing and Properties office seemed a touch optimistic. Furthermore, Eivindvik was almost as long a drive as Brennøy. Perhaps it would be best to start with Bringeland, who, by all accounts, had a copy of the contract in his office in the centre of Bergen. When I rang his number I got no further than his secretary, who after some to-ing and fro-ing was able to confirm that Bringeland could spare me five minutes at a quarter to ten. I accepted the appointment, finished breakfast and set off. The five minutes promised could soon become ten once I had a foot in his office.

On my way I bought my regular dose of newspapers and popped by my office to flick through them. The case had filled the front pages of the tabloids and had comprehensive coverage in others. *Crucified for the Environment* was one tabloid headline. *Killed by Eco-Warriors?* said another. But from reading the papers I could see that neither the name of the deceased nor any further details had been released yet. Most was speculation about how far NmV was involved. One of the articles in the biggest local newspaper was entitled: *We are not terrorists, says Ole Rørdal. Strilen* was the only paper to have photos of the crime scene, but it had little more than I had observed myself. One of the nationals had invested in a helicopter trip to Brennøy and was able to print a very impressive aerial photo in which the tall cross could be seen in all its glory. But the body had already been taken down, to the editor's undoubted disappointment.

I put all the papers in a heap on my desk, quickly went through the window envelopes I had brought up with me from the post box, confirmed that there were no important e-mails and then took the quickest route to Valkensdorfs gate.

There are no fixed rules and apparently no limits to how a solicitor's office should look. I had been to some that looked like anything from a broom cupboard to the audience chamber at the Royal Palace in Oslo. Experience had taught me to be sceptical about such offices. The broom cupboard revealed the total lack of any clientele, quite probably for professional reasons. The audience chamber indicated that fees were sky high, the same level as the importance with which the solicitors regarded themselves. You were safest – here as in most other areas of life – in the sober, middle layer, without visible extravagance as regards furniture, more partners than strictly speaking necessary and a battery of secretaries and ante-room ladies who made the barrier to the holy of holies practically impenetrable.

Bringeland & Kleve were located on the third floor somewhere in Valkendorfs gate, in common with most of the solicitors' offices in Bergen, at a suitable walk from the Courthouse. The secretary was a friendly but prim woman in her fifties of the ilk that usually rule most of the offices I have seen. I saw nothing of Kleve, and when I was ushered in to Bringeland he was putting a thick wad of paper in a briefcase and already appeared to be on his way out.

'I have only five minutes, Veum.'

'I'll get straight to the point then. Have you got a copy of the contract between Per Nordbø and Mons Mæland?'

He scrutinised me, suspicion glinting in his eyes. 'What do you want with it?'

'I've been asked to look into that case as well – and it would save me a trip to Eivindvik if you had a copy to spare.'

'Asked by whom, if I may be so bold.'

'I'm not sure if I ...'

'Then you can forget it!'

I reflected quickly. She hadn't mentioned any necessity for secrecy. 'Alright then: TWO.'

'The opposition, in other words.'

'I can assure you, Bringeland, I have no axe to grind. All I want are facts.'

He scowled at me, then shrugged his shoulders. 'Well, I suppose it can't hurt. The case is open and shut anyway, from my point of view.' He went to a filing cabinet, pulled out a drawer, chose a file, opened it and extracted a sheet. 'You can see it, but I'm not going to give you a copy.'

'Why not?'

'You can do as I did and contact the council in Eivindvik.'

He passed me the contract. I cast a quick glance at it, established that it had been signed by the shaky hand of the old man, Per Norbø, and that the signature had been confirmed by two witnesses: Bjørn Brekkhus and Gunvor Matre.

'Have you been in touch with them? With Brekkhus and Matre, I mean.'

'That's the contract you wanted to see, isn't it? I have nothing else to show you.' He had his coat on. He held out his hand.

Reluctantly I passed him back the contract and watched as he returned it to the filing cabinet. He pushed in the drawer and headed for the door. 'I'm afraid I have to go now. I'm due in court. Come on.'

I followed him out. On the way down the stairs, I asked: 'And Stein Svenson, how's he doing?'

'He's picking up. He had a nasty bump to the head and the doctor diagnosed mild concussion. He was told to stay at home until further notice.'

'And where is home?'

He sent me a scornful look. 'Aren't you a kind of investigator?'

'What did the police say, then?'

'They said nothing to me. He was questioned, but, as he said when they found him, he couldn't remember anything. Not unusual with concussion, the doctor affirmed.'

We were on the street and striding towards the Courthouse.

'I can find my own way, Veum.'

'I'm going in that direction anyway. So he didn't say anything to you, either?'

'Svenson? About the attack? Let me put it like this, Veum. We're quite sure it wasn't Mons Mæland. Otherwise the possibilities are legion.'

'You pointed a finger at Trond Tangenes while we were there.'

'Well ...'

'And Jarle Glosvik.'

'I have nothing else to say, Veum.' He stopped in front of the stone sculptures of the four cardinal virtues, watching over the entrance to the Courthouse. 'You can say hello to your employers from me and they can forget it. There will be no wind farm on Brennøy for the next ten years. I'll make sure of that.' Then he turned on his heel, dashed up the last steps and disappeared into the great hall.

I was left with the four stone figures: Force, his arm around a pillar, ready for action; Moderation, clutching a jug of wine in his hand – consolation for when the case was finally lost and there was no reason to continue any longer; Justice, with scales and sword – the scales to weigh the solicitors' efforts in gold and the sword to strike at the head of anyone who dared protest at the decision; and furthest to the east, Wisdom, with the serpent and the book, obviously poisoned by knowledge.

I was not at all sure which of them I trusted most. With a shrug of my shoulders I steered towards the street called Fortunen and down again to my office. If nothing else I should at least find out where Stein Svenson lived. I was sure he wouldn't mind a little visit from a concerned fellow-Norwegian.

20

Stein Svenson had an address in Bontveit, in what had once been Fana municipality. After a quick parallel check between the land registry and the local map I walked back up to Skansen, fetched my car and drove off. I had no intention of giving him any warning.

I followed the E39 to Lake Kaland and turned off at the Bontveit intersection. Thereafter the road rose steeply to Frotveit and on to the long valley between Livarden and Hausdalshorgi. Stein Svenson's tumbledown little smallholding, purchased, according to my information, four years before, was isolated, at the end of a forest road on the slope up to Mount Livgarden. The air was clear and pure, and up here in the mountains there was a touch of autumn in the air.

I turned into the yard in front of the two bedraggled buildings: a shed with what red paint there was hanging off it like dandruff and a small farmhouse that had been painted yellow not so long ago. I parked and sat in the car. In front of the houses there were two other cars. One was a three-year-old Saab 900, which was not the first car I would have chosen if I had a leading job in an environmental organisation. The second I had seen before. It was an Audi A4 with the same registration number as the one that had been parked at Naustvik on Brennøy.

I got out of my car, closed the door quietly behind me and walked carefully towards the house. From inside I heard irregular muffled sounds, like a fight in a cotton warehouse, and two angry voices: one loud and falsetto; the other dark and menacing.

I looked around for something I could use as a weapon. All I could find was a bit of plank lying on the ground by the steps to the front door. I doubted it would have much effect.

I tried the door. It was unlocked. I pushed it and the noises grew louder. Leaving the door open behind me, to keep my lines of retreat clear, I walked quickly through the porch, noticed an open door to the left, walked over and stood on the threshold.

'Hey, hey, hey!' I said, slowly increasing the volume, and not just to attract their attention. 'Let's cool it, shall we?' But I could feel my neck muscles tautening and my stomach churning.

Trond Tangenes had Stein Svenson pressed up against the wall and was holding him off the ground with his forearm. He hung there, his feet thrashing around wildly, ten to fifteen centimetres above the floor. Tangenes' other fist was primed to strike, and judging by the marks on Svenson's face he had already scored several direct hits.

Tangenes turned to face me. 'Keep your distance. This has nothing to do with you.'

I could hear he recognised me. 'Yes, it has. I have something to discuss with Svenson, and right now you're in my way.'

He bored his eyes into me. 'You'll have to move me then.'

Svenson was still thrashing around. 'Hey, lemme go, will you!'

Tangenes pressed him harder against the wall, and Svenson's face went red. 'He-ey …,' he whimpered.

'Shut your mouth!'

'Listen, Tangenes …'

He didn't like me knowing what his name was, that much was clear. I continued quickly: 'Everyone knows who you are. The police, Svenson's solicitor, me. Right now your fist is telling me that it was you who attacked Svenson on Brennøy. I would recommend you put him down carefully and come with me outside for a chat. And don't try anything. A lot of people know where I am at this minute.'

'Oh, yes?'

'Old rule of the mountains. Let people know where you are.'

I could see his brain working inside his thick skull. Then he made a decision. He loosened his grip on Svenson, let him slowly slide to the floor, grabbed his shoulders and shoved him hard onto the bed in one corner of the room, where he sat staring up at us and gasping for breath with the air of an aggrieved child.

Tangenes nodded towards the door. 'Out!'

I backed out slowly, keeping an eye on him and straining all my muscles as I went. In the yard I strode away from the house and turned round. He came after me and stopped four to five metres away.

He grinned. 'Are you frightened of me, Veum?'

'Has no one told you your breath stinks?'

He stopped grinning. His eyes narrowed. 'Get to the point. What was it you wanted to talk about?'

'I know that Jarle Glosvik is paying you.'

'Who?'

'Don't make me laugh. We all saw you talking on Brennøy.'

'Now you listen here, Veum. We know all about you.'

'We?'

'We know who you are, where you live, where your office is and …' He glanced at my car. 'What car you drive. Just like you, I keep my mouth shut about who employs me. Was there anything else you wanted?'

'It's very clear that Svenson is the target of your assignment, and that can only be for one reason: the lawsuit he is pursuing against the council with regard to the dubious property deal in 1988. My guess is you were hired to frighten him into dropping it.'

'You look a bit jumpy yourself, Veum.'

'You're wrong there. I know people like you are big mouths, but I've been round the block a few times and I'm not impressed. Let me return the warning, Tangenes. Go back to where you came from. You've been far too visible on this terrain. I would imagine Hamre gave you the same message when you spoke.'

Tangenes' jaw tautened. 'Cops are cops wherever they are in the world. So long as we stay off their hunting grounds they couldn't care less.'

'Don't be too sure about that. Hamre's not one of them. I know that from my own experience.'

Tangenes suddenly lunged towards me. I reacted immediately and ran.

He grinned. 'You're scared stiff. Boo, Veum! The bogeyman's coming to get you. Any other messages you wanted to give me?'

I kept a wary eye on him. 'No. Go home and say you haven't been here.'

He stood his ground, ruminating. Then he shrugged. 'Fine. I will. Where'd you like to meet next time? At your girlfriend's place? In Fløenbakken ...'

A chill finger ran down my spine. I could hear they had done their research. 'Keep well away, Tangenes! Do you hear me!'

He smirked. 'I'm not promising anything. Let's leave it like that, eh, Veum? We'll keep in touch, OK?' Then he turned, shot the house a final glance, rolled his shoulders back and strolled towards the parked cars.

I looked up at the house, too. Behind one of the unwashed windows I glimpsed the pale face of Stein Svenson watching us.

I stood without stirring until Tangenes had got into his black Audi, started up and accelerated onto the gravel road leaving a cloud of dust behind him. Then I ambled back to the house and went in to see Svenson.

The furniture in the small sitting room, which I assumed from the presence of a bed doubled as a bedroom, looked as if it had come with the house when he bought it: shabby, painted chairs – two of them overturned on the floor – and a wooden table that had seen its best years. The room was dominated by the piles of reading material, most of it on the floor: newspapers, magazines and books. On the table there was a laptop and a portable radio. That was the extent of the modern technology.

Svenson was waiting for me. He was unshaven. His short, red hair was tucked under a large bandage, and he was wearing a faded, dark-blue T-shirt over deep-green combat trousers. His face was not a pleasant sight. Swellings had appeared where Trond Tangenes' punches had struck home and he stood swaying in the middle of the floor, as if dizzy.

I watched and waited. When nothing was forthcoming, I said: 'What about: thanks for your help?'

'No one invited you, did they.'

'You would have preferred him to finish the job, would you?'

He sighed involuntarily and gasped for breath. Then he made an attempt to pull himself together. 'I need some coffee. Find something to sit on.'

He walked past me into the kitchen, and I could hear that he was running water into a kettle. I flipped up the two chairs with my foot and placed one of them at the table. The other I carried to the window where I stood for a while making sure that Tangenes didn't reappear.

As the water was heating he came to the kitchen door and glared at me. 'Who are you, actually?'

'We met on Brennøy. I was one of the people who found you after you'd been trussed up.'

He pinched the bridge of this nose. 'Yes, I remember you. You're from TWO, aren't you?'

'What makes you think that?'

'Because you keep trying to deny it.'

'I'm not sure I understand the logic, but …'

'And your name …?'

'Veum. Varg Veum. I'm a private investigator.'

'Right?' He appeared unable to absorb this. Then the water boiled and he went back into the kitchen. He clattered around, then returned with a mug in each hand. 'Only got instant, and nothing to put in it.'

'That's fine.' I took the mug. He made a move towards the table. I checked the window for a last time. All looked nice and peaceful. We sat down on the wooden chairs; his didn't seem comfortable, either. 'What did Tangenes want from you?'

'Tangenes?'

'The guy we turfed out.'

His eyes wandered. 'He said we should drop the lawsuit.'

'The land deal?'

'Yes.'

'Anything about the wind farm?'

'Nope.'

'Did he say who'd sent him?'

He started to shake his head, but stopped and groaned. 'Shit!'

'Sore head?'

'Well deduced. No, he didn't say who'd sent him, and I don't give a rat shit.'

'Are you going to follow his advice?'

He stared at me defiantly. 'You clearly don't know Stein Svenson. I don't buckle that easily.'

'Do you think it was him who attacked you on Brennøy?'

Carefully, he shrugged his shoulders. 'Don't ask me. I don't remember a thing.' He held the back of his head. 'But I do know this. Whoever it was, came from behind.'

'I should tell you something. The night before, I was woken by a heated argument outside my window. When I went to see who it was, I saw you and Ole Rørdal having a go at each other ...'

'Oh, yes? So? Are you trying to say that it was Ole who ...?' He pointed to his head and raised his eyebrows.

'You slept on the boat, and when Ole and Else passed underneath my window I heard Ole say very clearly: "We aren't terrorists!"'

'Right, and?'

'My conclusion is that the disagreement between you and Ole was about something he called "terrorism".' As he didn't respond, I added: 'Others might call it drastic action.'

His eyes were heavy and sad. 'I still don't understand where this is going ...'

'The murder of Mons Mæland, for example.'

'The murder of ... Are you out of your mind? Do you think anyone in an environmental organisation would go that far to promote their cause?'

'That's one of the main theories in the papers today.'

'The papers! Pah! Surely you don't bloody believe what they write? They've been after us ever since we set up.'

'Why?'

'We're not house-trained enough. We barge in where others fear to tread. We're the only bloody people who dare to say what these wind farms along the coast will really do.'

'There have been other critical voices, too …'

'Yes, but we … We take action, right?'

'Yes, exactly.' I leaned forward. 'And what sort?'

He sighed. 'Yes, drastic action. But murder? You're way off target.'

'Well, give me examples of the action you've planned then!'

'Why should I? So that you can run off to TWO and warn them?'

'I don't represent …' But upon mature reflection, that was exactly what I was doing. Instead, I changed the topic. 'This land deal, where did the idea come from?'

'Are we back to that?'

I nodded. 'Glosvik and Tangenes are not the only ones preoccupied by it, you know.'

'So? That could be called pretty drastic action, couldn't it?'

'Hardly drastic enough for it to be called terrorism. It would have to be something like hijacking a plane after sending an application in triplicate two weeks in advance.'

'You'll see – it will delay the whole process long enough for people to see the light before the farm is completed.'

'See the light about what?'

'Wind turbines! Isn't that what this is about?'

'Yes, probably.'

'Probably?'

'How did you get onto this land deal idea?'

'Get onto? We trawled through public documents and then this name cropped up. Per Nordbø. I knew we had someone called Nordbø in the family, so I kept at it and then we realised that, well, in fact I had a claim.'

'But the assertion that Per Nordbø was not of sound mind when he signed …'

'Yes, that was Bringe– …' He caught himself too late.

I nodded. 'That was Bringeland's idea. Thought so. How much commission have you agreed if the land ends up in your hands?'

He wouldn't answer the question. Instead he said: 'You can interview the people who signed the purchase agreement. The crown witnesses.'

'Bjørn Brekkhus and Gunvor Matre?'

'Yeah. Think that's their names … maybe.'

'I'll follow your advice. I'll talk to them.'

'Have fun!'

I took a sip of coffee. He did the same. We sat staring at each other.

'There's one other matter I was wondering about, Svenson. The first two times we met you asked if I was from Norcraft. Why?'

His eyes narrowed again. 'I asked, that was all.' I waited for him to go on, and he was unable to resist. 'I had a suspicion.'

'A suspicion about what?'

'That they would try to buy him off.'

'Buy whom off? Ole Rørdal?'

'It was likely they would try anyway, and Ole … Well, perhaps, he's not quite as strong as he appears.'

'Was this what was behind your disagreement?'

'Probably, yes. He'd suddenly started to lose his steel. Wasn't willing to go as far as … some of us wanted.'

'You suspected he'd been bought?'

He shrugged. 'How can I know? Anything can happen in this dirty business.'

I opened my mouth, but he interrupted. 'I've got nothing else to say.'

'Fine. So what now? Are you going to report the assault to the police?'

His eyes went walkabout. 'This today?'

'Yes, I wasn't thinking of the previous occasion. They already know about that one.'

'And what use would it be? Do you think they would be interested?'

I made a vague gesture with my hands. 'If it's relevant to the other case, they …'

'The Mons Mæland case, you mean?'

I nodded.

'I'll chew on it.'

'If you don't report it, I might. He threatened me as well.'

Svenson eyed me, undecided. 'OK. You can do what you like.'

'One last question, Svenson. Who do you think would have wanted to kill Mæland?'

'It'd be better to ask me who didn't have a reason to kill him.'

'Give me a clue. I never met him.'

'I've said what I'm going to say to the cops. They're investigating the case, aren't they?'

'Yes.'

'Face the facts, Veum. You're fighting against the wind turbines, too. As long as you're employed by TWO, anyway.'

'Svenson, they're *for* the wind farm, in case you haven't sussed it yet.'

He sent me a look that was an appropriate mixture of disdain and contempt. And, yes, maybe he was right. But I didn't need his sort to tell me so.

Before getting into the car, I rang Hamre. Surprisingly, he came through in no time. I told him what had happened, about the assault on Svenson and the threats Tangenes had made, both to me and to 'my girlfriend'.

'Come on now, Veum,' Hamre barked. 'Don't tell me you're investigating this case!'

'No, no. I've been hired to investigate the 1988 land sale contract, if you remember that?'

'I see. All right. Sounds harmless enough, but you keep your paws off the murder case.'

'Back to Tangenes.'

'Yes, I made a mental note. We'll send some patrol cars round a bit more often, in Fløenbakken and up at your place. Ring us if he turns up, Veum. Don't take the law into your own hands. You've never been much good at keeping off limits.'

'No?'

'No.'

I felt far from reassured. I immediately rang Karin at work. It was a while before she answered. 'Yes? Varg? I'm busy right now. Can you ring back later?'

'Yes. But don't leave the office until you've spoken to me. OK?'

'OK.'

We rang off. I opened the car door and got in behind the wheel. Frightened, Veum? Yes. But not for myself. If anything happened to Karin, however ...

I started up and drove towards town, slightly above the speed limit, but I was busy and if I was stopped and waved into the side I would have to pass on my regards to Hamre. That might help. It might not.

21

I left my car in the multi-storey car park in Markeveien, went down to my office, booted up the computer and started searching for the telephone numbers I didn't have. While I was at it I went into the Kvasir search engine and hunted for interesting names. Mons Mæland came up hundreds of times, Jarle Glosvik closer to thousands of times. I found a nice portrait photo of Stine Sagvåg, while Bjørn Brekkhus only featured in a few newspaper articles from the time when he was still Chief of Police. Ole Rørdal was high on the list, whereas Stein Svenson had only a few entries. Kristoffer had nowhere near as many mentions as his father, Else only a few and I couldn't find Ranveig anywhere. Neither Lars nor Kristine Rørdal produced anything of interest.

Finally I searched for Gunvor Matre. The sole entry for her was a brief address: 5970 Byrknesøy. There was ample evidence to suggest I should make another trip to Lindås and Gulen.

I sat staring into the distance, musing. Again I was haunted by the image of Mons Mæland hanging from the cross. There was something so graphic and brutal about this act that I was reminded of far more extreme action groups than those we were used to in Norway, with the exception of the neo-Nazis, and the remnants of that movement had never been interested in environmental politics, from my observation.

Religious fanatics had taken recourse to robust methods when the fight against the abortion law was at its peak, but, to the best of my memory, there had been no crucifixion. Lars Rørdal had been committed enough in his condemnation of the wind farm project, but I couldn't imagine he would ever go as far as stringing up one of his main adversaries. In addition, his consternation at the discovery of the body had seemed genuine enough.

Mons Mæland had been undergoing a change of heart, but those who were fighting *for* the wind farm wouldn't have gone to such extremes, either. Even a man like Trond Tangenes would have used far more subtle methods. A drowning accident, a hit and run, that kind of malarkey.

Could the motive lie somewhere else entirely? Someone settling one of life's outstanding debts?

I tried another name in the search box. *Lea Mæland*. But the result was negative. Not a single entry. She was definitively dead and buried, in Kvasir and everywhere else.

I would have liked to know what progress the police had made in their inquiries. The only person I could ring there was Atle Helleve, but I felt fairly sure that not even he would be very talkative at this stage.

I established the facts of the case. Mons Mæland had disappeared from his cabin on Radøy late Saturday night. On Sunday his boat was found drifting in the Radsund. On Monday I was given an assignment to track him down. On Wednesday we all found him, with Lars Rørdal as the first on the crime scene.

But how long had he been dead, and who had hung him on the cross? Was it one person or could there have been more?

Also, who had knocked Stein Svenson unconscious and tied him up? My main suspect was still Trond Tangenes, but could it have been someone else? And could he or someone else have hung Mons Mæland on the cross, if so? Was there any connection between these two events at all? Were there any other motives other than the dispute about the wind farm?

Could what happened when the land was sold – perhaps unlawfully – to Mæland in 1988 have been motive enough? In which case it would have to be Stein Svenson. But how did that explain the fact that it was him who had been assaulted and rendered *hors de combat* roughly at the same time?

So, *when* was Mons Mæland hung up on the cross? Wednesday morning? The night before? If the body was transported there, was it by boat, or some other way? Boat was the most likely option; it would have been far more difficult over land. But, of course, the police were checking this now, and they certainly would not answer any of the questions I might like to ask.

It was almost three o'clock when I rang Karin again.

'Oh, hiya,' she said, somewhat absent-mindedly.

'Can you speak now?'

'Yes, yes. No problem.'

'How is she?'

'She was pale but composed when I left her this morning. Kristoffer rang last night, and they agreed to have a kind of family council this evening. They have to plan the funeral of course.'

'It will probably take some time before forensics has finished with him.'

'Yes, I'm sure it will. But there must be other things they would like to discuss as well.'

'My understanding was that she wasn't exactly looking forward to it. You didn't …? She didn't confide in you at all after I'd gone?'

'No, Varg, she didn't. We sat chatting, but … Nothing that would interest you anyway, I can assure you. And after Kristoffer rang she had all that on her mind.'

'Hm. Are you meeting her today?'

'No, but I told her she only had to ring if there was anything. What about you? Are you busy?'

'Not today. But it looks like I might have to go to Gulen again tomorrow.' I told her about the assignment I had been given by Stine Sagvåg.

'Are you going to come up and see me?'

'Love to. My car's in Markeveien. We can meet there when you've finished.'

We arranged to meet and I clicked off. Then I rang Bjørn Brekkhus' mobile number. The only answer I got was a voicemail saying his phone was switched off or he was in an area without coverage.

When I rang his home number a woman answered. 'Hello?'

'Hello, I'd like to talk to Bjørn Brekkhus.'

'OK. Who's that?' I tried to place her dialect, but all I knew for certain was that she was from Eastern Norway.

'My name's Veum.'

'I'm afraid he isn't at home.'

'I've tried his mobile phone.'

'He often forgets to switch it on. The coverage where he is, is poor, too.'

'Where is he?'

'At sea, as usual. Can I ask him to ring you when he gets home?'

'Yes, please do. We met on Monday, so he knows who I am and what this is about.'

'Veum, wasn't it?'

'Yes.' I gave her my telephone number.

'Got it.'

'Thank you.'

I met Karin outside the multi-storey car park in Markeveien. As we drove to Fløenbakken I kept an eye open to check we weren't being followed, but I couldn't see anyone. After parking outside her block I told her to wait while I opened the door. I got out and scanned the area. Then I beckoned to her.

She looked at me with a worried expression. 'What is it, Varg? You seem so tense.'

'I don't want to worry you unduly, but … Let's go in first.'

Upstairs in her flat, I told her about Trond Tangenes and the threats he had made. Finally I gave her a detailed description of his appearance. 'If anyone rings at the door, don't open up unless you're sure you know who it is. And if you see someone vaguely resembling him, look for somewhere safe as soon as possible, talk to other people around you and ring me – or maybe just as good, the police. Hamre knows.'

She stared at me with big eyes and a grimace. 'I hope this isn't going to last long, Varg.'

'No, no,' I said, trying to make my tone lighter than I felt. 'In all probability they're just empty threats. His main aim was to do exactly this. To make us feel unsafe.' I patted her on the shoulder. 'It'll pass, sooner than you imagine.'

'Well …' She smiled, apparently confident. Then she shrugged and went to the kitchen. 'But we should have something to eat, shouldn't we?'

It could have been the perfect evening at home. Karin made a bowl of pasta and chopped up lettuce while I read the newspaper in greater detail than I'd had time to do in my office. After we had eaten we lay half-asleep on a sofa each until it felt to me that it was time to make coffee. We watched the news, first of all on TV2, then on NRK, but apart from some spectacular pictures of the cross on Brennøy the reports contained no more information than we already had.

She sat down close to me on the sofa. Then she looked up at me out of the corners of her eyes. 'Perhaps we should start planning?'

I put my hand behind her neck and gently caressed her. 'You're thinking about the wedding, are you?'

'Mm.' She smiled. 'And the honeymoon.'

'Well, we could kill two birds with one stone.'

'Meaning … ?'

'Well, Thomas and Maria are in Italy at the moment, and we don't have much family here, so …'

Her smile broadened. 'How romantic, Varg! An Italian honeymoon!'

'Yes, why not? In Venice maybe.'

'Now you're surpassing yourself. But I'm up for it. Bring it on!'

'And then we'll have to work out where to live. We won't need two flats any more.'

'No, something bigger maybe?'

'Maybe?'

She stretched up and kissed me. 'If only you knew how happy I am that we've got this far, Varg.'

'Me, too,' I mumbled to her lips.

It was almost nine when the phone rang. Karin lifted up the receiver and even from five metres away I could hear the shrill voice.

'Ranveig? What? Yes, I can hear you.' She looked at me and rolled her eyes. 'I see … Yes … Yes … Is it alright if I bring Varg along?' She arched her eyebrows in my direction, and I nodded. 'OK, we'll do that. Take it easy. We'll talk soon. Yes, yes. … Bye.'

She put the phone down. 'Yes, you guessed. She was hysterical. Obviously things didn't go so well with Kristoffer and Else.'

'No. Was she OK with me coming along?'

'Yes.'

'Shall we take the car?'

'That's perhaps the safest, in case we have to drive her somewhere.'

'A&E do you mean?'

'Yes.'

Five minutes later we were in the car covering the short distance to Storhaugen.

22

This time I drove right up to the house. I let Karin out before parking close to the fence that surrounded the property and getting out on my side. When we went to the front door we rang, but no one answered.

I grabbed the handle, pressed it down and pushed the door. It wasn't locked. We looked at each other. In my book, this was not a good sign.

I opened the door completely. 'Ranveig?' No answer.

Karin said: 'Oh, my God, Varg!'

'Let's go in.'

There was no one in the hall. I called: 'Ranveig!'

Still no answer.

I opened the door to the sitting room. She was lying on the floor by one of the windows with her mobile phone beside her, as if in a deep sleep. She was pale, and her breathing was coming in short, irregular wheezes.

I dashed over, bent down, held her left arm and felt her pulse. Karin followed, crouched down and placed a hand carefully against her cheek.

She blinked and looked up. 'Karin? What happened?'

'That was what *we* were wondering.'

'I must have fainted.'

I scrutinised her face. 'There was no one else here, was there?'

'No, I ...' She had difficulty focussing. 'I rang Karin and then ... That's the last I can remember.'

'Pulse seems normal,' I muttered to Karin.

'Can I have something to drink?'

'I'll get some water,' Karin said, getting up and going through the dining room to the kitchen.

'You haven't eaten something that disagreed with you, have you?' I asked tentatively.

She gazed at me bleary-eyed. 'Disagreed? What do you mean?'

'Well … Come on, let me help you up.'

With a strong grip around her waist I lifted her to her feet and supported her through to the big sofa. She slumped down, straightened her blouse and brushed off some invisible specks of dust from her tight, black trousers.

Karin came in from the kitchen with a full jug of water and three glasses. She put everything down on the black coffee table, quickly poured water for Ranveig and passed her the glass.

She gratefully took it and drank greedily. Then she took a deep breath and looked at us almost guiltily. 'Sorry …'

'No reason to be sorry for anything,' Karin said. 'The main thing is you're better.'

'Yes … I … It just got too much for me.'

The room went silent. The only sound to be heard was the jug against a glass as Karin poured herself some water and then me. Karin sat down beside her friend, wrapped a protective arm around her and sent me a concerned frown.

'Have you got a regular doctor?' I asked.

'No, no! … I mean yes, of course, I have. But please don't phone anyone. This was just an accident. I hardly slept last night. There's so much going on, and this evening … Else and Kristoffer. It was just awful.'

'Else and Kristoffer …?'

'Kristoffer phoned and asked if they could pop up. I was happy and said yes, of course. Had I known, though, I would have asked a solicitor to be present.'

'You've talked about the inheritance already?'

'That was how it started. Kristoffer said … with everything that's at stake on Brennøy … he wanted me to confirm that I would support the sale of the land to Norcraft, and that had to happen now, so there would be no further delays.'

'But I mentioned yesterday … Hasn't he understood that the sale in 1988 is being contested?'

'I told him, but he turned a deaf ear. Anyway, I had no say, he said.'

'No say?'

With a trembling hand she grasped the jug, poured herself another glass and drank, then wiped her mouth with the back of her hand. 'I hadn't deserved it, he said. It was my fault their mother disappeared, took her own life, he said, then he bored his eyes into me and said … if not worse.'

'If not worse?'

'Yes! That we had taken her life!'

'You and Mons? Did he say that to your face?'

'Yes. Because we'd found each other. Because we …' She threw her hands in the air. 'I mean … What I mean to say is … That we'd driven her to her death.' Then there was silence.

Karin and I exchanged looks. She warned me off, but I couldn't pass up the opportunity. 'What you're saying,' I said softly and in as gentle a tone as I could muster, '… is that you and Mons had started a relationship before Lea disappeared. Is that what you're telling us?'

She looked up into my face. 'Yes, that was how it was, but … The way he said it, the way he hurled these accusations into my face … Lea's disappearance was a terrible tragedy. It hung over Mons and me for all the subsequent years, and we never managed to free ourselves from the feeling of guilt. In many ways it destroyed what … what we had. To forget it we fled into another lifestyle … travelling a lot, spending money, yes … living! As though we had to live extra hard to justify to ourselves what we'd done. Do you understand?'

Karin followed this monologue with her big, blue eyes. It came as no surprise to me. This was what I had felt the previous evening: that there was something Ranveig was holding back, something she wouldn't say.

I nodded. 'I understand. And you still can't tell us anything about what happened to Lea?'

'No, Varg! You have to believe me. I know nothing. But you should know: She was a very complicated personality. Having children had a terrible effect on her. After both births she suffered deep depression, and the last time – when Else was born – things were so serious she had to be admitted to hospital. They feared she would do something to harm the child.'

'That serious?'

'Yes, that serious, Varg!'

'But she never did?'

'No, no. The doctors got her back on an even keel, but ... I don't know. Mons said she never really got on with them. With the children, I mean. Neither Kristoffer nor Else. So he had to look after them, read to them, put them to bed and so on.'

'Hm.'

'But of course we always talked about it, Mons and I did. About what must have happened. That she had decided to end it all when she heard about us two.'

'How did she find out?'

She swallowed. 'Mons was going to take care of that. He told her the same day she ... went missing.'

'And later he pocketed her life insurance money ...'

Loud intake of breath. 'If you mean that ... He could never have done anything like that! I know that for certain. He would never have stood the pressure.'

'Sure?'

'Absolutely sure.'

'But Kristoffer accused you ...'

'He accused us both! Of driving his mother to her death. But he can't ...' – her voice cracked – '... have a confrontation with his father any more!'

'No.'

I stood waiting for her to recover. 'What did Else say? She was here too, wasn't she?'

'Else!' She raised her hands to her face and made two circles with her fingers in front of her eyes. 'She just sat staring, without saying a word. Not one word! And when he left she just got up and followed him.'

'Mm ... He just left?'

'After spewing up everything he had inside him he banged the table, got up and said: "You'll receive a document in the post! If you don't sign I'll see you in court. Just you try it," he said. And brandished a fist at me.'

'Did you perceive that as a threat?'

'Yes, he was threatening me. That was exactly what he was doing.'

I tried to bring all the various threads together. 'But you don't think he could have ... what happened to his father ...'

Ranveig's expression was grim. 'I wish I couldn't believe it possible, but when I saw him this evening ... He's capable of anything!'

'Erm ...' I hesitated. 'Surely not, with all the people he has to convince around him. Do you think that sounds likely?'

She shrugged. 'No idea.'

'I certainly think you should tell the police about this.'

'The police?'

'Yes, unfortunately I can't do anything as far as this is concerned. I've been assigned to investigate the land sale in 1988, but this ... It's way beyond my remit. If I became involved I would only have the police on my back again.'

'Again?'

'Yes. It wouldn't exactly be the first time. Let me put it like that.'

'But ...'

Our eyes met, and I shook my head. 'No, I'm sorry. But if – I repeat if –something relevant to the case should appear I would, of course, take it up immediately – with the relevant party.'

She nodded, but I wasn't sure the message had got through.

Again a silence fell over the room. I shifted my gaze to the big painting, a classic Norwegian mountain landscape with autumnal colours and the sharp contours of a photograph. It looked so quiet and peaceful, far from all the mobile telephones and at a safe distance from everything that smacked of inheritance disputes.

Karin put her arm around Ranveig again. 'Would you like ...? Shall I spend the night here again?'

Ranveig was visibly grateful. 'Would you?'

'Naturally. It's good to be able to help.'

I couldn't exactly suggest staying as well, so with that the perfect evening at home had gone up in smoke, and the following night as well.

Karin accompanied me out, a reprise of the previous evening. 'I'm sorry, Varg, but I had to offer.'

'Absolutely. I spend most of my nights alone anyway, so …' I pouted my disappointment.

'Not for long,' she said with a smile, leaned forward and kissed me. 'You've earned a bonus – next time.'

'A bonus? What might that be?'

'I'm not going to give it away, am I!'

'The trick worked. I feel better already.'

'Till next time then …' Another kiss before she gradually let go of me, a lingering reluctance, which made me feel even better.

'Remember: Don't forget to keep your eyes peeled as you set off for work tomorrow morning.'

'I won't. I haven't forgotten.' Her expression was serious as she closed the door, and I waited on the step until I heard she had locked up properly.

I went to my car, got behind the wheel and drove home. I had made up my mind now. I knew where I was going the next day.

23

Once again I caught the ferry from Leirvåg, but this time I didn't drive off at Skipavik but at the next stop, Sløvåg. The extensive industrial site there cut brutally into the landscape, but over the first brow of the hill I came to a far more idyllic part, along cultivated, autumn-yellow fields leading to Eidsbotn. From there I followed the road along the Eids Fjord, past Dalsøyra, down through the steep, narrow Undal Tunnel to Leversund, past Haveland to northern Gulen, where I turned west towards Eivindvik.

In 1961, when I was doing my final exams at Bergen Katedralskole, I was tested orally on Henrik Wergeland's poem about 'Eivindvig'. Inwardly, I had sung the praises of my teacher, Dahl, for his thorough analysis of the poem in Norwegian classes. I knew all about Provost Dahl, the priest at Eivindvik, and the final line of the poem, about how Dahl had nurtured young Strileland minds, was etched in my brain for ever. *Our* Dahl had squeezed a modicum of intellectual curiosity out of Bergen lads and lasses with more passionate looks for one another than the potato-pioneering priests of yore. The oral exam went well. Dahl later became a famous literature professor. I didn't get to Eivindvik until the end of the 80s, also then in connection with a case I was investigating.

The beautiful white timber church that meets you as you arrive in Eivindvik is from 1863, eleven years after Provost Dahl's death, so it couldn't have been there he had nurtured young Strileland minds. To the west of the church stand two stone crosses – a sign of early Christianisation, and it was here, in this region, that the historic legislative assembly of Gulating was held, where some of the oldest laws in the country were passed.

Today Eivindvik was a quiet, sparsely populated municipal centre with a hotel – we were never quite sure whether it was open for business or not – a quay where the old ferry had long stopped plying its trade and a council building that looked more like a children's school from the 60s, up on the ridge opposite the old rectory. However, it would be hard to find more beautiful surroundings, with Mount Kvitbergnova to the north and Mount Fonnefjellet to the south of the sound. Between the mountains idyllic Eivindvik nestled in the warm September sun.

Before I left Bergen I had made sure that the Housing and Property office would be staffed this Friday. I was received by a middle-aged man with a none too neatly arranged comb-over, who had dug out the contract between Per Nordbø and Mons Mæland, dated February 1988, in advance of my arrival. I was immediately able to identify it as a copy of the one I had seen in Bringeland's office.

'Could I have a copy, please?'

'No problem,' said the man with the comb-over, taking the contract with him to a side room, where I heard a photocopier starting up. Without being asked, he took out an official stamp to confirm that the copy was genuine, stamped the document and signed it himself before slipping it into an envelope and giving it to me. Exemplary administrative conduct, I had to concede.

'I'm afraid there's a small fee. Copy charge.'

'And it is … ?'

'Twenty kroner.'

'That's fine.' I took out my wallet and paid. Then I said: 'Could I ask you a question?'

He nodded and looked at me expectantly.

'Do you remember this case yourself?'

'No, I can't say that I do. This concerns a property on Brennøy, and I didn't know the people concerned. Anyway, the contract was signed in February 1988, and at that time I was in fact off sick. For a couple of months.'

'But one witness, Gunvor Matre, was supposed to be employed at the nursing home here.'

'At the nursing home? Yes, I remember her vaguely. But she left. She wasn't from Eivindvik, I don't think.'

'So she doesn't live here any more then?'

'No, logically she must have moved.' Then he seemed to remember something. 'Hang on ...'

He went over to one of the filing cabinets, found a file, opened it and nodded. 'That's what I thought ...' He came back to me with a pensive expression on his face. 'She bought a lot on Brennøy, too.'

'A lot?'

'Yes, a little piece of land. That was the year after, January 1989, and by then I had been back in the office for quite some time. That was how I remembered.'

'Could I ... ?' I held out my hand.

'Yes, yes, be my guest.'

He gave me the sheet and I read what was on it. It concerned the sale of a plot on Brennøy. The seller was Mons Mæland. The buyer was Gunvor Matre. The signature was witnessed by two people. One was Bjørn Brekkhus, the other Jarle Glosvik.

'Where is this on Brennøy?'

He took back the document, checked the property number, found a map of the area and began to search with his finger. 'Here: this must be the chapel, unless I'm very much mistaken. And this is Gunvor Matre's land.'

He showed me where on the map, and I leaned over. I immediately saw where it was. The small, red house we had passed on the road towards the cross.

'Bit strange, don't you think?'

His expression was blank. 'Well, a sale's a sale. So much happens on that front.'

'May I have a copy of this, too?'

He nodded, and the procedure was repeated: photocopier, stamp, envelope, fee.

'The Deputy Chairman: Do you think he'll be in his office today?'

'I believe I saw him earlier in the day. It's two doors down from this one.'

I thanked him warmly and left the office. Deeper into the bowels of the council building I came to a door with a sign saying *Deputy Chairman*.

I knocked. Straight afterwards I heard footsteps across the floor. The door opened, and in the doorway stood Jarle Glosvik, staring impatiently at me.

'Yes? What do you want?' Then he recognised me, and his eyes narrowed. 'Oh, yes. You're the person who … don't think we've been introduced.'

'No. My name's Veum. Varg Veum. Have you got a moment?'

'I have got one or two. Come in.'

He showed me into a very ordinary office where the only thing to brighten it was a large photograph of the building on one wall, taken as far as I could see from a plane flying north-east. The furniture was simple and practical and signalled that, in this regard, the council was as sober as the taxpayers in Gulen could expect.

Glosvik sat down behind the desk and motioned with his hand to two chairs, one on either side of a little table, where visiting administrators could put their piles of documents if they were too heavy to hold.

After I had taken a seat, he said: 'Veum … I couldn't really place you when you were on Brennøy, I must confess.'

'No?' I had a rejoinder on the tip of my tongue, but decided to be rather more tactical than was my wont. 'I'm a private investigator and I was there because my assignment was to track down Mons Mæland.'

'Yes, he'd been missing for some days, I'd been told. It was a dramatic turn of events. It's still whirring away inside me.'

The 'me' he referred to was small and compact. His hair was dark blond, in need of a trim, his face was round with fleshy lips and narrow eyebrows. He was wearing plain, everyday clothes: brown trousers, blue pullover and a white shirt with a faint check woven into the material. 'But now he's been found, so that can't be why you've come to see me.'

'No. I've been given a new assignment in connection with a matter that came up on Brennøy.'

'Came up? What matter would that be? No doubt the environmental organisations are behind this. If you only knew the sort of accusations they hurl at us. We aren't worth the ground we walk on, according
to them!'

'Really?'

'And all we work for is the good of the council and the community.
This is about the local economy above all else. Income from property,
new workplaces, tax breaks, money for the sale of power. If we can get
these wind-power projects off the ground – and not just on Brennøy but
in other places in the municipality, as well as Solund and further north
in the county – all the indications suggest that life will be better for
those who live here: the health system, social services, schools, roads
... For me, this is a "to be or not to be" question for the whole region.
The difference between poverty and wealth, and at the same time huge
progress for people all over the globe in the fight for the environment.'

'But you knew that Mons Mæland had changed his mind?'

'Changed his mind? What about?'

'The wind farm. Word is he may have been about to change his mind
at the time of the land sale. And I have this from reliable sources: his
son, Kristoffer, for one.'

He glared at me furiously. 'Oh, really? This is news to me, I have to
admit.'

'So, in other words, the environmental organisation was interested
in keeping Mons Mæland both alive and at the head of its company.'

'Yes, but did they know?'

'Absolutely sure they did.'

'So then ...'

'Then the perpetrator could equally well be on the opposing side,
among the potential developers.'

'We-ell ...' He raised both palms. 'I can see that. But one thing I can
tell you, Veum: Such actions are way beyond the scope of official politics in the municipality of Gulen.'

'*Official* politics, you say!'

'Now, don't try and be funny, Veum. There are much stronger powers at work here than we in Gulen can access. But I assume you didn't come all the way from Bergen to Eivindvik to tell me this.'

'No, my real business was with the Housing and Property office.'

'Oh, yes?'

'The sale of land that is being contested.'

He flushed with annoyance. 'Yes, what a case that was! Solicitors … You can have them for free, as far as I'm concerned!'

'Solicitors? Free? Which planet do you inhabit?'

'Yes, I know what you mean. What an idea to come up with, ten years after the event! But they won't get far with it; I'll make sure of that.' Then his face changed, something sly and feline entered it. 'I hope the solicitor didn't hire you, did he?'

'No, not at all. But I've been given a copy of the contract … well, not given; I paid for it …'

'Yes, yes, get to the point!'

'And it looks relatively genuine. It was witnessed by the then Chief of Police in Lindås and a nurse from the home here.'

'Relatively genuine? What's relative about it?'

'Well, it transpires this nurse … you clearly know her yourself – Gunvor Matre.'

'Yes. What about her?'

'The following year she bought a little part of Mons Mæland's land on Brennøy, this time witnessed by the Chief of Police in Lindås, Bjørn Brekkhus, and you yourself.'

'Yes? I remember that. You're not going to question Mons Mæland's sanity as well, are you?'

'No, no. Not initially. But the sale itself is a bit odd.'

'Odd? It was an old house, right by the chapel, and it had no value in itself, at least not with reference to the wind farm. It's where Per Nordbø lived while he could still look after himself.'

'And the price?'

'Erm, that must be in the contract, isn't it?'

'Yes … 75,000. Seems quite reasonable, doesn't it?'

'You're not talking about a plot in the heart of Bergen, Veum. This is

the reality in Fringe Norway. I would imagine 75,000 kroner was probably a pretty normal fee there, even with an old house on the plot.'

So you found nothing strange about the contract when you witnessed it? Or now?'

'What should be odd about it?'

'The only thing I know about Gunvor Matre is that she was one of the
witnesses on a property transfer that has turned out to be very significant.
A year later she buys a slice of the same property. If someone subsequently
questions whether Per Nordbø was of sound mind when he signed the
contract, someone might also wonder whether *fru* or *frøken* Matre has
been persuaded to sign with the promise of later remuneration.'

He took stock of me. 'Are you aware that this is a particularly serious
accusation you're making, Veum?'

'I'm not making any accusations at all. I'm just suggesting the kind
of thing someone might spread. Especially now that a solicitor has
entered the arena.'

Jarle Glosvik sighed heavily, half-turned in his chair and gazed out
of the window. 'Is it any wonder we have trouble recruiting new people
for posts as local politicians? When folk who don't have a clue about
the problems we confront here in the so-called provinces are constantly putting spokes in our wheels?' Then he turned to me again, with
a hang-dog expression. 'Were there any other glad tidings you wanted
to bring me today, Veum?'

'Let's conclude this business first, shall we. I assume when you witnessed this contract in 1989 it was in good faith. What would *fru* or
frøken ...'

'If we're going to be precise, it's *frøken*.'

'I'll make a note of that. What did she want with a property on
Brennøy?'

'She had her roots there and had always wanted a retreat facing the
sea. So she had the opportunity to spend some of her savings on this
purchase.'

'You're from Byrknesøy, I understand.'

'That's correct.'

'Almost everyone I've met on this case has roots somewhere there, I've been told.'

'Yes, and so? Where did the wealth of this country come from? Had it not been for fishermen and farmers Norway wouldn't exist. Without Western Norway we would have been a wasteland. Fish in the old days, hydro power for most of the century, oil the last decade and for a while yet – and then wind – and maybe wave power in the future. Tell our friends at Storting that, Veum. Without Western Norway there would be no Norway.'

'I don't mix with that kind of person on a daily basis.'

'No, nor me.' He got up and came round the desk. 'Now I've got other matters to attend to.'

I got up, too. 'Besides politics you run a business, I gather.'

'It's no secret, Veum. Full-time politicians are city folk. Here we need to have something on the side to live.'

'Any jobs in connection with the wind farm?'

He flushed again. 'I'm deaf in that ear, Veum. Say it again and I might have to contact a solicitor myself.'

'Would you like me to recommend one?'

He snorted.

'And there was one other thing, Glosvik.'

'Yes?' He scowled at me.

'Let's stop beating about the bush, shall we. We all saw who you were talking to on Wednesday. Even I had the pleasure of bumping into him the following day at Stein Svenson's. We both know who we're talking about.' As he didn't answer, I added: 'Trond Tangenes.'

He gulped. His eyes hardened. 'Who?'

'Don't make yourself appear any more stupid than you are. He as good as admitted it himself, at Svenson's. He was there carrying out an assignment for you.'

He opened his mouth, as if to say something, but closed it again without uttering so much as a syllable.

'You've talked at great length about local council finances and so on. Probably true, most of it. But what about your finances? Work for

entrepreneurs is hard to come by at the moment, isn't it? You're depend-
ent on things improving. For you personally it would be an enormous
lift if the wind power project got under way. Or am I mistaken?'

'What do you want, Veum?'

'This is what I want. Listen to me. Not only did Trond Tangenes
physically attack Stein Svenson. He also issued unveiled threats –
against me personally and against someone close to me. Am I making
myself clear? Do you understand what I'm saying?'

He observed me without speaking or showing any emotion.

'So let me spell it out for you. If anything serious happens, either to
me or my partner, I will hold you responsible, Glosvik. Personally. I'll
hang you out to dry, so high that your reputation won't only be ruined
throughout Gulen, I'll have your name on the front page of the biggest
bloody papers in the country. I will stop at nothing. And remember
this, Glosvik. You have a position to uphold, which is much more than
I have. In other words: Tell your mongrel to stay on its mat. Now. Have
you understood?'

His staring eyes were glazed, the blood vessels in his temples swollen
and his jaw muscles visibly groaning. Then he reacted. He went to the
door, slammed his hand down on the handle and opened it. He stood
there as silent as the mountain ranges in the landscape outside.

I followed. I stopped in front of him. 'Have you understood, I asked?'

'Get out, Veum. We have nothing more to discuss.'

For a few seconds we stood glowering at each other. I could see that
deep inside him my message had hit home. Whether it would lead to a
positive outcome it was still too early to say.

It would be wrong to say we parted as friends. But I hadn't been
pampered by fate in that respect. He stood there until I was well down
the corridor. Then he withdrew and slammed the door hard after him.
I found my own way out.

There was one man I felt a strong need to contact. Before getting
into my car I rang Bjørn Brekkhus. He still wasn't answering his mobile.
When I phoned his landline it was the same woman who had answered
the previous evening.

She could hear who it was and said at once: 'He got your message, but all he said was: "What good is it now?"'

'So that was why he didn't ring back?'

'I assume so.'

'Is he available now?'

'No, he's gone to Brennøy today.'

'Really?'

'We found out what had happened to Mons Mæland. He and Bjørn had been friends ever since their younger days. He said he wanted to see the spot where the crime took place.'

'He hasn't got roots there as well, has he?'

'Roots? On Brennøy? Not at all. His family's from Masfjorden, if you go back a few generations.'

'Tell me: Did you also know Mons Mæland?'

'Not very well. But I'd met him on various occasions.' After a short pause she said: 'There's something you should know.'

'Oh, yes.'

'I've been in a wheelchair for the last fifteen years. Our house has been completely adapted so that I can cope indoors without a problem. But I don't do much gallivanting, if you know what I mean.'

'So your husband won't stay overnight on the island?'

'Oh, no. I'm expecting him home for a late dinner, at around eight.'

'Well, please mention that I rang again and that I'd appreciate it if he returned the call.'

'I'll do that.'

We finished the conversation, I stuffed my mobile into a pocket and I had already made my decision. Brennøy was up next, no question.

24

I was lucky with the ferry at Sløvåg and drove onto the deck just before the gate closed for departure. Ten minutes later I drove ashore at Skipavik. The weather was still as beautiful. The sky was high and blue, and the air so clear that you had the sense that you could see as far as Iceland if you were high enough up.

Driving down onto the quay in Brennøy, I recognised the black Mercedes of Bjørn Brekkhus, parked carefully outside Naustvik Hotel & Harbour. In approximately the same place as the last time were the unwashed, red Opel Kadett and the white VW. I parked next to Brekkhus. So that we wouldn't miss one another I went to the reception cabin, opened the door and stepped inside.

There was no one in reception, and no one was sitting in the café area. The tables and chairs were back in place after the re-arrangement for the police interviews two days ago. Behind the glass counter there were some waffles and the coffee in the jug on the warming plate was steaming.

From the floor above came some sounds I was unable to define until I was standing at the bottom of the stairs, and even then I wasn't a hundred per cent certain. Someone could have been watching TV, of course. It could have been a discreet wrestling match or it could be … something else.

The investigator in me shoved all my usual good manners aside and drove me noiselessly up the stairs, step by step, until I was at the top. The door to the office where I had spoken to the police previously was ajar and there was no longer any doubt. That was where the commotion was coming from, and now it had assumed a definitive character of … something else. There was the slap of skin on skin, flesh on flesh, in regular rhythmical movements, accompanied by semi-stifled groans.

I should have politely withdrawn, of course. Whenever my ledger is closed, this entry is unlikely to end up on the credit side. Softly, I tiptoed to the door, leaned forward carefully, held my breath and peered through the gap between door and jamb.

Kristine Rørdal was lying prone across the desk. Staring ahead in dark ecstasy and tossing her head with every thrust her body received from behind. Her top half was fully covered, but someone had pulled down her trousers and was pumping away between those milky white thighs with determined strokes. She didn't seem to be objecting, and when I heard his voice I realised that every right was on his side.

'This is for your sinful life! This is for your bastard! You bitch! You whore! You tart!' It was Lars Rørdal giving us all the variants of loose women he had in his repertoire.

'Yes!' groaned Kristine, rolling her eyes. 'Yes! Yes! Yes …'

Without a further sound I cautiously withdrew. Step by step, down to reception. I opened the door, careful not to make any noise, stepped outside and closed it quietly after me.

I stood breathing out until I had my respiration back to normal. What I had experienced had made an impression on me, in several ways. But the detective in me had focussed on what Lars Rørdal had said. *'This is for your bastard!'* Was he talking about Ole? And, if so, who was the father?

I was in two minds as to what to do next.

I could wait for ten minutes or so and take a punt on them having finished, perhaps make sure that my arrival created more noise than before, bang the door, ring the bell in reception and ask in a loud voice if anyone was there. Or I could do what I had actually come to do: try to get a conversation with Gunvor Matre and Bjørn Brekkhus, preferably both together.

The latter was probably the better idea. I glanced at the abandoned fish hall where we had found Stein Svenson, confirmed that there were no boats moored today and then made my way up the slope to the chapel.

Once there, I found myself confronted with another decision. For a moment I stood eyeing the small, red house with the white curtains. I recalled the glimpse of a woman's face the first time I had walked past. Now I knew that in all probability it had been Gunvor Matre.

The house looked sombre and forbidding. There was nothing to suggest she had any visitors. I continued through the copse and over the rocks to the cross. I was still a long way off when I saw the tall, erect figure of Bjørn Brekkhus. He was staring up at the cross, as motionless as if he had turned to stone. He was unaware of my presence until I was right next to him.

25

He was standing close to the cross. To get there he had stepped over the cordon the police had left, secured around some sizeable boulders they had found.

'Veum? What are you doing here?'

I stayed the other side of the cordon. 'I tried to ring you. Again.'

He looked at me suspiciously. 'And you were in such a hurry that you followed me here?'

'No. I had business here anyway. What about you? Why are you here?'

He ran a large hand through his slicked-back, steel-grey hair. 'We saw the news item on Wednesday evening. And read the papers the next day. How unbelievable that it should be Mons! When Ranveig rang to tell us, it came as a shock … I couldn't believe it could be true. Him going missing was bad enough. I would have understood it if he'd drowned, as Lea did. But this grotesque act …' He turned back to the cross. 'It's incomprehensible, stringing him up on a cross, like some common thief.'

'Or a saviour.'

'What?'

'We probably connect Jesus the Saviour with the cross rather than the two thieves.'

'You know what I meant.'

'Yes, of course …' I had this incurable weakness: I could never take a word at its face value. I always had to split it down the middle.

'Who could have done it?'

I shrugged. 'I don't know.'

'But you were here when they found him?'

'How do you know?'

'Ranveig said.'

'Yes, I was as good as in the front row. But it was Lars Rørdal who found him.'

'Lars?'

'Yes, do you know him?'

'Oh, yes. Can't deny that.' His eyes glazed over. 'There was a time ...' He looked around him. 'In my younger days, I often pootled around these islands in a boat, Veum. When you get as old as I am and you know your sojourn on earth is finite you often hark back to the time when you were young and full of hope and had the best years in front of you. And now that's one hell of a long time ago.'

'Mons and you were childhood friends, I'm told.'

'Actually, it was more like teenage friends. I was four or five years older than him. But we were both boat enthusiasts, and when you chugged around like we did ... You know, there were dances on the moles and quays, and not just official ones. Someone had a battery-operated gramophone. That was all that was needed. Or someone had brought along an accordion or just a guitar. On rare occasions a band came over from Bergen, but then that was at a youth centre and a closed arrangement. I can remember that the Stringers came here once and a band called the Harpers ...'

'The Harpers, yes. I knew those boys.'

'And young people came from all over, north and south. Now and then there was the odd dust-up, and as I was over twenty I was often used as the law-enforcement man. You wouldn't believe it today, but Lars, he was a bit of a bruiser in those days. And more often than not he got involved in fights over Kristine.'

'Kristine?'

'Oh, yes, she was quite a looker, I can tell you. There were loads of boys drooling over her, but Lars guarded her like the crown jewels.'

'They were together even then?'

'Yes, at least they got together then.'

'Mons also had a soft spot for her, didn't he?'

'Yes, but they became friends again … afterwards.'

'After what?'

He hesitated. 'I don't know …'

'Come on. Spit it out. Don't you mealy-mouth me.'

'Well … OK. Once, one late summer's evening on the quay in Solei-botn, I think it was, there was a dance at the harbour. Kristine suddenly disappeared, and Lars was absolutely desperate. He thought something had happened to her. She was in the bushes having a pee, we said. But no. He sent a group of us to look for her, in all directions, and, well, it was me who found them.'

'Kristine and Mons?'

'Yes, they had scrambled up a slope, crawled behind some bushes and … well, I think you understand.'

'They were screwing?'

He raised both hands. 'She had her knickers round her ankles, that much I can say. And they didn't protest when I told them to go back down. They looked pretty sheepish, I can tell you. I packed Mons off ahead so that Lars wouldn't get suspicious and afterwards I accompanied Kristine safely back to the dance. Straight afterwards she and Lars went off in his boat. Early that autumn Lars converted, and they never went dancing again, neither he nor Kristine. By the following year they were married and had Ole.'

'And what's the time scale here?'

'Erm … early 60s. 1962–3.'

'And later …'

'Later? What do you mean?'

'Did you meet Lars and Kristine again?'

'Only sporadically. I rarely came out here. And if I did, it was by boat. But Mons and I kept in touch.'

'And Lars and Mons: do you know if they stayed in touch?'

'As long as Lea was alive they did.'

'Oh?'

'Yes, that wasn't so surprising. After all, they were related.'

'Related? You mean … ?'

'Lea was his sister.'

'Lea's maiden name was Rørdal?'

'Yes.'

'But … Did she also go to these harbour dances?'

'No, never. They came from a deeply religious family, both of them. Lars broke out, as I said, before finding his way home, as he put it.'

'But how did she meet Mons then?'

'It came about because he spent his summer holidays here. As you can imagine, this match wasn't very popular in her house. Our Inner Mission is not that far from the Taliban, Veum. They refused point-blank, but she stuck to her guns, and for some years after the wedding I don't think she had any contact with her family at all. But as time passed, things eased, especially when the children were born. Nevertheless, we shouldn't ignore the fact that the psychological afflictions she suffered in later life had their origin in this breach with her family and the feelings that must have produced in her.'

'Now I understand even better why he was so shaken after finding Mons. Lars Rørdal, I mean, on Wednesday.'

A picture was beginning to emerge here, which as yet I couldn't fully interpret. Lars, Kristine and Mons. Mons and Lea. Kristine, Mons and Lea. And Lars again.

'Did you ever talk about those times, you and Mons?' I asked.

'About when we used to go to dances? Only superficially. The way you talk about old times and mutual acquaintances.'

'But today you came out here … ?'

'Yes. As I said, I wanted to see the scene of the crime.'

I pointed to the cordon. 'You're supposed to stay this side.'

He looked down, as though it was the first time he had noticed. 'They've done all the investigating they needed to do.' He looked up again. 'Do you know whether they have any suspicions?'

'The police?'

'Yes.'

'You're closer to them than me. I imagine you would know. You have contacts, don't you?'

'Yes, I do, but I haven't asked anyone. Anyway, it's limited what they're prepared to say to outsiders, even if you're an ex-colleague. 'And you, Veum? Did you find anything while you were searching for him?'

'Hmm ... In brief, yes and no. There were conflicts in the family, that's obvious. Ranveig was a red rag to a bull as far as both children were concerned. There was the feud about this wind farm. The environmental lobby was against it – or at least parts of it. The power companies were for, naturally enough. Mons Mæland had changed sides, as Ranveig told us when we were at their cabin. And then there's the old land deal which has come under the spotlight.'

'The land ...?'

'That's actually why I've come here today. To talk to Gunvor Matre. But it suits me very well that you're here, too.'

He frowned. 'Oh, yes.'

'Have you heard about this? During the survey on Wednesday it came out that someone called Stein Svenson, who is a kind of provisional second-in-command at NmV – Naturvernere mot Vindkraft, in case you didn't know – has let it be known via his solicitor, Johannes Bringeland, that they're going to query the legal status of the 1988 land sale.'

'I see ...'

'As you perhaps remember, you and Gunvor Matre were witnesses at the signing of the contract.'

'Yes, that could well be right. She was a nurse from the home where the vendor had been admitted.'

'His name was Per Nordbø.'

'Yes, something like that.'

'But you witnessed another sale in which Gunvor Matre was involved.'

'Did I?'

'The year after. When she bought the plot by the chapel off Mons Mæland. You and Jarle Glosvik signed.'

'Yes, now it's coming back to me. But I just had the contract shoved into my hand by Mons. I had to sign that the man was in his right mind.'

'And was he?'

'Absolutely! But what on earth has that got to do with all this?'

'I was given this assignment by another client. So let's take you first: You maintain that Per Nordbø was in his right mind when he signed over the land in 1988?'

'I certainly do. Otherwise I wouldn't have signed.' He pointedly stretched out his left arm to check his watch. 'But now I've got to get back. I have a ferry to catch.'

'Yes, I spoke to your wife. She was going to keep your dinner hot, she said.'

'Right ...' He stepped across the red-and-white tape, turned round and cast a final glance at the cross, at the small skerries and the vast sea beyond, then sighed heavily, shook his head and went on his way. The light from the afternoon sun fell over us, pale and colourless, as I joined him.

'I spoke to Ranveig last night,' I said.

'Uhuh.'

'She made a confession.'

He glanced at me. 'About what?'

'She confessed that she and Mons had already started a relationship before Lea went missing.'

He slowed his pace. 'She and Mons: did Lea know about them?'

'According to Ranveig, Mons had told Lea the night before she disappeared.'

He came to an abrupt halt. 'For heaven's sake, man! This changes everything. There was never any talk about it at the time.'

'You never investigated this aspect?'

'No, we had to believe ... Mons assured us there had never been any disagreements between Lea and him, that they had a normal ... She always went for a morning swim and there must have been an accident. But now ...' He threw his arms in the air. 'Naturally enough, we'd considered suicide. Had we known this, we would have considered other options, and I personally ... I would have had to stand down from the investigation because of my long-standing friendship with Mons. I'm sure you understand.'

'The case isn't time-barred.'

'No, but what good would it do? Lea died sixteen years ago. Mons is dead now. Ranveig …'

'Yes, she claims she doesn't know anything. She says Mons and she always feared that it was suicide, precipitated by what they had done. And from what I know now, Lea had broken with her family to marry Mons. And she had experienced serious post-natal depression. How bitter must it have been for her to discover that her marriage had broken down too? Completely. How difficult it would have been for her to go back home – after all that. Perhaps putting an end to it all was a simpler solution?'

He looked at me glumly. 'So why rake everything up again after all these years?' Slowly he started to walk on. You've upset me, Veum. I had the wool pulled over my eyes, by the person I regarded as my very best friend.'

I said nothing. We were silent until we were on the road between the chapel and the red house belonging to Gunvor Matre.

'Aren't you coming in?' I asked him.

'Why should I? I don't know her. I've only met her once, the time we signed the contract. Besides … the ferry.'

'There are several ferries.'

'That right, Veum? Sometimes I actually feel the very last ferry has gone. And that we're stranded here forever.'

'Here?'

'Here,' he said, downcast, and in one long, lingering glance he took in everything from the vaulted sky and the sea to the small cluster of houses and the bridge superstructure over to Byrknesøy, the top of which we could glimpse above the chapel roof.

Then he nodded and went down to the car park. I stood watching for a moment, then left the road for the path to the red house. This time a curtain definitely twitched, and I hadn't reached the house before the door opened and she was standing in the doorway waiting for me.

'Gunvor Matre?'

She nodded briefly. 'And you are … ?'

'Varg Veum.'

'And what is it you want?'

'A little chat … about what's happened.'

'You mean …?' She glanced towards the trees hiding the cross and the mountain plateau.

'Amongst other things.'

For a few more seconds she eyed me with suspicion. Then she stepped aside, looking quickly down at the other houses to see if there was anyone watching what was going on. 'You'd better come in. But take off your shoes. I've just cleaned.'

I did as she instructed, like the well brought-up man that I am.

26

She had not only cleaned the house; it was as though she had sterilised it. But the detergent had been green soap. It had a characteristically strong smell and reminded me of my early childhood when my mother cleaned at the weekend and everywhere smelt exactly like this.

Gunvor Matre was an energetic little woman with round cheeks and snowy-white hair tied into a tight bun behind her head, making her face look even rounder, like a Buddha's. She was wearing a plain, dark-blue dress with a white hem by her knees. Age-wise, I put her at about seventy, but in good physical shape, the way old nurses often are.

The little sitting room she showed me into was simply furnished in an old-fashioned way. She had some yellowing family photographs on the walls, but even those of children looked to be from the early 1950s, judging by the clothes. The furniture consisted of two upholstered armchairs in red and grey, a small coffee table and a dark-brown side-board. On the table was a narrow white runner embroidered with a grey cross-stitch pattern. She had placed a blue-black flower vase containing a sprig of heather on top. In one corner there was an antiquated television set, and in the adjacent kitchen, which faced out onto the road, I glimpsed a portable radio on one of the shelves. There was a cup of coffee on the table. I guessed that was where she spent most of her time, in exactly the right spot behind the transparent, white curtains.

I took a seat in an armchair.

'Cup of coffee?'

'Yes, please.'

She had coffee brewed and ready, and it didn't take her long to pour us both a cup.

Occupying the other chair, she looked at me with her alert blue eyes. 'Terrible business,' she said.

'No doubt about that.'

'And then Mons Mæland. A man like him.'

'Yes, you knew him, didn't you?'

'I wouldn't say that, but he made a very good impression on the occasions I met him.'

'Did you notice anything on the night or the morning when it must have happened?'

'If I noticed anything?' She shook her head. 'The police asked me the same question. But I didn't see or hear anything.'

'Were you awake?'

'At night? No, but I'm a very light sleeper. I would have heard if anything unusual had been going on. I've told all this to the police. Who are you? What do you want?'

'Varg Veum, as I said. I'm a private investigator, hired to find out about the land sales you were involved in, in the late 80s.'

'Land sales? Involved in?'

'Yes, this house for example. You bought it from Mons Mæland in 1989, is that right?'

She bristled with defiance. 'Yes, and?'

'The previous year you witnessed the signing of a contract by the man who originally lived here, Per Nordbø, transferring the whole of this area in the north of the island to Mons Mæland.'

'Yes, nothing wrong with that, was there?'

'Not if Per Nordbø was in his right mind when the sale was carried out. Someone has decided to contest it.'

'Oh? Who?'

'Well, a distant relation, Stein Svenson. If that name means anything to you.'

'Svenson? Isn't he one of these environment people?'

'Yes, that's the one.'

'So he has his own opinions about this and that, I suppose.'

'Yes, but, back to … Was Per Nordbø right in his head when this sale went through?'

'As right in the head as you and me, *herr* Veum! I'd had him as a patient for two and a half years. He was unsteady on his pins and couldn't stand for long. But his head was as clear as a bell. He read four newspapers a day and could follow everything they watched on TV.'

'You don't need to be very clear-headed to do that.'

'He *was* clear-headed. He knew what he was doing when he sold the land to Mons Mæland. He was happy that the person who bought it had roots here, he said. And he had no heirs himself, so, well, that's how it was.'

'And you knew what you were doing when you bought this house from Mons Mæland the year after?'

'What's that supposed to mean? We discussed it the very first time we met, when he was in Eivindvik and was negotiating with Per. He had no interest in this house. He had a cabin somewhere, and he had no plans to move out here. It was the land he was interested in, the investment potential. He had foresight, Mons did, I can tell you that.'

'Yes, you can say that again. But you've got roots here too, I'm told.'

'Yes, not on this island, but across the bridge.' She nodded in that direction. 'At the end of the fjord. But after the bridge came … It's nice and quiet here. If, like me, you've had a long life working for the health service you enjoy every moment you have, the peace and quiet over a cup of coffee, the radio.'

'And the chapel across the way.'

'I'm not one of them.'

'No?'

'No. I've seen too much illness and death over the years to believe completely in the infallible creator they worship over there.'

'But you know Lars Rørdal and his family?'

Her eyes glinted. 'Oh, yes, that's not a big family.'

'No?'

'No, it's just him and Kristine, since Ole went to Bergen.' After a little pause she added: 'And no one knows for sure who *his* father was.'

'No?'

'No, and please don't repeat this, but that Kristine was a lively young thing, I remember. A town girl and used to a bit of everything. Then she suddenly fell pregnant, and they got married, quick as a shot, Lars and her. Well, they'd been together for a while, it wasn't that. But there have been no children since, and you can interpret that in lots of ways, I've learned. But *she* proved she could have children.' She sighed dramatically, and I saw a glint of schadenfreude in her eyes as she added: 'They didn't get the son and daughter-in-law they wanted, those self-righteous Rørdal parents, but that's what it's like now in these much-trumpeted modern times.'

'So no theories about who could be the father?'

'No, you'll need to tap other sources for that information. The people they were with at the time.'

'Mons Mæland ... could he be a candidate?'

She sent me a funny look. 'Mons Mæland? Well, the Mælands came here on holiday. But surely you don't mean ... Could Lars be ...?' Her eyes automatically found the cross. 'No, you can't mean that. They were related, in a way.'

'I don't mean anything at all. It's subject to the police investigation.'

'Yes, that's ... But I don't suppose that was ... What did you actually want from me?'

'I wanted to talk about the land deal, and you've answered my questions there. The rest was what we might call "chit-chat".' I lifted my cup in the air as if to emphasise what we were doing.

'Yes, please don't repeat it, as I said.'

'The other person who signed when you bought this property, Jarle Glosvik. How well do you know him?'

Again the repressed schadenfreude shone in her eyes. 'Oh, you know. We come from the same village. But he's had his problems, Jarle has, I understand.'

'In politics, do you mean?'

'No, I was thinking more about ... It's not so long ago that I heard he was close to going bankrupt. He's working hard to keep his head above water, they say.'

'So it would be very important if the work here gets off the ground?'

'It would certainly be important for the land he has on Byrknesøy, but you can't ignore the fact that it would bring work for his firm over here, too.'

She sat staring into the air, with a thoughtful expression on her face. 'Are you saying that … ?' She didn't the complete the sentence, and I didn't follow it up, either. But I felt fairly sure that we were both thinking along the same lines.

I drained my cup. 'Well, thank you for the coffee and chat.' I took out one of my business cards. 'If something occurs to you, you can find me here.'

'Occurs to me? What about?'

'Well …' I hunched my shoulders to say I didn't know, either.

She accompanied me to the door, and we said polite goodbyes. I set a course for Naustvik, confident that the lovers' tryst on the first floor would be over by now.

27

When I was back down in the car park, both Bjørn Brekkhus' black Mercedes and the battered Opel Kadett were gone. However, a new car had arrived, a Saab 900 I thought I recognised. The last time I had seen it was in Stein Svenson's yard. Now it was parked down by the old fish hall where we had found him two days ago.

I walked down there, pushed the door open and shouted: 'Hello! Anyone here?'

As no one answered, I went in. The big room was as empty as on the previous occasion, but the footprints on the floor showed what had gone on after Svenson had been found. I crossed the room and opened the door to the room where he had been. It was empty as well.

I left the building, closed the door behind me and crossed the car park. At reception I knocked politely and waited for a couple of seconds before opening the door and entering.

Kristine Rørdal was standing behind the desk with shiny eyes, rosy cheeks and dishevelled hair, or perhaps that was how I perceived her, as I knew what she had been doing a couple of hours before.

She looked up in surprise. 'Veum?'

'Hi. Is Stein Svenson here?'

'Svenson. No. Why?'

'His car's outside.'

A puzzled expression formed on her face. 'No. He hasn't been here.'

'You haven't had any visitors?'

'Visitors? No.' But she tossed her hair back and blushed as though frightened I could see right through her. 'What do you mean?'

'Well, nothing except that when I parked a couple of hours ago there were two cars here. Is the red Opel Kadett … ?'

'Oh, yes. That was Lars. He ... popped by.'

'Popped by?' I held her eyes and smiled. Now her blushing was so obvious she was annoyed. 'Yes! There was something he had to do. What business is that of yours actually?'

'And a black Mercedes. Did he pop by too?'

'That must have been Bjørn Brekkhus. Yes, he popped by and had a cup of coffee before ... He was going to see the crime scene, he said. The cross.'

'You and he are old friends, aren't you?'

'From way back, yes. He's become ... older.' She stroked her hair as though what she had said reminded her that several years had passed for her, too.

'Have you got a cup of coffee for me perhaps?'

'Yes, of course. Find yourself a table.'

She got up, left the desk and went to the coffee machine behind the glass counter. She was wearing practical clothes today as well, a lumberjack shirt and loose, blue workman's trousers, but her female charms were no less winsome now that I – in a way – had seen her in action, with her rump in the air and trousers round her ankles.

I watched her as she crossed the floor with a cup of steaming coffee. 'Black, if I remember rightly, wasn't it?'

I nodded. 'You didn't tell me when we were talking last time that you and Mons Mæland were related.'

'Related? We weren't ... ah, you mean, related by marriage, yes.'

'Yes, I didn't mean blood-related.'

'No.' She looked down. 'Lars and Lea were brother and sister, that's correct. But Lea broke away and left home. I mean the ... milieu she came from. The chapel. Belief in God. They didn't get on that well. And then she disappeared.'

'Yes. Sixteen years ago.' I waited for her to go on. 'But you're the aunt – through marriage – of their children. Else and Kristoffer. Don't you have any contact with them, either?'

'No, not much. But we'll have to go to the funeral now. Do you know when it'll be?'

'I haven't heard. I'm sure it'll be delayed a bit by police investigations.'

'You mean … ?' She sat down at my table as though it had suddenly become difficult for her to remain upright.

'Yes, there'll definitely have to be a post-mortem examination. Often with this type of death the deceased will be buried in such a way that he/she can be exhumed later, should there be any fresh developments.'

'But … so no one knows how he actually died?'

'One person does. At least one, perhaps I ought to say. You must have seen the newspaper articles?'

'Only the local ones. But I can see the environment movement is in the spotlight …'

'Have you spoken to Ole since it happened?'

'No. He went back to Bergen after his police interview. But he couldn't possibly have done that sort of thing.'

'Couldn't he?'

'I know my own son!'

'Yes. You two have only got him, have you?'

'Yes. And?'

'Nothing …'

'Why did you come here actually?'

'To talk to Gunvor Matre. About a land sale in 1988. Do you know her?'

A flash of displeasure crossed her face. 'The owl, yes.'

'The owl?'

'That's what we call her. She sits by the kitchen window watching everything that goes on from early morning to late at night. For all I know, she might sit there at night as well. Once a week she catches the bus to Byrknes to do her shopping. If you happen to meet her on the road she smiles sweetly and looks at you with those prying eyes of hers. She's a good old-fashioned gossipmonger. I would never believe a word of anything she has to say.'

'Have you known her for a long time as well?'

'I vaguely remember her from the summer holidays when I was small, even though she was a lot older than us. But she kept her beady eye on us then, too. Old maid, mum called her, I remember. They often go like that.'

'Is there anyone she's friends with?'

'Not as far as I know. She doesn't even go to the chapel, so …'

'But Mons Mæland sold her the house and the plot up there.'

'Yes. God knows why!'

'A favour between friends. That's what it seems like …'

'Friends, Gunvor and him? That sounds very unlikely.'

'Business connection then?'

'Also unlikely!'

'Well, they signed a couple of documents together, so they have met each other, I would assume.'

That was as far as I got. The front door crashed open. In the doorway stood Ole Rørdal, scanning the room. Then he rushed in. He focussed his eyes on us, for a second or two an expression of surprise spread across his face, as though he had caught us red-handed, then he shouted: 'Mum! Have you seen Stein?'

Kristine got up. 'No, I … That's what Veum asked me.'

His gaze landed on me. 'His car's outside.'

'Yes.'

'Come on!' He beckoned to me.

I pushed my coffee cup away and quickly joined him. Behind me I heard Kristine shout: 'Ole, what's going on?'

'I don't know. But it could be a matter of life and death!'

In the car park he pointed to the quay. 'Down here! And follow the beach to the bridge. We've got to stop him!'

Ole set off at a run. I panted after him. When I was alongside I gasped: 'What's up?'

'I'm frightened he's going to blow up the bridge!'

'What!'

'I can't speak!' He was fighting for breath. 'We've got to hurry!'

From the quay we jumped down onto the rocks that followed the line of the sea under the bridge. I was forced to keep my eyes on the ground so as not to slip or stumble. Ole was clearly faster and more sure-footed than me, shorter and used to running on this terrain from childhood.

The bridge across Brennøy Sound grew in size as we got closer. Suddenly Ole stopped. His lungs rasped as he struggled for breath. Then he raised his voice, which cracked in the middle after the hard run. 'Ste –iiiin! Don't!'

Directly beneath the bridge stood Stein, partly bent over. In front of him was a black plastic bag, which he was stuffing under the foundations of the bridge. An aerial protruded from the bag, and in his hand he was holding what from a distance looked like a mobile phone. When Ole shouted he looked up and turned his face in our direction.

'Don't do it!' Ole shouted, swaying from side to side as though unable to move forward.

I stood beside him, panting. 'What's that he's got?'

'Plastic explosives,' Ole groaned. 'And an electrical detonator. One touch of a key and …'

Stein Svenson had stood up straight now. From under the arch of the bridge he stared at us, phone in hand.

Ole set off again. 'Wait for me, Stein! Listen to me.'

I made a grab for him. 'Ole …'

He didn't answer, just ploughed on. After some hesitation I followed, some four or five metres behind.

'Stein! We've discussed this so many times. No good will come of this!'

Stein Svenson stared at his former brother-in-arms. 'That's what you say. But you've been bought lock, stock and barrel!'

'Lock, stock … What nonsense are you talking, Stein!'

'Norcraft! Don't you lie to me!'

Ole didn't slow his pace. 'I've never taken a bloody øre from those guys!'

'Oh, no?'

'No!'

'Stay there!' Stein Svenson shouted. Ole was only a few strides away from him now. 'Don't you come a step closer!'

I came to a halt. Ole came to a halt. I could see from how he held himself he was weighing up the pros and cons. He didn't hesitate any longer. I opened my mouth to stop him, but it was too late. With an immense spring he launched himself forward, tripped over a rock and staggered towards Svenson as he reached for his mobile phone. They collided, fell headlong, I watched their bodies entwine, and then – all of a sudden – doomsday.

I never found out what happened: whether it was an accident in the heat of the moment, whether he really pressed a key or whether it was Ole trying to wrest the phone from his grasp.

A ring sounded from within the black plastic bag and then – without any form of warning – it detonated with a roar. The explosion was so powerful that we were hurled backwards by the blast. For a fraction of a second I saw both men in the air, before losing sight of them. Around us there was a hailstorm of stones and concrete, gravel, soil, moss and heather. Instinctively I doubled up and put my arms over my head to protect myself from the deluge. I landed with a bang on one of the rocks down by the sea, rolled around and lay still. In my ears the echo from the explosion sang like shrill cymbals and I felt adrenalin pumping through my veins, driven by tumultuous turbines. All the breath had been knocked out of me, and now it was returning, in long, searingly painful wheezes.

Then there was silence. All I heard was the distant screams of ter-rified seagulls. At first I lay still, amazed that I had survived. Then I moved my arms and gently lifted my head. Not far away, Ole Rørdal was doing the same. Bleeding from various cuts to his face, he groaned and held one arm; otherwise he seemed unscathed.

I struggled to my knees and then to a standing position as I looked around me. My forehead stung and so did my left cheek, somewhere. I touched it and got blood on my fingertips. Stein Svenson had been less lucky. He was lying in a strangely distorted posture, underneath a huge piece of concrete, with fractured steel girders protruding from the side, like the severed wings of a bird that had crashed to the ground. Only his legs and the lowest part of his body were visible. The rest lay under the concrete block.

I raised my eyes. The explosion had blown apart one concrete pillar on our side of Brennøy Sound, and the weight of the deck had broken off part of the bridge, making it tilt dangerously to one side. Above us there was a large, open crack in the carriageway. There was no doubt that Svenson had achieved his aim, even though he would never be able to enjoy the sight of his handiwork. It would be a long time before anyone would drive over Brennøy Bridge again.

28

For the second time in a very short time Jakob E Hamre of the Bergen Police arrived on Brennøy in Gulen by helicopter. As he stepped out of the side door and crossed the car park he clapped his eyes on me and said: 'We have to stop meeting like this, Veum. Before this week I'd never been to Brennøy. Now this is the second time in as many days, and you're here this time as well. What's more, you look dreadful. What the hell's going on?'

Behind him appeared Helleve, Solheim, Annemette Bergesen, Kvamme and Pedersen. Ole Rørdal stood in front of the Subaru four-wheel drive with his arms wrapped around his mother, who had sunk into a kind of phlegmatic apathy after the first shock, when she went storming down the quay screaming as if she had been hit by debris. In a crowd at the top of the quay, still at a safe distance from the centre of events, stood a tiny handful of islanders, those who had been at home at this time of day from the look of things. On the margins, not speaking to anyone, I saw Gunvor Matre.

The police viewed the damaged bridge, shaking their heads. From here, the result of the explosion looked even more dramatic, as if the very umbilical cord from Brennøy to the rest of the world had been cut.

'Jesus!' Solheim said. 'That must have been quite an explosion.'

Helleve scrutinised my face and gravely shook his head. 'That could have been curtains for you, Varg.'

'That was how it felt as I sailed through the air.'

Hamre looked at me in amazement. 'And it was Stein Svenson who set it off?'

I nodded to where the explosive had been placed. 'He's down there, under a block of concrete.'

'Right. Do you think it was suicide?'

'No. We got to him too quickly. I'm sure the idea had been to move to a safe distance before triggering the explosion, but then Ole Rørdal and I turned up, and Ole ...'

'Yes?'

'He tried to wrestle the mobile phone, remote control ... whatever it was in his hand ... from him. And that was when the plastic explosive went off. So unbelievably bloody loud.'

He regarded me sombrely and sighed. Then he turned to Helleve. 'Has the Chief of Police stopped all the traffic? No one will cross that bridge again.'

'And my car's here,' I groaned.

Hamre smirked. 'Robinson Crusoe, I presume! Perhaps you getting stuck here is the best thing that could have happened, Veum.'

'Hellooooo!' a voice cried from the other side of Brennøy Sound. Lars Rørdal had driven his battered Opel Kadett down to one of the quays there. Now he was standing on a pontoon with his hands funnelled round his mouth and shouting to us, like Moses by the Red Sea. But it was impossible to hear what.

Kristine and Ole went onto the quay, waved to him and I heard Ole call: 'We're fine! Talk later!'

Lars Rørdal called back, but it was still impossible to decipher what he was shouting.

Hamre cleared his throat beside me. 'We'd better take a peep at the crime scene. Afterwards let's assemble in the cabin lounge, like last time. Could this have been what they were arguing about on Tuesday night, Veum?'

I nodded. 'Very likely. It may even cast some light on the attack on Svenson the same morning – or whenever it happened.'

He puckered his lips in thought. 'Possibly.' He turned to his officers. 'Come on. Let's go for a walk.'

We went down to the quay together, crossed the rocks by the sea and to the place where Stein Svenson lay under the heavy concrete block. 'Bloody hell!' said Hamre. 'We're going to need a crane ...' He turned to Helleve. 'Suppose it will have to be a seaborne crane, will it? Can you requisition one ASAP? I reckon they might have one in Mongstad. In which case, it's not so far away.'

We stood in a semi-circle studying Svenson. I could feel my stomach turning over. It had been enough of a shock to find Mons Mæland strung up on a cross facing the sea, but I had never met Mæland; I had only a vague personal impression of him. With Svenson it was different. It was no more than a day since I had been to his house, the tumbledown smallholding in Bontveit, asked him questions about the conversation between him and Ole Rørdal and discussed the matter of the land deal. Nothing would come of that now, unless Bringeland decided to run the case on behalf of the estate, in view of the agreed commission.

I couldn't say that I had liked Svenson. I hadn't found him particularly likeable. But he had been active and alive. Now he would be lying under a slab of concrete until a crane arrived to lift it off him, although that would not make him any less squashed than he already was.

'Well ...' Hamre motioned to Pedersen and Kvamme. 'You'd better start recording whatever data you can find. At least there's no doubt about the course of events or the cause of death in this case, but we'll have to document it as best we can. I'd be very interested to know what type of explosive was used and where it came from, for example.'

Pedersen nodded. Kvamme's eyes scoured the ground.

'The rest of us will go back up. Annemette? Will you fetch the first-aid box from the helicopter? You'll have the honour of sticking plasters on our friend, the Master Detective.'

Annemette Bergesen grinned. 'With the greatest of pleasure.'

'It's not ...,' I started.

'It's an order, Veum,' barked Hamre, and his colleagues laughed soundlessly behind his back while Helleve went to shake my hand, as if to suggest that now I was in the force, too.

As we went up to the quay we heard the sound of a small boat with an outboard motor docking. The engine was switched off, Lars Rørdal stood up in the boat and threw a rope to Ole, who tied it to a small bollard. Then the preacher grabbed the edge of the quay with both hands and hauled himself up. He had barely stood upright when Kristine threw herself in his arms, let out a scream and burst into tears. Ole stepped back as though embarrassed by his mother's emotional outburst. Lars looked at him over Kristine's shoulder and asked him a question. Ole answered, Lars' jaw dropped and glanced towards the bridge, horrified.

'There has to be a connection,' Hamre said as we climbed onto the quay.

'What do you mean?'

'Between these events. Mæland's murder and this … what shall we call it? … act of terrorism?'

I patted his arm. 'There's one thing you should know before we go up to …' I turned my back on the Rørdal family so that they wouldn't be able to read my lips.

Hamre stopped. 'Oh, yes …'

'I've heard rumours that Ole Rørdal is not Lars' son. One of the paternity candidates is said to be Mons Mæland.'

His eyes narrowed as he glanced over my shoulder at Kristine, Lars and Ole. 'And how old is Ole Rørdal?'

'Thirty-five by my reckoning.'

He slowly shook his head. 'In other words, we're talking … How much water has passed under the bridge since that happened, eh? I know you're a bit of a terrier for digging up rotten bones. The deeper they're buried, the better. But what the hell's a potential paternity suit thirty-five years ago got to do with a crime today – not to mention …' He flapped an arm at the bridge. 'This?'

'Revenge is mine, saith the Lord, they say in the circles Lars Rørdal moves in. Or something like that.'

'I know you're well versed in biblical matters, Veum.'

'But what if the Lord didn't avail Himself of the opportunity? In the end someone might have given Him a helping hand?'

'So you think I should rattle skeletons in the Rørdal family cupboard? You're inventive, I'll give you that.'

I pointed up at the chapel. 'On the wall there is a quote from the

Bible. Something about destroying your own house and inheriting the wind. That might be …'

'Veum, sorry to have to interrupt you, but actually I don't have the time for these theological reflections.' He gently pushed me aside. 'I have a job to do. But you're welcome to join us. We haven't finished with you … yet. Besides you need a few plasters.'

Then he passed by me, went to the Rørdal family, said a few words to them and pointed up to the cabins. I shrugged my apologies to Helleve and Solheim, who had both stopped to hear what I had to say, then followed Hamre. Behind us, Annemette was on her way up from the helicopter with the first-aid box under her arm.

Lars looked pale and shaken. Kristine's cheeks were tear-stained and her eyes red-rimmed. Ole met my gaze with the same ghastly realisation as when we had both got up and seen Stein Svenson under the heavy slab of concrete. His face was covered with crusts of blood and he was still holding one arm. Otherwise he looked physically unscathed.

Hamre said: 'Can we go in?'

Kristine nodded.

'I'm in shock,' Lars said. 'Deep shock.'

'Yes, aren't we all?' Hamre said. Then he turned round, annoyed, and searched the skies, to the south-east. Another helicopter hung in the air over Byrknesøy heading their way. 'Bloody media. Now we've got them above us again.' He pointed to Solheim. 'Bjarne, keep them at arm's length, from the crime scene and up here.' Then he faced Helleve. 'Where the hell are the local police?'

I noticed Lars Rørdal twitch at every expletive that was uttered, but he kept his counsel, watching the policeman exercise his authority with a mixture of disgust and alarm.

Helleve held his mobile phone up in the air in front of him. 'I've got them on the line. They're coming over by boat as well. They just have to erect barriers at the entrance to the bridge. And the crane's on the way.'

'Good.'

Annemette Bergesen had gone over to Kristine and now

accompanied her into the building. She cast a glance in my direction. 'Are you coming, Varg?'

'Yes, I just have to make a quick call.'

Before I joined them I phoned Karin and told her what had happened before she heard on the radio news and elsewhere.

She reacted instantly. 'Oh my God, Varg! Are you hurt?'

'Just a few scratches.'

'Sure?'

'Yes, yes. I'm just going to get some sticking plasters.'

'But surely this can't be connected with the other business, can it?'

'The police think so, but we'll have to see. Are you still at work?'

'Yes.'

'And there have been no sightings?'

'No, no.'

'I was wondering … This morning I found out that Lea Mæland was born a Rørdal. If you could be bothered, would you mind searching for her name and see what you can dig up?'

'Dig up? What do you mean? She was declared dead about fifteen years ago.'

'Yes, but you know how my brain works …'

'Yes, indeed, I've definitely learned. When are you coming back?'

'No idea. My car'll be stuck here for God knows how long. I'll have to hitch a lift in Hamre & co's helicopter.'

'Goodness, I can feel my body going numb.'

'You're not the only one.'

We hung up. The second helicopter was still hovering in the air above us, uncertain whether to land or not as the one that had brought the police was still on the quay. Through one of the side windows I glimpsed a camera, already preserving the damaged bridge for posterity, no doubt. Once again we were going to end up on a nationwide TV channel this afternoon and evening. I had no personal pressing need to be in the spotlight. I quickly followed the others into the cabin.

29

Kristine Rørdal poured coffee for the police officers. Resuming a fixed routine seemed to be a source of succour.

Annemette Bergesen attended to the cuts on my face with skilled hands. When she had finished she surveyed the results with satisfaction and mumbled: 'You probably won't be offered any major film roles this week, Varg.'

'Nothing new there then.'

'No?'

'No.' Then she nodded, took her notebook and made a beeline across the floor for Kristine. It was clear that she had been instructed to interview her first.

Ole Rørdal sat at one of the tables by the window with Atle Helleve. The interview was already in progress. His father stood behind the reception desk, somewhat dispirited, as though he didn't quite know what to do with himself. He exuded an air of lumbering loneliness, an adolescent ungainliness that I couldn't make tally with the eloquent preacher I had met on Tuesday morning, nor the fiery lover who had been pumping away at his loyal spouse a few hours ago.

Hamre beckoned to me. First though I had to … 'Veum. Over here.' He led me to the furthest table from reception. We took our cups of coffee with us.

We sat down at the table. Hamre leaned forward and said in a low voice: 'Run this by me one more time, Veum. What are you doing here again – and what can you tell me about what's happened?'

In brief outline, I reported back on my new assignment regarding the land deal in 1988, told him about my trip to Eivindvik and the information I had gleaned there, and how it had led me to Brennøy to have a chin-wag with Gunvor Maltre.

'Did anything come of it?'

'Not a lot. Everything to do with the contracts seems to have been above board, at least if we can believe the witnesses involved. So far only Bringeland the solicitor and Stein Svenson have made any objection, and the latter, well …'

'He's dropped the case. I think we can safely say that. Did you meet anyone else?'

'By the cross I met the second witness from 1988, the ex-Police Chief in Lindås, Bjørn Brekkhus.'

'Yes, I can remember him. What was he doing there?'

'He and Mons Mæland were close friends, from their younger days. He wanted to see the crime scene, he said.'

'And where is he now?'

'He went home a couple of hours ago. His wife's in a wheelchair apparently.'

'Any more?'

'Well, when I came back here I popped in to …'

'Again? You'd been here earlier in the day, hadn't you?'

'Yes, but briefly. No one was here …'

'No one?'

'Not that I noticed. But Kristine Rørdal said her husband had been there … before.'

'Right …' Hamre looked moderately interested. 'Go on …'

'On my return I noticed Svenson's car, which I recognised from the previous day.'

'Yesterday?'

'Yes, I went to see him in Bontveit. We discussed that yesterday, Hamre. That was where I bumped into Tangenes.'

'Ah, yes, that's right. But you haven't seen him today?'

'No. I asked Kristine if she'd seen him. She hadn't. We chatted and then her son, Ole, came in and asked exactly the same question. He said we had to hurry and I had to go with him. We ran down … He obviously knew where to go. We found Svenson preparing the explosive. The rest you know.'

He sat staring into space for a moment. Then he carried on: 'But what links all these people? And by that I mean not only what's happened today but what happened on Wednesday as well.'

'Well, you can go right back to the very beginning when Mons Mæland and Kristine née whatever spent their summers here. And they met Lars Rørdal and Lea, his sister, who both lived here. As children, and later as teenagers. They even went dancing together, on the quay, because Lars hadn't found salvation yet, even though the home he came from was pretty strict. At some point Kristine became pregnant, Lars took responsibility and married her. Later Mons and Lea also got married.'

'But she's dead?'

'Yes, she disappeared in 1982. Apparently she went swimming in the sea and was never seen again. You could talk to Bjørn Brekkhus about that. He led the investigation at the time.'

He nodded.

'But there are some who claim that Lars couldn't be Ole's dad. At any rate, he and Kristine had no further children. And, according to what Brekkhus told me today, Mons could easily have been the guilty party.'

'Yes, but this is thirty-five years ago ...'

'Yes, I know.'

'Let's concentrate on the potential links between Stein Svenson and Mons Mæland.'

'You know them already. On the one hand, there's the land deal, with Svenson representing the possible heirs. On the other, there's the political struggle, with him standing up against the plans for a wind farm here and, the way I see it, willing to resort to much more fanatical methods than, among others, Ole Rørdal, who in this regard compared it to terrorism.'

'That's your interpretation.'

'Yes, as I said. You'll have to see what Ole says about this. Mons Mæland's daughter, Else, is also in NmV, by the way, and according to her she had persuaded her father to change his mind, too, before he disappeared.'

'And then there's ...' He held up one hand and counted on his fingers. 'Mons Mæland's son, Kristoffer, and the family company. There's Norcraft with Erik Utne. There's TWO with Stine Sagvåg. All supporters of the wind-power project.'

'You're forgetting someone. The Deputy Chairman, Jarle Glosvik and his political pals at the council. He was the one who hired Trond Tangenes.'

Hamre looked at me, scepticism gleaming from his eyes. 'Glosvik and Tangenes? Does that sound likely?'

'Glosvik runs a local business with iffy finances, I've been told. For him personally it would be of the utmost importance that the wind farm here becomes a reality. That's why he went for the heavy artillery with Tangenes.'

'Have you got any evidence for this, Veum?'

'Sort of evidence. Circumstantial, as you usually call it. I feel fairly sure I'm right though.'

'OK, but it's hardly likely that either of these characters would have taken Mæland's life, is it.'

'Harrumph.' I rolled my shoulders as a sign that I couldn't answer.

'Yes, of course you're an old anti-capitalist, I know, but in peaceful little Norway ...? If Russian capital had been in the picture we could have discussed this, but ...'

'TWO is an international company today,' I found myself saying, until it struck me that this was my employer I was talking about.

'Yes, OK, but ...'

'Perhaps you'll have to go back thirty-five years after all, Hamre?'

He viewed me with displeasure. 'Hardly. We found Mons's car in Lindås yesterday morning, parked neatly on a forest road not far from Hundvin.'

'I see. Any sign of an attack?'

'Nothing. It was unlocked. Forensics is going through it now with a fine toothcomb.'

'By the way ... Cause of death? Have you got any further?'

He forced a weak smile. 'You'd like to know, wouldn't you. But ...

Well, alright. The preliminary autopsy result suggests he was strangled. Furthermore, he'd been wrapped in what we believe must have been a plastic bag and kept chilled. Either in cold storage or dropped in the sea.'

'Drowned then?'

'No. Strangled.' He held a hand to his throat. 'Clear signs of strangulation round the larynx.'

'Strangled with bare hands?'

'No sign of a rope or the like at any rate. They used the rope to hang him.'

'They?'

'Yes. The perps, that is. It would have been quite a job for one person to hoist the body, although it can be done of course, if there's something to stand on.'

'And for the time being you have no suspects?'

Again that weak smile. 'If we had, we would hardly have told you.' He got up. 'But we should be getting on with the job in hand. If you remember anything that might be of significance for the case, I hope you'll contact us. If it were up to me, I'd like it to be Svenson who killed Mæland and what happened today a form of atonement.'

'In which case you'd be assuming he committed suicide, but then it's very improbable that he could have calculated where the slab of concrete would fall.'

'Mm ...'

'And who knocked Svenson unconscious and left him bound hand and foot in the abandoned fish hall?'

'Good question, Veum. Very good,' said Hamre, looking very thoughtful. Then he beckoned Lars Rørdal over.

'One last thing, Hamre. As you saw, my car's on this side of the sound. Would it be possible to thumb a lift home with you?'

'Had it been up to me, you would be staying here. However, then we'd have to come back and collect yet another body, so it's fine. We'll be here for quite some time, just so that you know.'

'I'll find some way to pass the time. Thank you.'

He mustered a thin smile. Lars Rørdal had joined us and was waiting impatiently. I nodded to him as I passed. Behind the reception desk Kristine was in conversation with Annemette. Ole Rørdal and Atle Helleve still hadn't exhausted all they had to talk about. So I went outside, strolled down to the quayside and took out my phone.

After some reflection I rang Stine Sagvåg. She was no less shocked than I had expected. 'What is going on there, Varg? This is simply catastrophic.'

'Do you mean from a human or a business perspective?'

'Both. This Stein Svenson ... I don't know much more about him – only trivial details. But how could he be so desperate ... ?'

'Someone went to great lengths to stop him doing this on Wednesday, if you know what I mean.'

'Yes. They were absolutely justified then. In stopping him, I mean. And now you're telling me the bridge is destroyed as well. This could delay the project for years.'

'Not impossible.'

'I feel like swearing.'

'Don't restrain yourself on my account. I can tolerate most swear words.'

'Oh, shut up.'

If that was the worst she could come up with, it would take a little more powder to blow my kneecaps off. 'As far as the assignment's concerned, one party has gone now, for good. Furthermore, neither of the two people I've spoken to has admitted that anything in any way shady took place. So unless someone submits a demand for Per Nordbø to be exhumed and examined to establish an advanced state of senility I feel sure that we – that is to say, you – have a strong case against Bringeland.'

'Good. I'm happy with that.' In a cool, business-like fashion she added: 'Send us an invoice and we'll regard the case as terminated.'

'Thank you. See you another time.'

'Maybe,' she said, and rang off, without giving the impression that a reunion would be a top priority on her side of the Langfjellene mountains.

Such was life. I'd had two assignments in the course of a short week, and I couldn't say either of them had been concluded to the complete satisfaction of either employer. I was on the point of admitting that Hamre was right. I should go round with a flag warning everyone I met: Beware of Veum. Death is nigh …

The crane from Mongstad had arrived. The guys on board the boat manoeuvred their way to the rocks where Svenson lay. I had no interest in seeing what he looked like after they had raised the concrete. Instead I walked in the opposite direction, sat down by the water's edge and watched the gulls hovering, to all intents and purposes, aimlessly above the sound. But I knew this was an illusion, too. They were always hunting as well. In this respect we were relatives. But, unless I was much mistaken, they would have better results to show for their work than I would at the end of this day.

30

With the ease and grace of a dragonfly the helicopter took off from the quay. For a few, brief instants it hung in the air over Brennøy, and in a swift sweeping scan I saw the whole of the tiny island community, separated from Byrknesøy now for an indefinite period. Outside Naustvik, Kristine and Lars Rørdal stood watching us from below. Ole also had a seat in the helicopter, and the two of them looked strangely abandoned in the car park, along with a handful of cars that would evidently have to be lifted by crane to the mainland. Further up the island we could see other buildings: the chapel, Gunvor Matre's red house, the dark belt of forest and furthest away, on the rocks in the north-west, the cross, in sharp profile against the bluish-grey sea beyond.

Then the helicopter dipped slightly as it increased speed before straightening up and heading for Bergen. Leaving Byrknesøy behind us, we flew over the southern tip of Sandøy, thereafter straight past Mongstad. A tanker was moored by the vast oil terminal. On the side of the ship, painted in large, white letters was: TWO. From the tall chimney ashore burned the eternal Olympic flame, except that in modern Norway O stood for oil and not Olympic, and no Olympic champions had ever brought so much gold to the country as the floating black-and-yellow remains of plants and animals that the mill of time had left behind on the sea bed off the Norwegian coast.

As we passed Lygra, I leaned forward to the window, located the cabin in Lurefjorden and pointed it out to Hamre. 'That's Mons Mæland's cabin. And there's the quay in Feste, where his car was parked.'

Hamre nodded and pointed in the opposite direction. 'And over there is Hundvin, where the car was found.'

I followed his finger. As the crow flies, it wasn't far. What had he been doing over there? Had he had a meeting with someone or had he been transported there – after someone had killed him?

Hamre turned right round in his seat and fixed me with a glare. 'But don't you get involved, Veum. Not even slightly.'

I nodded, without saying a word, without promising anything, and I saw his eyes flash before he turned round and sat staring ahead for the rest of the trip.

After a short telephone conversation with my insurance company I arranged to pick up a rental car in Flesland. A Corolla, so that I would feel safe, even if it was a much newer model than my own.

Ole Rørdal came back to Bergen with me. He was going to his office in Lille Øvregate, he said. I went home. From there, I called Karin.

'Oh, thank God. You're home.'

'Yes, I was lucky and could take advantage of Hamre's helicopter service.' I quickly brought her up to speed on events, then asked: 'Did you find out anything about Lea, née Rørdal?'

'Not much more than we already knew. Went missing in 1982. Assumed dead in 1983.'

'Assumed?'

'Yes, that's what it says here.'

'Well … have you got any plans for the weekend?'

'Yes, I have actually. Ranveig asked if I'd like to join her at her cabin. She doesn't want to go there alone.'

'No, I can understand that.'

'She wants to go through Mons' papers. To see whether she can find something useful for what she imagines is going to be a row over the estate with Else and Kristoffer.'

'When are you going?'

'I'm going to change into something more practical, then we'll do some food shopping and make dinner when we're there. I think it will do her good to think about something different.'

'Probably.'

'I'd much rather spend the weekend with you, Varg,' she added quickly.

'Me, too. With you, I mean. Now I don't know quite what to do. My assignment's as good as finished, but I think I'll phone Else. After all, she knew Svenson.'

'OK.'

'And Karin, I don't think you should worry too much about Tangenes any more. I've spoken to his employer, and I think he got the point, so to speak.'

'Good,' she said lightly, unable to conceal the tinge of nervousness in her voice. 'Look forward to seeing you on Monday then.'

'Yes, have a good weekend.'

'Same to you. I'll be thinking about you.'

'I know you will.'

After hanging up I called Else Mæland. Her voice was tearful as she answered. I said my name and asked if she wanted an eye-witness's report. She did.

She opened the door herself when I rang the doorbell this time. Her face was tear-stained, and she was holding a little towel in her hand. It was clear that she had tried to wash the tears from her cheeks but without complete success. Her eyes were bloodshot, and there was a tightness to her mouth as she desperately tried to hide the quivering of her lips. She looked shockingly young, like a confirmand who has just experienced the bitter facts of life for the first time. When she saw the plasters on my face she burst into tears again. So all her efforts had been in vain.

I went inside and placed a comforting hand on her shoulder. She hesitated for a moment, then she came close, buried her face in my chest and cried without restraint. I put my arms around her, stroked her back and mumbled softly: 'There, there … There, there.' Obviously this death had meant much more to her than the death of her own father.

I cast my eyes around. There was complete silence in the flat. Not a sound to be heard apart from the wracking sobs of the woman in my arms.

After some minutes the sobbing subsided. She gently detached

herself and looked at me, ashamed. 'I'm sorry, but … this is too unbear-
able to think about.'

I nodded. 'Is there no one else here?'

She looked around. 'No, they're out … at a party probably. Come in.
I've put the kettle on. Would you like a cup of tea?'

'Please.'

I followed her into the kitchen, where she pulled out a chair from
under the tiny table by the window, which on this side of the house
faced the stream of traffic in Ibsens gate. But now it was Friday evening,
and the gaps between cars passing were longer than in the rush hour,
straight after work.

She took tea bags from a kitchen drawer, put one in each of the two
large mugs and poured hot water from the white kettle. 'Sugar?'

'No, thank you.'

'I think I've got a few biscuits if you're hungry.'

'No, I'm fine.'

'I haven't had a bite of food since I heard.'

'Who told you?'

'Ole rang and said.'

'Your cousin.'

'Yes.'

'You didn't mention a word last time we spoke – or on the island –
about you being related.'

'No. I thought you knew.'

'I considered you a couple.'

'Ole and me?' She gaped in surprise.

'So it was Stein and you?'

She blinked several times, as if to hold back the tears. Then she gave
a nod; it was barely perceptible.

'I happened to be standing by the window when Ole and you passed
by on Tuesday night. I'd seen Ole and Stein arguing on the quay, and
I heard Ole say as you passed: "We're not terrorists for Christ's sake!"'

She looked at me, expectantly, without saying anything.

'Were they arguing about sabotaging the bridge?'

She seemed to be mulling over the question, but it was more likely she was weighing up how much she was willing to tell me. 'Yes, it probably was. Ole was against it.' Then she hurriedly added: 'I was, too.'

'Ole might have been thinking about his mother's business.'

'Ole thought about everyone! They'd fought for years and years to get a bridge, and when the very last bridge comes, in a few years' time, over Brandanger Sound, they'll be part of the mainland, the whole of Outer Gulen. Blowing up a bridge was like ... was like ... smashing their own spine. The whole community's.'

'But Stein wasn't bothered about that?'

'No.'

'So how did the argument finish?'

'It didn't! Stein was annoyed and refused to go back to the cabin. He insisted on sleeping on board the boat instead.'

'And the next morning he was gone. Until we found him later in the day, all trussed up.'

She didn't meet my eyes; she stared down at the table. 'Yes ...'

'Yes?' I repeated, more insistent now. 'That might not have come as much of a surprise to you?'

Now she did look up. 'Oh, yes it did!'

'So what is it you're not telling me?'

She swallowed. 'I ...'

I waited. When she didn't go on, I said: 'You slept on the boat as well, didn't you.'

She looked at me and blinked hard once. In a frail voice she answered: 'Yes ...'

She had gone back to the cabin with Ole, got into bed, but she couldn't sleep. So she had got up again and returned to the boat.

'How much later was this?'

'Well, half an hour maybe.'

'And there was no one else about at this time?'

'No, who could there be?'

'Well ...' Trond Tangenes, for example. Or some others.

However, she hadn't seen anyone, and when she had returned to the boat she had climbed on board, gone down to Stein, who was in bed but couldn't sleep, either. 'I stayed there until the morning. But I went back to my room before anyone else had woken up.'

'Why? You're adults. You were then as well.'

'There had been enough arguments as it was. Ole didn't like us being ...'

'Lovers?'

'Together.'

'In other words, you were the last person to see him before he was attacked?'

'Probably. But the attack ...'

'Yes?'

'Does it matter now? After all that has happened since? Stein has ... gone, and so has Dad ...' Her eyes searched mine helplessly. 'I simply don't understand what's going on here.'

The doorbell rang. She jumped, and I could see her hesitation. She half-stood up and looked at me as if my being there made her feel guilty. The bell rang again. Then she decided and went out. I got up from the chair. Afterwards I heard a voice in the hall. It was Kristoffer, and he would hardly be expecting to meet me here.

31

She had already told him I was there, and there was no sign of surprise in his face when he came through the door, only measured curiosity. 'Veum …?'

'Yes, I'm sort of reporting back.'

'About what happened on Brennøy today?'

'Yes.'

'Ah, I can see you were hurt, too.'

'Nothing that a couple of plasters can't remedy.'

Kristoffer shook his head. 'It's incomprehensible what these groups can get up to! As if what we're doing is damaging to society, when it's just the opposite – something future generations will thank us for.'

Else came alongside him. 'Would you like a cup of tea?'

'Yes, please.'

'Well, you go into the sitting room and I'll be right in. Veum, if you take your cup …'

I nodded and followed Kristoffer into the sitting room. It was furnished as rooms in collectives often are, with a jumble of furniture bought from Fretex, the Salvation Army shop, and an impressive sound system along one wall the only modern feature.

Kristoffer turned to me. 'What are you actually doing here, Veum?'

'I was there when the explosive went off. Your sister wanted more information than she had gleaned from the news. Of course she knew the deceased.'

He sighed. 'Yes …' Then a twitch seemed to go through him. 'You were there, you say? Today as well?'

'Yes, I'd been given an assignment – by someone on your side of the debate – to sniff out what was behind these allegations of irregularities when the land was sold to your father in 1988.'

'Stine Sagvåg?'

I neither confirmed nor denied his guess.

'Well … And what did you find out?'

'So far there's absolutely nothing to suggest the sale shouldn't have gone through, and now that Svenson's dead … I don't think it's the biggest problem you have with regard to public opinion.'

'No? What do you think is then?' His tone was sarcastic.

'Logistics, above all else, now that the bridge is in ruins.'

'We'll work that out.'

'And, in addition, a man has sacrificed his life in the fight against the wind turbines. And you're just going to motor on as before? Good luck, I say. I'm afraid the wind is going to get a lot stronger. Just wait until you read the newspaper headlines tomorrow morning.'

He clenched his teeth. 'If we'd known this when we bought the land, then …'

'Do you remember anything about it?'

'When Dad bought it in 1988? Nothing at all. I was eighteen and probably had other things on my mind.'

Else came in from the kitchen. This time she had brewed the tea in a pot. She poured us all a cup and then sat down. 'You still haven't told me what actually happened,' she said quietly.

'No, that's true. We were distracted.'

I told them in the simplest possible terms what I had seen, without going into any detail about the meetings with Bjørn Brekkhus and Gunvor Matre. They sat silently listening to the description of Ole's arrival, how he and I had run to Brennøy Sound and the bridge, Ole's attempt to stop Svenson and finally the moment I would never forget, when the explosive ignited and we were hurled through the air, all three of us.

Else sat with widened eyes, which filled with tears when I came to the explosion. Kristoffer's face became sterner and sterner.

After I had finished, Else said: 'But Ole and you … Was he injured?'

'No more than me. Stein was unlucky and was …' I paused, 'crushed by falling concrete.'

Else breathed in sharply. 'Falling concrete!'

I nodded.

'Environmental terrorism pure and simple!' Kristoffer exclaimed. 'That's what I'd call it.'

Else looked at him. 'He was desperate, Kristoffer! It was his commitment that made him act in such a desperate way.'

'Commitment! But this is an *environmental* matter, Else! How many times do I have to say it? The wind farm is for the good of the environment.'

Again she looked terribly young. 'Yes, but not everyone believes that ... As if it matters what we believe today.'

For a while we sat without speaking. I took a swig of tea. It tasted of apple and cinnamon. Through the windows we heard the sounds of children playing in the yard. Else looked utterly drained. Kristoffer had sunk into himself; was he wondering what strategy he should choose with regard to public opinion and his contacts at Norcraft and TWO so that the project could be completed without any major delays?

I broke the silence. 'You went to Ranveig's yesterday, I heard.'

Else glanced at her brother, then answered: 'Yes, and? There's a lot we have to get cleared up.'

'It wasn't the most tranquil of meetings, I understand.'

'Tranquil! That woman has a lot to answer for, I can tell you that.'

'Yes, she got that point. She said you threatened her.'

'Threatened?' Kristoffer leaned across the table. His sister placed a hand on his arm, but he wasn't to be held back. 'I'm sorry to have to say this. What she and Dad have on their conscience ... If we end up in court there'll be a washing of dirty laundry she'll regret having started for years to come.'

'And you're referring to ... ?'

'To the circumstances surrounding my mother's death. Even if she was difficult to deal with, she definitely didn't deserve this.'

'You mean it wasn't an accident?'

'They killed her!'

'Kristoffer,' Else chided softly, but he ignored her.

'They either indirectly drove her to her death – or they did it on purpose.'

'Ranveig said that your father could never have done such a thing.'

Kristoffer scowled. 'And her? Or someone else?'

'Another person?'

'Let me tell you something, Veum. Something we've discovered. *I've* discovered. It started in 1984, two years after she'd disappeared.' He glanced down for a second, as though reflecting. 'A few weeks ago I managed to access my father's account, through a connection in the credit branch . That is, he accessed it. And he gave me some startling information.'

'Which was … ?'

'Four times a year, from 1984 onwards, Dad transferred a fixed sum to a bank account in Sweden. Over the years it has totalled an amount close to a million Norwegian kroner.'

'Goodness me!'

'You can say that again. I asked my contact to check who the account belonged to. I was given a name. A certain Stig Magnusson, who resides in Malmö.'

'Did you confront your father with this information?'

He blushed. 'How could I do that? How could I reveal that I had wriggled my way into his account? That would have brought my contact into disrepute as well. But I told Ranveig yesterday.'

'She didn't say anything about it.'

'No? Don't you find that strange?'

'Yes. Or … Maybe not. What did she say?'

'She denied everything. Had no idea what the money was, she said. Had never heard about it.'

'And?'

He splayed his hands. 'Well? What do you expect? Her to lay all her cards on the table, sixteen years after the event?'

'All her cards? What do you think these payments are for?'

'You know, job-related stuff. Dad was in contact with a variety of people. I don't know if you knew, but this Trond Tangenes who appeared on Wednesday had done some work for us, too.'

My neck tautened. 'I see! Did you have him go to Brennøy this time as well?'

'No, no. What damn good would that do? My understanding was Glosvik was behind that.'

'Yes, that was my understanding as well. So, what did you use him for?'

'Well, debt collection. Outstanding claims. That kind of thing.'

'Uhuh. And what's your point?'

'This Stig Magnusson. What if he was the same sort? What if Dad got him in to do work he wasn't man enough to do himself?'

'Are you thinking about your mother?'

'I don't know. But close on a million kroner, Veum. That's a lot of money.'

'Yes, I wouldn't have said no to such a payout. If I had earned it, that is.'

'Exactly. You have to earn a sum like that.'

'Have you tried to contact Magnusson?'

'No, but I rang the police. That is, I rang Bjørn Brekkhus, who led the investigation at the time. He was like an uncle to us when we were small. Wasn't he, Else?'

Else smiled sadly and nodded confirmation.

'I rang him to ask if they had known about Magnusson back then. "No", he said. But ... By 1984, in reality, the investigation had been shut down for some time. Had they known this then ... But now there's nothing he can do.'

'What did he recommend?'

'Actually he recommended I forget the whole business. If not, I should contact Magnusson directly.'

'And did you?'

He sighed. 'No. There were too many other things to take care of, and then Dad's disappearance ...'

'Did anything happen in 1984 that could shed some light on this?'

'No. The account just showed a mass of bank transfers. Properties bought and sold. The payments could have been a perfectly normal business transaction. But not that long afterwards and not regularly, four times a year.'

'What about a loan, on the black market?'

He sent me a doubtful look. 'Yes ... Maybe. But in that case it's odd Dad didn't share the information with the rest of us.'

'He wanted to spare you the agony perhaps. Or he was embarrassed that he'd had to resort to such measures. Who knows?'

'And then he came into money that year, of course.'

'Oh?'

'Mum's life insurance policy paid up. I think that was in 1984.'

'I see. When did you talk to Brekkhus about this?'

'A week ago. The end of last week.'

'Well, you've got an inheritance dispute ahead of you, so I'm sure all the dubious entries in life's ledger will come up, both moral and pecuniary.'

'I'm looking forward to that,' he said with a caustic little smile. Then he indicated Else, and said: 'But now I've got something to discuss with my sister, a private matter. Is there anything else on your mind?'

There was. But I chose to keep it to myself.

I drained my tea. Else accompanied me to the door without even the most fleeting of glances. Ranveig had been right about her. When her brother was around she didn't say a lot. Perhaps it wasn't so surprising that she had gone to others to register a protest – against what her brother stood for.

Before getting in the car I looked for Ole's mobile number and rang him. He answered quickly, in an irritated tone. 'Yes?'

'Varg Veum here. Are you still at the office? I'd like a word, if it's possible.'

'What about?'

'Stein Svenson.'

'Is there any more to say about that case?'

'I think so.'

'Alright then. Fine. You know where to find me.'

As I got back behind the wheel I said to myself: When will you learn to drop a case, Varg? Will you ever learn? As I started the car I answered my own question: No. Never.

32

Ole Rørdal opened the door, greeted me mutely, poked his head out and looked down the staircase I had come up.

'I'm alone,' I said. 'If that was what you were wondering.'

He answered with a dark glare. 'A journo might have used the opportunity to sneak in, right? The phone hasn't stopped ringing since I got back. I doubt there's a paper in the land that hasn't rung me, plus the TV and radio. I must be the most popular man in Norway today …'

'Good exposure for your views.'

'Not like this.'

'No.'

'Come in.' He stepped aside and let me in.

I looked around. Everything was as it had been before. The room was as untidy, but the piles of paper on the shelves were, if possible, even higher. On a small, portable TV the evening's programme faded as another newsflash was expected. One of the three computers was also on, and a coffee machine with a jug of a murky liquid chugged away on the worktop.

His mobile phone rang on the long, untreated wooden table. He grabbed it, looked to see who it was, cursed and pressed the OFF key. 'There we go. Can't get me now. Secret number. So you know who it is …'

I nodded. The country's biggest newspaper did that, apparently to protect its writers from angry calls.

'This is – God forgive me for my sins – the worst day of my life, Veum!'

'You feel it was your fault?'

'It was my fault he died, yes. And yours …'

'I went with you because you asked me to, Ole.'

'Yes, I know. I didn't mean it like that. But if he'd had the time he needed he would have retreated to a safe distance. But when we caught him off-guard he realised it wouldn't be possible and he and I crashed into each other and that triggered the explosion.'

He slumped down at the table. The shadow of hair on his shaven skull was darker than when I was here last, his beard was pointing in all directions and his suede shirt hung outside his trousers. 'This has sent me into a deep depression, Veum. What I feared most has happened. Despite discussing it at length beforehand. Now our cause will be discredited for years. Just wait till you see the headlines tomorrow. *Planned Environmental Terrorism! Environmental Terrorism's Suicide Bomber!* I'm expecting the worst. But, whatever cause we fight for, it shouldn't cost you your life!'

I went to the coffee machine, found a clean cup and asked if he wanted any.

'No, thanks,' he mumbled. 'Think I've had enough.'

I poured myself a cup, examined the contents with suspicion and sampled it warily. The coffee was bitter and lay on my tongue like ash. With my back to the worktop and cup in hand, I said: 'So that was what you were arguing about on the quay on Tuesday night?'

He nodded. 'Yes.'

'Svenson wanted to blow up the bridge. You go in for more peaceful methods.'

'You could put it like that, yes.' He looked up. 'I've had a Christian upbringing, Veum. Consideration for others is important for me. We have to think about the community out there. Folk have to live their lives whether we have wind turbines or not.'

'You wouldn't use violence then?'

'Violence?' He peered up at me. 'Only if necessary. In self-defence, for example.'

'Or to protect your own interests.'

'What do you mean?'

'Svenson asked me several times if I came from Norcraft. He suspected that you'd been bought.'

His jaw dropped. 'Did he say that to you? He was off his chump. I'm not for sale to anyone, I can promise you that.'

'So, you've heard that before?'

'That was what he used as an argument when we were discussing the bridge.'

'But you stopped him in time, didn't you.'

He glowered at me. 'What do you mean?'

'I'm still talking about what happened on Wednesday morning. My theory is that it was you who attacked him, tied him up and thus prevented him from doing anything drastic. For that day anyway. Am I right?'

He didn't answer.

'Mm, I can even imagine he saw who attacked him. But he refused to say, so as not to compromise the whole organisation. That's the other variant. But the guilty party in both versions is … you.'

'I can see you have a fertile imagination,' he sneered. 'But I don't think much of your notion as to how conflicts in ethical organisations are resolved. And just how are you going to prove this?'

'Prove?' I queried. 'I don't need any proof. I've got an eye-witness.'

'An eye-witness! Who?'

'Your cousin, Else Mæland.'

'You're bluffing!'

'She spent the night with Svenson.'

'Yes, but she was back in the cabin well before …' He angrily broke off. Then he blushed scarlet, and I could see the sinews along his jawbone swelling with anger. 'Before I got up, I meant to say.'

'So that was what you meant to say,' I retorted. I didn't elaborate. Experience told me that this was one of those tipping points when things could go either way. Either he would see through the bluff or he would crack and admit everything. But he was a hard nut, harder than most.

I ratcheted the pressure up a notch. 'You didn't know that they were an item … Else and Stein?'

'Of course! They're … He was young and free. Both of them. What business was it of mine?'

'And you know she went back to the boat that night?'

He threw his arms in the air. 'I saw them, didn't I!'

'What did you see?'

'Her going back.'

'And ... ?'

'And nothing! When I ...' He cast around in the room as if searching for something.

'Just admit it, Ole. It'll all come out anyway.'

He took a very deep breath before releasing it. 'Alright then! What does it matter now? I went on board the boat in the morning, woke up Stein and said I had something to show him. Something we could use in the campaign. He was still dopey and went over to the empty building by the quay with me. Once inside I told him: "I'm sorry, Stein, but you've forced me to do this." And before he could react I hit him over the head, tied him up and left him there, in the old fish hall.'

'And how long were you planning to leave him there?'

'Until the survey was over, of course. No longer. But there was all the business with Mons Mæland and then you found him.'

'You weren't frightened he would give you away?'

He shook his head. 'No, I was sure he wouldn't. He knew as well as I did that it would be the end of our whole organisation. We talked about it the day after, that we would agree to disagree. We made peace, in a way. But then ...'

'Yes, how come this peace didn't last?'

'If only I knew the answer to that, Veum! I tried to talk to him earlier in the day. Drove up to Bontveit, where he lives. But I couldn't see any sign of him or his car. I guessed he had gone to Brennøy to carry out his plan anyway. And when I saw his car on the quay I realised I was right.'

'I suppose you could say that after what you did on Wednesday he no longer trusted you.' I noticed the big poster on the wall behind him. 'Don Quijote and Sancho Panza had split up for good.'

'I know! That makes me feel all the guiltier, don't you understand?'

'Of course ... of course I understand. This wasn't how tilting at windmills was supposed to end, but if my memory serves me right he also suffered defeats, the sorry figure of the knight errant.'

Ole gawked at me. 'Who?'

I nodded towards the poster. 'Don Quixote.'

'Right ...' He still didn't seem to know who I meant.

'Tell me, Ole, this land deal. The case Stein was pursuing against Mons Mæland. Were you involved in that?'

'No, no. But I thought he had a good case. I supported him to the hilt, hoping it would lead to a postponement of the decision.'

'Will you carry it on, on his behalf?'

'Doubt it. I really haven't thought that far ahead.'

'It'll be a case with new protagonists. Have you any idea who could be behind the murder of Mons Mæland?'

'One thing I can tell you for sure: it has nothing to do with us. Not even Stein was that crazy.'

'I'll have to take your word for it. Anyway, he had an alibi, didn't he?'

'Yes, he did.'

I left him sitting at the table, sunk in his sombre thoughts. I had a clear sense that it would be a while before we heard any more about NmV and Ole Rørdal, and that from now on the fight against wind power would be left to other players.

I drove home, made myself a simple meal, switched on the television and caught up with the various channels' presentations of the events on the island. Hamre, Erik Utne and Jarle Glosvik made statements, while Ole brusquely refused to be interviewed. Of course, the latest news was linked with the unsolved murder case, and the report more than implied that Stein Svenson, who as yet was anonymous, could have been connected with that case too, a contention that Hamre parried with the argument that it was far too early in the proceedings to draw any firm conclusions.

It had been a long and eventful day, and I sat slumped in front of the TV as a variety of light entertainment programmes tried, and failed, all of them, to make Friday evening a lively experience. In the end, I switched off the television, poured myself a small glass of aquavit and took a CD from one of the piles. Duke Ellington's Blanton-Webster band, as it is known, from 1940–42, played *Jump for Joy*. The notes oozed through my tympanic membranes like cream, although I felt no need to do any jumping myself. We came closer to reality, however, when a few tracks later someone asked the question: 'What good would it do?'

Before going to bed I rang Karin on her mobile. All I got back was her voicemail telling me that the subscriber had either switched off their phone or was in an area where there was insufficient coverage. I knew the latter was not true. I could accept the first possibility. She often switched off her phone at weekends when she was free and didn't want to be disturbed. Whether I liked it or not was another matter, but there could have been other reasons for my sleeping so badly that night.

The next day stole upon me like a thief with a long face and was as welcome as an alcohol-licensing inspector after midnight. I tried to phone again, but she didn't answer this time, either. Again I told myself there wasn't any reason to be concerned.

Before shaving I gingerly removed the plasters and cleaned the cuts from the day before. I applied a new plaster on one of them and looked a great deal more presentable.

After breakfast I got into my car and started the engine. The weather had turned. The clouds hung so low there was a risk of them settling around your neck, the rain lashed against the windscreen and, as I crossed Nordhordland Bridge, a strong gust of wind caught the car, making me force the wheel in the opposite direction to keep a straight course. This was no day for heading off on pleasure trips, but then strictly speaking this wasn't one.

33

I left the arterial road at Seim and followed the minor one to Lygra and Feste. The route went through rolling countryside, sometimes through dense forest, sometimes past cultivated fields. At regular intervals Seim Fjord appeared down to the right and you didn't need much imagination to picture Harald Fairhair sailing in one of his long ships to the King's Sæheim estate at the end of the fjord more than a thousand years ago. At this moment on a Saturday morning there was no traffic on the fjord, other than a cabin-owner tuning up his outboard motor and a marine research vessel lying still in the middle. Deep in these waters resided a mysterious jellyfish by the name of periphylla periphylla, a reddish-coloured sea creature that had made the old fjord its hunting ground; it had no natural enemies and therefore proliferated. At night, just under the surface of the water, you could see the red flashes it transmitted. During the day it sought the depths and the darkness, as though suffering from a bad conscience.

At Tofting I branched off towards Lygra, the old island community that became part of the mainland in 1973, but where Olav, the so-called saintly king, and other kings held their assembly in olden times. Now they had a newly opened heathland centre all of their own and a view of the oil flame in Mongstad twenty-four hours a day, like so many other places in the region.

The closest village shop was in Feste, so to find where Bjørn Brekkhus lived, I had to ask for help from a passing stranger on the byroad to the white timber church. He was a kindly old boy in wellies and a dark-green sou'wester pulled well down over his forehead. He pointed and explained, and not long after I was turning in by a single-storey detached house that could have been in Bergen, had it not been for the size of the plot. There were no other cars parked in the drive, but there was a light in the west-facing windows, through which the afternoon sun, if it was out, must have poured into the sitting room. Today the rain was pounding against the windows and the whole house reminded me of a diving bell hauled onto dry land to wait for better times.

I parked the car, opened the door, ducked my head and ran the few metres to the front door, where I found shelter inside a slim porch. I rang the bell and immediately afterwards a woman's voice answered from the intercom nearby. 'Who is it?'

'It's Veum. Varg Veum. I'd like to have a chat with Bjørn Brekkhus.'

'He isn't at home right now.'

'Is that *fru* Brekkhus?'

'Yes, it is.'

'Perhaps we could talk instead?'

'What's this about?'

'Mons Mæland,' I said loudly. 'Amongst other things,' I added, more to myself than *fru* Brekkhus.

After a short pause, she said: 'Come in.'

The lock buzzed, and the door slowly opened inwards. I waited until it was fully open, then I stepped inside.

The spacious hall was empty, but through an open door I heard a low hum. I looked in that direction and a small woman appeared sitting in a motorised wheelchair. Dressed in everyday clothes, with completely white hair that looked light and downy and her head sticking up, she resembled a baby bird. Her bent nose completed the image.

She stopped in front of me and held out a hand. 'Lise Brekkhus.'

'Hello.'

She looked at the rain dripping off my leather jacket with an amused expression. 'Wet out, is it?'

Good job you don't have to go out, I thought. 'It certainly is.'

I saw her looking at the plaster on my forehead, but she didn't make any comment.

'You can hang it up there.' She pointed to a wardrobe. The hall was decorated simply, with a copy of an old chart on one wall, a water-colour painting of small, blue-and-purple skerry flowers on the other.

She watched me as I hung up my jacket. Then she adroitly spun her wheelchair round and motioned to me. 'In here.'

I followed her through the threshold-less doorway to the large sitting room. It was fitted out in timeless simplicity with stylistically matching furniture, bookshelves from IKEA, TV, radio and stereo. The pictures on the wall were of the same kind as those I had seen before, each with a maritime flavour: water-colours of sea birds and skerry flowers, paintings of ferries and fishing smacks. On the coffee table there lay a pile of newspapers and some books with a library binding. One of them laid apart from the rest, with a bookmark poking out from the middle.

She performed another pirouette with the wheelchair. 'Can I offer you anything? Coffee? Tea?'

'Yes, please. So long as you're going to have something yourself, then ...'

'I like having company,' she said. 'But I think I'll go for tea at this time of day.'

'Then I'll have the same.'

Pleased, she nodded, swung towards the doorway again and disappeared in the direction of what I assumed was the kitchen before I had a chance to ask if I could help. I sat alone in the sitting room with the slightly uncomfortable feeling that a confirmee might have had visiting the local priest for the first time and finding only the priest's wife at home. What on earth were we going to talk about?

It was conspicuously quiet outside. No agricultural machinery at work. A small freighter sailed past down in Lurosen fjord, but so far away that all you could hear was a low chug. Some herring gulls were flapping their wings and wailing in the strong wind as the white-crested waves snapped at them from below.

There were some binoculars on the window sill. I looked across the sound towards the island of Radøy. Over Lurøy I glimpsed the steeple on the rebuilt prairie church by the Immigration Centre in Sletta, but the angle was wrong for Mons and Ranveig's cabin. Even with the binoculars it would be impossible to see.

Lise Brekkhus trundled back in. She had attached a tray to one arm of the chair. On the tray there was a teapot, two large cups, a bowl of sugar and a little dish of dry biscuits. On a separate plate there were some slices of lemon. Effortlessly, she placed everything on the coffee table. All I did was move the cup closer after she had poured the tea, take a slice of lemon and some sugar and stir it with the teaspoon.

When everything was ready and we were sitting there with a cup of tea in our hands like two members of the parish council in the process of setting up their own faction, she addressed me with an air of curiosity. 'What was it actually you wanted to talk to me about?'

'In fact, I wanted to speak to your husband.'

'Yes, but you said you could talk to me instead.'

'Yes, I did, you're right.' I carefully tasted the tea. It was dark, strong and good. 'I don't know how much your husband has told you.'

'As little as possible, as usual,' she said lightly, though with a touch of acid.

'Did he mention my name?'

'The name was Veum? Varg Veum? Was it?' She grinned. 'Funny name.' As I didn't respond, other than with a nod, she continued: 'No, he didn't.'

'Then I'd better introduce myself. I'm a private investigator.'

'Detective?'

'Yes, I prefer investigator though. It sounds less dramatic.'

She nodded and motioned for me to continue.

'I was invited over there by a friend …' I nodded towards Radøy. 'Last Monday, by Ranveig Mæland. It was my job to try to trace her husband, Mons, who had disappeared. Your husband was present.'

She sent me a chilly look. 'Yes, I know. Ranveig slept in our guest room on the Sunday night. Bjørn and Mons were old friends. We knew Lea too. Before I became …' She made a gesture towards her thin legs. 'Like this.'

'What …?'

She sighed. 'It's a form of muscular atrophy. It's been gradual, it started over thirty years ago, but I've always known it would end like this. In a wheelchair.'

'How long have you …?'

'The last fifteen years. Now you didn't come here to talk about me, did you.'

'No, sorry. But … well, enough of this. I was asked to locate Mæland, and I did, for that matter. I'm sure you've heard about it.'

'Yes, it was dreadful. I couldn't sleep the following night. He was crucified, in a way.'

'Yes, it was a shocking experience for all of us there.'

'Did you actually find him?'

'I can't say I did, no. In fact, that was his brother-in-law, I found out subsequently. Lars Rørdal, if the name means anything to you.'

'Yes, it does. Lea's brother, isn't he?'

'Yes. Do you remember when Lea went missing?'

She seemed almost indignant. 'Do I remember? We were there … Well, I wouldn't say we were bosom pals – Bjørn and Mons were – but at any rate we met a couple of times a year. The boys were huge fishing fans, you know, so there were often extravagant fish suppers on the menu to use up some of the catch. We've eaten fish six days a week ever since, and everything is freshly caught, if I might say so. By Bjørn, of course,' she added. I waited, and she picked up the thread again. 'Lea … Yes, it was terrible. But … that was sixteen – seventeen years ago, wasn't it?'

'Sixteen.'

Her eyes glazed over. 'I was already beginning to get so weak then that I wouldn't go out any more, but I hadn't got this then.' She tapped the wheelchair. 'I hadn't seen her for more than a year, I think, so … It had an awful impact on us, of course, and Bjørn was deeply involved. In the investigation, I mean.'

'She was never found, though …'

'No, she wasn't. But everyone thought she had drowned. After a few years she was declared dead. There are rules and regulations for that kind of thing …'

'Yes, there are indeed. Did your husband ever talk about the case?'

She looked pensive. 'He did, yes. My goodness, it's so long ago, and we were friends, as I said. But Lea … She wasn't easy. But I can't say … At that time my mind was on myself and my own fate.'

'Yes, I can imagine.'

'I'd finally been diagnosed, even though the symptoms had been obvious for many years already.'

'And then Mæland re-married …'

'Yes.' Her lips became thinner. 'Ranveig. Bit too fast for some people's taste. It didn't matter to Bjørn. He was there just as often as before.'

'There?'

'Yes, across the sound, in their cabin. Even if Mons worked in property and was really an entrepreneur he wasn't much of a handyman, according to Bjørn. So he often went out to their cabin and helped them with practical things, even when they weren't there or it was just Lea …'

I waited. I had a hunch there was more coming.

'Private investigator, did you say? You uncover a lot of dirt then?'

'Now and then, yes. But I don't do matrimonials, for example. I'm a social worker by profession and I used to work in the social services.'

She leaned back and scrutinised me carefully. 'Why don't you do matrimonial cases?'

I shrugged. 'Maybe because I want a peaceful life. Most cases of that kind have two sides. Very often three.'

'Don't all cases? Sleaze, property deals and so on?'

'Yes, but then there are more people involved. More people are cheated then, too. Not just one or two.'

'Hm.' She didn't seem convinced. 'Well, I can tell you, Veum, that I have no trouble seeing things from the other side.'

'I'm not sure I understand.'

'No?' She sneered. 'The investigator is not one of the sharpest knives in the drawer after all …'

'It's quite a while since I've been whetted.'

'Well … let me put it like this … When you're in my shoes you have to be honest, both to yourself and to others, if you're going to survive.'

She paused. Again I waited. Then she continued: 'There are no feel-ings left in this old body of mine. I don't have a lot to offer a man. I have ...' She looked away. 'Books. TV. The radio. Newspapers ... Bjørn religiously goes to the library and borrows stuff for me. Comes back with huge piles. Not everything's to my liking, but I read virtually eve-rything anyway. I'm sure I could do you a talk, if you were interested. About literature, I mean. As far as the physical side goes ... Well, I have nothing to offer, as I said.'

I intimated that I understood. I wasn't entirely without talent.

'He might have gone after other women ... I would completely understand that ...'

'Is it your impression that he has?'

'He's never said anything, but in a way it has been understood and ... We know the ways of the world. Learn to read the signs. You become even more sensitive when you're like me, almost immobile.'

'I think you're coping very well,' I said, indicating the teapot and the cups.

'Round the home, yes. Brewing a cup of tea or coffee. You can do that too, can't you?' The acid tone was back.

'So let me ask you straight out. Are you suggesting that your husband ... that he went behind his old friend's back?'

Again she leaned backward and fixed me with a sharp look over the bridge of her nose. 'Yes. For example.' Then she leaned forward and eye-balled me. 'But I know nothing.'

Yet again she changed position. This time she straightened up and looked through the window, where the rain was beating down as relentlessly as before. Her gaze went in the same direction that mine had a little earlier – to a cabin that was not visible. Then she whispered: 'Sometimes I saw his boat until it vanished, into the inlet there. When he came home and I asked where he'd been, he would say, fishing in the fjord. And he always had fish with him. He always had fish.'

'But ...'

'He'd always been attracted by Lea. It wasn't hard to see. I think. With her background. She came from a proper Low Church background in

Gulen – yes, you know yourself. Lars Rørdal is one thing. His parents were even worse. Real puritans. Running away and marrying Mons … I think that made her in Bjørn's eyes an angel, descended from heaven. And I'll admit it. She was as beautiful as any of God's angels. Long, blonde hair barely cut since she was confirmed; clean-cut, attractive face, but, as I said, not easy. It was as though … I don't know … as if she had expended all her energy detaching herself from the religious milieu on the island. I think, no, I know, there was a passion in Lea that made her both strong and … dangerous.'

'Dangerous? Do you mean with reference to the children?'

'Children?'

'Yes, I was told she was admitted to hospital after her last birth because it was feared she might do something to the new-born child.'

'Yes … Post-natal depression. But that wasn't what I meant. No, she was a danger to whoever she met. Dangerous in the sense that she didn't know her own strength, the power she could exert on men.'

'You mean she had power over your husband, too?'

'I know he was smitten, bewitched, definitely attracted to her, like every other man. And when she disappeared, you should have seen the hours he put in. He worked round the clock. There wasn't a cubic metre of sea in Lurefjorden, Radsund, right up to Alverstraumen, that wasn't searched. He came home late at night and left again early the next morning. Often, when a body was found in the sea – even many months afterwards – it was as if, it's sad to say it, some hope was kindled in his eyes. Not that he thought she was still alive. But that he would finally have it confirmed. That she was gone for good. That he could go back to his life. You understand … a bit like a relative.'

I nodded. 'Yes, I understand what you mean.'

'And then when Ranveig turned up …'

'Yes? She doesn't have the same radiance.'

'No? Well, you're the man.'

'She's good-looking and nice enough, but she's not the way you describe Lea. She certainly hasn't got that kind of charisma.'

For a moment or two she seemed content. Then she said:

'Nonetheless, he's there as often as he was before. Where do you think he is now, for example?'

'Oh, yes. Is that where he is?'

'I don't know, to be frank. He goes to sea as much as he can. Sometimes he doesn't come home until late at night. Now I can't even be bothered to look for him any longer ...' She nodded towards the binoculars on the window sill. 'I would guess that he's visiting the widow, though.'

'But the widow isn't alone,' I mumbled.

'No?'

'My friend's there with her, too.'

34

The shop in Feste was a lot busier on a Saturday morning than it had been on the Monday. Despite the poor weather it was clear that cabin-owners had found a way across the sound. I glimpsed the tall shop-keeper at the back of the room. Behind the cash desk sat a dark-haired woman. At a table to the left was a handful of old-timers drinking coffee. An elderly woman was busy cutting off the tops of yesterday's unsold newspapers to send back for a refund; she smiled sweetly as I entered.

I ambled over to the shopkeeper, who obviously recognised me. 'Hello again. Anything I can help you with?'

'I was just wondering … You don't know if anyone could take me across the sound, do you? I want to see the Mælands.'

'Oh, they were just here this morning, shopping. *Fru* Mæland and another woman.' He scanned the room. 'You could ask Hageberg over there. He's got to go that way anyhow, and I saw he came by boat.' He nodded towards a stocky man with grey hair and stubble. He was second in the queue, wearing full oilskins.

I thanked him, walked past the cash desk and stood waiting until Hageberg had paid for the items in his basket, mostly foodstuffs. He was a bit taken aback when I told him my name and repeated my question. But he nodded good-naturedly, shook hands and introduced himself as Hans Hageberg. 'Of course I can take you across the sound. No problem.' He eyed my outfit sceptically. 'But you're not exactly attired for the occasion.'

'No, I'm aware of that.'

'I've got an old rain cape in the boat. You can borrow it. Come on.'

I followed him to the pontoon, and he led me down to a small, plastic boat with a curved windscreen and a wheel at the front, and no other mod cons except for a blue tarpaulin that could be pulled back to cover the driver's seat and the closest seats behind.

Hageberg stepped on board and put his shopping in a large cooler bag on the floor before turning round, stretching out his hand and helping me on board. The light boat rocked beneath us, but balance was restored as soon as we sat down, him in the driver's seat, me beside him.

'Mæland, did you say? Yes, I know exactly where he lives. But … I read in the papers yesterday what happened. Afterwards we heard who the victim was. Do we know any more about what lay behind it?'

'Not as far as I'm aware,' I answered, which was the truth, at least if by 'we' he meant the police.

'It was one hell of a story, if you'll pardon my language.'

'You can say that again.'

During the chat he had loosened the mooring ropes. 'Right, let's go. Hold on tight.' He backed out from the pontoon and headed north through Radsund. With the southerly wind behind us we didn't notice the waves much, apart from the occasional sudden jump.

As we turned into the quay beneath the red house we saw the same two boats as before. As well as the sea-going boat we had taken last time, there was a compact blue-and-white day cruiser with a powerful outboard motor, which I assumed belonged to Bjørn Brekkhus.

Hageberg slowed his speed and made an elegant turn into the side of the sea-going boat. 'Will you grab it?' he said to me. I stood up and grabbed the railing of the boat beside us. Hageberg stopped the engine, and I carefully pulled us towards the other vessel.

I looked up at the cabin. Karin had come out on the steps by the entrance and stood sheltered by the little porch. I waved up at her. She waved back.

'They're in anyway,' Hageberg said.

I turned to him. 'Thank you very much. That was very kind of you.' I took off my rain cape and passed it to him.

'If you need a lift back, just give me a buzz,' he said and gave me a business card, which was soon soaked in the rain. 'You've got my mobile number there. I'll be around for an hour or so, fishing.'

I put his business card in my inside pocket without looking at it. 'I assume I'll be able to get a lift back, but ... once again, thank you for your help.'

He smiled. I clambered over into the big boat and from there up to the quay. Then I walked quickly up the path towards the cabin. Karin was waiting for me, with a slightly odd expression on her face, as though she was both flattered and also slightly irritated that I had turned up here ...

I jogged in under the porch and gave her a hug.

She looked at me, gently stroked the scratches on my cheeks and the plaster on my forehead. 'Thank God that was all it was!'

I nodded reassuringly. 'I was lucky, but ... I've been trying to ring you. You didn't answer.'

She gave a resigned smile. 'Yes. In my haste I left my mobile at home. But you could have rung Ranveig. She has hers ...'

'Yes, of course, but ...'

She ogled me mischievously. 'Was it so terrible being alone at the weekend.'

'Well ... I had to come here anyway. I wanted a little chat with Bjørn Brekkhus.'

'Oh, yes, in fact he's here.'

'Mm, his wife intimated he might be. When did he come?'

She shrugged. 'Half an hour ago. Something like that. He's been trying to get us to go fishing, but ... in this weather ...'

'No, I wouldn't have been tempted, either.'

'We saw the boat from the window and wondered who it was. It was only when you moored that we saw it was you. Who was sitting next to you?'

'A kind soul I met in the shop.'

'We don't have to stand here. Come in! I'm sure we can rustle you up a cup of coffee.'

She turned, opened the door and stepped in. I followed her.

Ranveig Mæland and Bjørn Brekkhus were sitting at the low pine table, each with a cup of coffee in their hands. There was a third cup where Karin had been sitting. A candle had been lit in the mini-Viking ship, and several of the little lamps on the wall shone, a cosy contrast to the rain-swept atmosphere outside. Brekkhus had hung up his rain gear in the hall and was wearing a grey-and-black Icelandic jumper and green military fatigues. In his belt he had a sheath, from which protruded the red shaft of a knife. He was equipped for a fishing trip. Neither of them appeared to be jumping with joy at the sight of me.

'I'll find you a cup,' Karin said, and went to the kitchenette, found a cup and poured some coffee in it from the Thermos flask. 'Anyone else want a top-up?'

They both said yes.

Then I sat down at the scarred table as well. It struck me that we all had our own scars: Karin after Siren, Ranveig after Mons and Bjørn Brekkhus after one thing and another. I didn't even want to think about mine.

'What … ?' Ranveig began without completing the question.

'I've just left your wife,' I said, looking at Brekkhus. 'But actually it was you I wanted to talk to.'

It could have been an absolutely normal Saturday morning chat in a cabin, a pleasant chat between old friends. But this wasn't. This was something else. This, although none of us was aware of it, was the beginning of the end.

35

I should have kept my mouth shut of course. I should have waited until we were all safely back on the mainland. Or I should have rung Hamre first. At any rate, I should definitely have kept my mouth shut.

Brekkhus looked at me with that cold, appraising police stare of his. 'And what was it you wanted to talk to me about?'

I glanced at Ranveig. 'Would you like everyone to hear?'

Ranveig looked at him and then at Karin.

Karin said, without much conviction in her voice: 'We can go for a stroll ...'

'I have nothing to hide. I don't know what you want to talk about, Veum.'

I held his eyes. 'No?'

He didn't budge an inch. 'No.'

I should have kept my mouth shut. I should have insisted that Karin went back to Bergen, phoned Hageberg and got him to pick us up. But I couldn't resist.

'We can start with the information you received from Kristoffer at the end of last week. About the payments Mons Mæland had been making four times a year since 1984 to an address in Sweden.'

'Yes, what about it? Firstly, there was nothing I could do about it, being a pensioner. And secondly, the most likely reason was an outstanding demand, a loan on the black market. You know what it was like in the 80s. There were no limits to how you borrowed money.'

'And you didn't tie these payments to Lea Mæland's disappearance two years previously?'

'Again ... this news came fourteen years too late, Veum. If we'd known this while the case was still active, but now ...'

'Stig Magnusson is the name of the recipient.'

'Yes, I …'

'You had investigated that much then?'

He blushed. 'Yes, that much, but no more.'

I glanced at Karin. She was quiet, listening. Then I turned to Ranveig. 'You were also told this when Else and Kristoffer went to see you.'

She blinked. 'Yes …' Then she opened her eyes wide, as though it were only now she grasped what I had said. 'You can have no idea of the allegations he made!'

'Kristoffer?'

'Yes … That Mons had hired … That we …'

'Ranveig,' Bjørn Brekkhus cautioned.

'Is it any wonder that I'm having a breakdown? That I rang … ?' She glanced at Karin, and her eyes filled with tears.

I could still have chosen to keep my mouth shut. I could have stopped the conversation there and then, swallowed what they said, taken Karin with me and gone back to Bergen and left them to themselves and their thoughts. But I didn't. I ploughed on relentlessly, as though I had some special vocation in life.

'But you admitted, when Karin and I were with you at home that evening, that there was already a relationship between you and Mons … before Lea disappeared.'

She stared at me through tear-stained eyes. 'Did I? *What* did I admit?'

'You haven't forgotten, have you? Perhaps it started with a slip of the tongue, but … you told us everything. That you were in a relationship with Mons and that he was going to tell Lea the weekend she disappeared. An alert police officer in such a situation would …' Here I sent a fleeting glance at Brekkhus. 'He would say you had a concrete motive for wanting her gone.'

'You surely can't mean to say that … But … I've told you before. Mons could never have done such a thing.' Then in a weaker voice she added: 'And nor could I.'

'No, so maybe that's why he contacted someone he had used before … in Sweden.'

'No, no, no! That's not true. It's as I told you before.' Then she seemed to pause to reflect, and added: 'As far as I know anyway.'

'As far as you know? He could have hidden it from you, you mean?'

She chewed her lip. 'Yes, perhaps … yes, maybe.'

I turned back to Brekkhus. 'Do you follow my thoughts? The motive is obvious? But … perhaps you were too close to Mons and Lea to see it clearly from outside. You should have declared yourself partial perhaps, from the very first moment?'

'Partial! Investigating a missing person? What a fatuous thing to suggest!'

'What about your relationship … with Lea?'

This time he blushed scarlet, and his mouth twisted into an ugly snarl: 'Relationship! I didn't have any bloody relationship with Lea!'

'Your wife said …'

He rolled his eyes. 'So it's Lise … Her illness has gone to her head. She no longer has any control over her imagination.'

'She said you were very taken by her. By Lea. Everyone could see it.'

'Taken? Taken? … What's that supposed to mean? I didn't have any relationship with her. She was … the purest person I'd ever met. She was … and these two, Ranveig and Mons … They went behind her back.'

Ranveig sat with her head bowed, following him with her gaze. It was a gaze that came from deep, deep inside her, like the gaze of a whipped child, a cowed slave. She opened her mouth to say something, but no sound emerged between her dry lips.

'So, you reached the same conclusion?'

'Yes … I confronted Mons with it.'

It happens almost every time. Every confrontation comes to a point when one person has said too much and there is no way back. And then it's definitely too late. Then there's no sense in holding back, for either of you.

'You confronted him with it … Last Saturday maybe?'

His jaws moved soundlessly. I saw it in his eyes. He knew now. He had said too much. There was only one way to go. On.

'We agreed to meet … on the island.' He looked out through the window.

'At Hundvin?'

'Yes?' His eyes quizzed me.

'The police found his car there.'

'Oh …'

'You didn't know?'

'No.'

'Well … What did he say?'

'He denied it! At first he said there hadn't been any money transfers, but when I told him what Kristoffer had come to me with, and I discovered the man's name, he gave … more or less the same explanation I gave you.'

'A loan?'

He nodded.

'But you didn't believe him, did you.'

He looked in front of him, a week back in time. 'Instead he went onto the … offensive.'

'Physically speaking?'

'Verbally at first. He … he told me not to go round bloody accusing him, me, when I was … If I thought he didn't know, that he hadn't realised …' He watched Ranveig from the corner of his eye.

She was following closely, visibly swallowing, but she said nothing, only stared at him, as though everything he said was new to her too. And for all I knew it might have been.

I looked at Karin. Her mouth was half-open, but she didn't seem to be as surprised as I had expected.

'Now let's get things straight,' I said. 'You never had a relationship with Lea, did you say?'

'No, I didn't, for Christ's sake. She was … pure.'

'Ranveig, on the other hand … Are we talking about the Madonna and the Whore syndrome here? You had no scruples about having a relationship with her, did you?'

'No, she … ' I couldn't quite interpret the look he sent her, but it was a strange mixture of devotion and contempt.

I leaned forward. 'I appreciate that you have a difficult situation at home, Brekkhus. No one could possibly have any problem understanding ... Even your wife understood. That you sought ... solace ... elsewhere.'

'Solace!' he snorted contemptuously.

'Sex then.'

Ranveig rotated her head in a slow circling motion as though relaxing her neck muscles. Still she said nothing.

'Perhaps we could come back to what happened in Hundvin ...'

Brekkhus glowered at me. 'He went for me. I had to ... defend myself. I grabbed him round the throat. He kicked and punched. I had to hold him tighter. We ended up down by the water's edge. I ... I don't know what came over me. I think, above all else, it must have been the fury at losing ... Lea. He knew more than he'd ever told me. I held him tight with his head half under the water, gripping his throat ... until he went ... still. He probably drowned.'

I gently shook my head. 'No, he was strangled. You killed him with your bare hands.'

'Right! But it was self-defence.'

'You'd better save that argument for your lawyer. What interests me most is what happened afterwards. How did he end up on the cross on Brennøy?'

He pinched his lips.

'I'm happy to give you my interpretation, Brekkhus ...'

I had their full attention now, not just his but that of the two women as well. 'Allow me to assume the following scenario. You know you've sullied your hands, whatever explanation you might give. It's ... early Saturday evening? You have to get rid of the body. You can't put it in his car. It would soon be found. You can tie something heavy round his legs and sink him in the sea, of course. But bodies like this always float to the surface in the end. The rope rots. The bodies rot. And they're not necessarily carried away by the current. Down there, it's not very strong. You have to do something with the body. My guess is you choose another bay a safe distance from where the car was parked, and do exactly that. Pack him in plastic and sink him in the sea, tied to a weight as a temporary solution. Saturday evening, Ranveig rings and reports him missing. Did she know you two had arranged to meet?'

As he didn't answer I addressed her. 'Did you know?'

'No,' she said quietly. 'I suppose I didn't want to know ... Everything I've said is true. We had a disagreement, and Mons went on his way.'

'Perhaps it wasn't the wind farm you disagreed about though?'

She didn't answer.

'It could have been the situation that had arisen after he found out – or realised – that there was something between Bjørn and you?'

Still she said nothing.

'You admit it? Bjørn didn't object when I implied the same a few minutes ago.'

She looked at him with such hate-filled eyes that he had difficulty meeting them.

'You repeated your exploits? Seventeen or eighteen years ago you had a relationship with Mons behind Lea's – his wife's – back. Now you've done the same behind Mons' back. In a way, all one can say is that he got a taste of his own medicine. And perhaps the similarity between Lea's fate and his own is even greater. Perhaps they both met their ends here: him by his friend's hand and her by an unknown Swede's ...'

She nodded. Once again her eyes filled with tears. Now she didn't even try to hold them back. They formed snail trails down her pale cheeks and collected under her chin, where they hung until they became too heavy and fell onto the front of her T-shirt.

I turned my attention back to Brekkhus. 'You were frightened that Ranveig would have a nervous breakdown, that the relationship between you would be discovered and reveal that you had a motive to kill Mons if – or when – he was found. But you could see a different scenario, a different scapegoat. Which would force the police to concentrate their activities away from you. I think you knew most of what there was to know about Mons Mæland and Brennøy. You yourself had been a witness to his purchase of the land. You knew about the confrontations between him and Kristoffer. Another thing: you knew, although no one else did, that he had another son on Brennøy ...'

Ranveig raised her head and glared at me. I nodded to her and said: 'Ole Rørdal.'

'Ole Rørdal!'

'It's a long story, and perhaps it's no longer important. The important thing was that the experienced policeman here knew exactly what information of this kind would tell detectives if they got wind of it. For him it was important to secure the body, make sure it was found quickly and made as spectacular an impression as possible. He knew about the cross of course. I imagine Mons must have told him about it while they were still friends. It had been there quite a while after all. And he went to sea at all hours. According to his wife, he could be away till late if the fish were biting ...'

Brekkhus stared at me with dark eyes. 'You have a lively imagination, Veum, I'll give you that. Surely you don't expect anyone to believe this rubbish?'

'Imagination? Rubbish? You took Mons Mæland's body, wrapped him in a tarpaulin and transported him to Brennøy. You approached from the uninhabited side, carried him ashore, tied the rope around him and strung him up on the cross. Afterwards you went home, late at night – if I am to believe your wife, and I think your former colleagues will, too. A couple of days later you went there and walked all over the crime scene so that you could spread confusion at any potential trial, if anyone found your footprints there. The fact that innocent people might come under suspicion for what you had done didn't enter your head, even though there might have been immense political repercussions. But ... I don't suppose you're a fan of wind power, either. Or was it the opposite? That you relished the thought of discrediting your opponents?'

I should have seen it coming, but I had been too preoccupied by my own tentative reconstruction of events. I should have noticed him tensing his legs beneath him and arching his back as he stared at me with eyes that became darker and darker with every word I uttered. I should have noticed where he had his hand.

With a roar of suppressed anger he jumped up, his sheath knife in his right hand. In his left he held Karin, pulled her up from her chair, dragged her backwards, held her tight and pressed the blade against her throat. 'Don't move, Veum! Or I'll kill her!'

Ranveig half-rose from her chair. 'Bjørn! Don't …'

'Stay where you are! You, too!'

She slumped back down.

Karin stared at me, her eyes black with fear.

Inside me I felt a dull fury grow, a fury so violent it could make me do even more stupid things than I had already done.

I should have kept my mouth shut of course. Now all I could do was watch his every move as he dragged Karin to the door, the knife held to her throat, while he stared back without blinking, as if to ensure I did as he ordered.

Once he was out of the door I leaped to my feet. I looked at Ranveig. 'Call the police! At once. Ask for Hamre if you can't get anywhere. Tell him what's going on.'

She nodded, fumbled for her phone on the window sill and began to press the keys blindly. 'Wh-what's the number?'

'The emergency number. 112 for Christ's sake.'

I dashed out. They were already halfway down to the quay. Neither of them was wearing a coat, and it was raining as hard as before.

Brekkhus looked up at me, holding the knife in the air as they staggered downwards. 'You stay there! Or I'll kill her!'

I stopped. I looked across the sea. Hans Hageberg's boat was in the middle of the sound. I put my hand into my inside pocket, took out the card he had given me and reached for my phone.

I kept my eyes trained on Brekkhus and Karin. As he stooped down for the mooring ropes she grasped her opportunity. She screamed, hit out and kicked. But he didn't let go. He yanked her closer and punched her in the face, so hard that her head flew back and her knees buckled. It seemed to me I could hear the crunch of bone from where I was standing. For a moment she appeared to try to struggle up. Her upper body rose, but her head didn't want to join in. She collapsed on the quay, motionless. Undaunted, he bent over her, picked her up, threw her over one shoulder, grabbed the aft rope with one hand and jumped on board.

My insides were tied in knots. Without looking where I was going I charged down the steep path. I skidded towards the gravel on the wet rocks, fell headlong and staggered to my feet again, my hands stinging from breaking my fall. But I didn't get there in time. The engine erupted into life and seconds before I arrived at the quay the boat was on its way with Bjørn Brekkhus at the wheel. I couldn't see Karin anywhere. She was lying on the floor, incapable of doing anything.

36

My pulse pounding in my throat, I dialled Hageberg's number. As it rang, I watched from afar. He was on his way to the shore.

Hageberg answered. 'What the hell's going on? I could only see it from the distance.'

'Do you think you could cut him off?'

'At that speed? It won't be easy. But I can give it a go.'

I watched as he changed course and headed north-west.

Ranveig was halfway down the path from the cabin. She was holding her phone in her hand. 'Varg! What shall I say to them?'

'Have you got Hamre on the line?'

'No, someone else, but …'

'Tell them to send a police boat. Or best of all a helicopter. Alert the Police Chief in Lindås! Tell them what's happened and they'll know what to do.'

I kept an eye on the two boats, but I could see that Hageberg was too late as well. Brekkhus had pulled back the throttle and set a course even further west.

Then Hageberg came on the phone. 'I couldn't catch him! What now?'

'Could you come here? We've called the police in.'

'Will do.'

He turned the boat and headed straight for us, the sea surging round the bows. But he was still a good distance away.

Ranveig staggered onto the quay. I looked at her. She was pale with shock. 'I had no idea he could … I've never seen him like that. Did he knock her to the ground?'

I nodded grimly. 'Charming suitors you choose for company, I must say.'

She paled further. 'You provoked him. You should never ...' She
didn't complete the sentence, but I knew what she was going to say.
She was right. I should have kept my mouth shut. Of course I should.

Then it was as if the truth hit her like a delayed tidal wave. 'But that
he ... that it was him who ...' Her voice cracked. 'Mons ... because of
me.'

'That probably wasn't why,' I said, in an unnecessarily brusque tone.
'It's more likely it was because of Lea. That was what made him lose his
head.'

'How could Mons have ... How could he have brought in a ... what
do you call them? ... a hired killer?'

I should have answered her, but there wasn't time. Hageberg came
alongside the quay, put the engine into neutral, manoeuvred his way in,
grabbed one of the bollards and dragged the boat alongside.

He looked up at me. Before he could say anything I had jumped
down into the boat. 'After him as fast as you can!'

Ranveig was left on the quay. Hageberg looked at her. 'She's staying
here.' I shouted up to her: 'Tell the police ... no, I'll ring them. Take
care of yourself.'

'Ready for the off?' Hageberg asked.

I grabbed the railing of the boat and held on tight. 'Give it all you've
got!'

He let go of the quayside, shoved off, put the engine into gear and
increased the speed with a strong hand. I looked back at the shore.
Ranveig stood erect on the quay, like an abandoned stowaway, one of
life's random victims.

I trained my eyes on the sea ahead. Brekkhus was level with
Lurekalven now and holding a steady course north-west.

Hageberg glanced at me. 'Have you any idea how far he's likely to
go?'

'To get into open sea he has to go through Kilstraumen, doesn't he?'
'Yes.'

Suddenly I knew. 'I wouldn't be surprised if he was intending to go
to Gulen.'

'To Gulen!'

'Brennøy. Can you make it that far?'

'That far? We can make it to Iceland if the weather's kind and we have enough petrol. What's this about?'

'We're chasing a killer.'

'A killer … Jesus Christ! The time I was a bouncer at Chianti years ago could come in handy now.' He grinned mischievously and upped the speed a notch.

We went on in silence. I dialled the number for the police station and asked for Hamre. He was out, I was told, but I got Helleve on the line instead.

'Yes, we've just had a hysterical *fru* Mæland on the line,' he said. 'Could you give us some more information, Varg?'

I gave him what I had and asked if they had managed to requisition a helicopter to Brennøy.

'For the third time this week? Well … that'll smash the budget. But I will admit … you do have a persuasive argument.'

'What's it going to be?'

'I'll try and get hold of Hamre. We'll do the best we can. At worst we'll take the decision ourselves.'

'Could be a case of life and death!'

'Better get going then, eh?'

We rang off, and I looked at Hageberg. 'Are we keeping up?'

'He's got one hell of a motor on that tub of his. I'm afraid mine doesn't measure up to it.'

'Which means?'

'He's probably doing somewhere between 40 and 50 knots. I'm doing somewhere between 20 and 25, wind and conditions taken into account.'

'So he'll reach Brennøy long before us … ?'

'He'll get to hell faster than us, if that's where he's planning to go.'

'I hope not,' I mumbled, staring through the windscreen.

As we passed the narrow Kilstraumen peninsula the boat in front of us was out of sight, but its wake spread across the sea like a bride's veil. Forty to fifty minutes after setting out we were at the end of Fens Fjord. Far to the west we had Holmengrå lighthouse. North of us was Byrknesøy. Then we caught a fleeting glimpse of Brekkhus' boat again. He was as good as on the other side of the fjord and heading straight for Brennøy, as I feared.

'What's he trying to do?' Hageberg said.

'No idea,' I said, looking upwards, not in prayer but in the hope of seeing a helicopter heading in the same direction as they were. But there was nothing to be seen, nothing to be heard.

'I hope I've got enough petrol,' Hageberg said, checking the console with a concerned frown. 'I hadn't bargained for a long trip like this.'

When we were just off Byrknes we saw Brennøy in front of us, but once again the boat was out of sight. I peered up through Brennøy Sound, where the damaged bridge reminded me of a modern work of art: sprawling form, no real content. The bridal veil continued further west. 'Keep to the far side. Look for the cross.'

'The cross?' Hageberg said, opening his eyes wide. 'Oh, God. Where Mæland was strung up?'

'Yes ...'

I stared ahead of us. At last I heard what I had been expecting: the thrum of a helicopter. I turned round and looked south. It hung in the air, lights flashing, somewhere over the Lindås peninsula, heading in the same direction as we were, only much faster.

We moved through the narrow sounds on the far side of Brennøy. I saw the tree-clad heights behind Naustvik. Hageberg had slowed down. 'I don't know the waters here, Veum.'

The dark cross towered up against the sky. Bjørn Brekkhus' boat was moored by the smooth rocks in the sound. But Brekkhus ... And Karin ...

Now I could see him. He was heading for the cross, with Karin over his shoulders. I cursed him roundly. 'Could we take a risk? Accelerate?'

Hageberg regarded me with concern.

'Any damages that occur ... we'll cover! I can give you a guarantee ...'

He nodded. 'OK.' Then he pushed the lever forward again, and the boat responded instantly.

Brekkhus had hurled Karin to the ground. He was standing behind the cross, and I saw at once what he was planning to do. He threw a rope over the cross and down the front. Then he took the loose end, bent over Karin and pulled.

I yelled as loudly as I could: 'Brekkhus! Noooooo!'

I was sure he heard me. He must have heard our boat behind him. Now the helicopter was close as well. It hovered over the cross, unable to find anywhere to land. The noise was deafening, and Brekkhus made a furious gesture, as if warning us all to keep away. Then he went behind the cross and pulled the rope.

Hageberg shouted: 'Look out! We're going to hit land!'

I didn't care. I clung to the railing and as the boat smacked against the rocky shore I jumped onto land, felt my legs firmly beneath me and charged up over the crag towards the cross.

Brekkhus had managed to tie a knot around the foot of the cross, and Karin was dangling helplessly from the middle of the upright with the thick rope around her neck. The look he sent me was one of triumph, but beyond all rationality. He had blown all the fuses he probably had. Of what had once been the Chief of Police in Lindås there was only a shell left. But he stood between me and the cross, and he didn't appear to be willing to let me pass.

I went straight for him. He was a large man, and I knew nothing but the coarsest methods would do. I drew back my fist, as if preparing to punch him, enough for him to take up a defensive pose. Instead I stopped in apparent mid-swing and kicked him hard in the knee. As he screamed out in pain I stepped back and kicked him again, this time in the crotch. He doubled up, and I punched him in the face with all the pent-up fury I possessed, hitting him somewhere between his ear and his temple and watched him slump forward, as heavily as a felled ox.

Then I grabbed the rope, desperately tried to loosen the knot, but it was too tight. I bent down over Brekkhus, who was lying beneath me on the ground, holding his crotch and whimpering. I took the knife from his sheath, cut the rope, grabbed it and gently lowered Karin to the ground. I lunged forward, held her tight, loosened the rope around her throat and searched for a pulse. It was there, so weak that I could barely feel it. Her face was white, her mouth gasped for air and her eyelids quivered, but so faintly the movement was only just perceptible.

Hageberg ran up from the rocks carrying a boot hook. The helicopter was still hovering above us. I recognised Helleve's face through a window. He motioned for them to land a bit further along the headland.

When Hageberg arrived I nodded in the direction of Brekkhus' body. 'Sit on top of him!' I was blind to everything except Karin, who lay lifeless in my arms.

37

The intensive care ward at Haukeland Hospital was efficient and well-organised. For a week I had more or less lived beside her bed. I had been home to change clothes, I had been to the police station for questioning and I had popped by the office, where I had quickly answered emails and phone messages. The rest of the day I had spent at her bedside, with her hand in mine, staring at her apparently sleeping face and up at the screen above her head. Every now and then doctors or nurses stopped by to check her condition. During the first days she was taken out for X-Rays, MRI scans and other examinations. I seized the opportunity to grab a bite to eat in the huge canteen in the middle of the building. For breakfast and supper I was given food in her room. She ate nothing. She received all her nutrition intravenously, from the drip hanging beside her bed.

One of the doctors had patiently explained to me what the various lines on the screen meant. The top two green lines measured the heart's activity, how many beats there were a minute and whether the rhythm was normal. A flashing red light marked every heartbeat. Whenever there was a flash there was also a little beep. The white wavy line showed how much oxygen there was in her blood and the number to the right, the percentage. The red line showed her blood pressure, and the numbers to the right were what the doctor called systolic and diastolic pressure. The yellow line showed the blood pressure in her lungs and the blue wave the body's carbon dioxide levels in the air she expelled. The orange number at the bottom, to the left, showed the body temperature. It was sky high, but the doctor reassured me that the monitor was American and therefore measured everything in Fahrenheit.

I listened politely to everything he said, but understood that what I had to keep my eye on was the heart activity at the top of the screen.

Karin was in a coma on the seventh day. She hadn't woken up since she was brought in by helicopter, and regardless of whether I squeezed her hand, stroked her cheek or tried to talk to her, there was no response.

I thought I had heard that coma patients could hear what was being said around them. I asked the doctor about that, and he nodded gravely and said there were reports of patients who had woken up from comas, but it was impossible to say whether that would apply to all patients. 'But what if I talk to her?' I asked. 'It wouldn't hurt,' the doctor said, patting me on the shoulder and strolling off to see other patients.

'Is she going to survive?' I had asked several times. They had given hesitant answers. 'To be honest, we don't know,' one of them had said. Then she had added: 'But I think we should be prepared for the worst.'

Who was we? I had thought, suddenly irritated. You and me? But the feeling passed. Instead I was gripped by a sense of dejection. I cursed myself. I should have held my counsel of course, then none of this would have happened. It was my fault she was here, in deep slumber, on the margins of life, in the borderland with the unknown.

I had tried to explain everything to her. I had sat with my head bowed, face to face with her, as though it were life's most intimate secret I was confiding. 'The red mist must have come down,' I had said. 'I mean … That's the way I see it. He considered his best friend's first wife, Lea, as … I think she must have been the love of his life. At home he had a partner who was growing feebler by the day. Across the sound he had an angel sent from heaven, a creature he held as a romantic idyll, so much so that when she disappeared she left a void in his life he never managed to fill. Witnesses – his own wife – have claimed he was possessed as he searched for the missing woman. Later he started a relationship with the same friend's new spouse, a relationship that was revealed at the moment he received confirmation of what he had always feared … that Lea's death was no chance occurrence but hastened by her husband's summoning of a hit man, if I can call him that.

It ended in a violent altercation, Mæland fell into the sea and Brekkhus laid a complex plan to get rid of the body and point the finger of blame in other directions. But then Ranveig contacted you, I appeared on the scene and gradually, as I dug deeper into the case, I came closer and closer to what Brekkhus would have preferred to keep hidden for perpetuity. After his arrest he was questioned at great length. His lawyer claims Brekkhus was not responsible for his actions at the moment in question. Brekkhus himself maintains he was suffering from total blackouts, both when he was dealing with Mæland and … with you. He remembers nothing, he says. He's been in such interviews before, but on the opposite side of the table, so he knows the rules of the game. But Hamre pushed him hard. They have to build on the circumstantial evidence for the first case. But they have two solid witnesses for what happened to you. Three, if we count Ranveig. He won't get away with this, Karin, I can promise you that. And if he did …' I clenched my fist. 'Trond Tangenes is chickenfeed compared with what I'm going to do …' But as I said it I knew I was lying. I would never be able to do what he had done to her, not to anyone, not even to myself …

Later I had chatted, partly to her, partly to myself, about the years we had shared, the places we had been, the people we had met. We had known each other for 27 years and we'd had a relationship for the last eleven. Along with Thomas and Beate, she had been the most important person in my life, for the last eleven years more important than Beate. Now I was going to lose her.

The nurses had been coming more and more often in the last few hours, frequently in tandem. They checked the equipment with great care. One of them gently pulled the duvet up over her calves. Whereupon one exchanged a serious look with the other. They sent me an encouraging nod and quietly walked out again while talking in whispers to each other.

There was a silence in the room. I sat looking at her without saying a word.

Sitting at someone's death bed does something to you, too. I was sixty-five, fit and in good health. But I knew I had many more years behind me than I could expect in the future. For every day I was alive I was irrevocably approaching what would be my own final moment, the day I would exit time, suddenly in an explosion, or quietly and peace-fully in my sleep. I'd had several close shaves. I had been knocked down and beaten up, stabbed in the stomach with a fork, slashed with a knife, shot in the shoulder, but I had got up again every single time, perhaps rather more sluggishly the last few times than earlier in my career, but nevertheless … In the words of the old Norwegian summer revue song: 'The next day he was happily standing on his balcony watering his flowers.' I didn't have a balcony, or indeed many flowers, but I had used up my allocation of cats' lives. The situation was more parlous for the woman lying in bed beside me.

Outside the room the wind was howling round the houses like a demon and the rain was beating against the windows as it had done for the whole of last week. Now the two nurses were in the room for the third time in an hour and I realised the moment had come. One of them smiled sadly at me and said: 'She's approaching the end …'

With tears in my eyes I leaned over Karin and held her hand tight. 'Karin,' I whispered, 'Don't give up! Come back! It wasn't supposed to …'

But she didn't respond. She lay with the same peaceful expression on her face she'd had during her whole stay at the hospital, as though she had long accepted what was going to happen, as though she was well on her way over the bridge to the unknown pastures beyond.

Then a deep sigh swept through her. For the first time in a week she opened her eyes and looked up at the ceiling. She moved her lips and said something, in such a low voice I barely understood. Then her eyes rolled again, and she sank back into herself forever. 'Nineteen zero three forty-four,' Karin said, and died.

38

Two weeks after the funeral I flew to Copenhagen, took a taxi from Kastrup Airport and caught the ferry across Øresund to Malmö. To the south I could see the new bridge over the sound taking shape, but the official opening was still at least eighteen months away. In my inside pocket I had an address in Malmö. It was the last piece of the jigsaw puzzle.

There were not many people at the funeral. Karin had no close family left, but a few distant relations made an appearance: an old aunt, a couple of female cousins and one male cousin. Most of the others were colleagues from the National Registration Office and Inland Revenue, some neighbours I was on nodding terms with and some I couldn't identify, perhaps some of her old school friends. I had expected Ranveig Mæland to turn up, but she didn't. Both Helleve and Hamre were there. They came over and offered their condolences afterwards, but neither of them mentioned the case. All Hamre said was: 'We'll catch you later, Veum.'

The urn was placed in Møllendal ten days later. Only I and an employee from the church warden's office were present. From her grave I could see the roof of the block where she had lived for as long as I had known her. Now her flat was empty. I had no idea who would inherit it. Perhaps it would be her aunt, perhaps one of the other relatives. I had dropped by to collect what was mine, a few books I knew she was particularly fond of, a few CDs we had enjoyed listening to and a photo album of the last years. In the end I stood looking around and it struck me: nothing had any meaning any more. That is the degree to which humans animate – give substance to – their surroundings. When you are gone everything becomes meaningless. I had dropped by before, when she had been away on her travels, to water flowers and make sure everything was OK. Even then there had been a strange empty feeling. I certainly didn't belong there when she wasn't present. But now she wasn't on her travels. She would not be coming back again. The dust could slowly settle. The flowers could wither and die. In fifty years' time hardly anyone would remember her. Other than to our nearest and dearest, we mean nothing. Memento mori, I said to myself. Remember you will have to die too… Then I locked the door for the very last time.

I alighted from the hydrofoil just in front of the immense Kockums Crane, which stood like a modern version of a city gate in the old ship-yard when you arrived across the sound from Copenhagen. I caught a taxi to Malmö Concert House, which I had been informed was a suit-ably discreet place to be dropped, not far from the address I had found on the net. The Concert House was a long, modern building, domi-nated by white marble tiles and matching window panes that reflected the façades of the buildings opposite in Föreningsgatan.

I crossed the street heading for a big, red-brick building which, according to the inscription above the entrance, belonged to the Nils Rosenquist Foundation. An oak chestnut tree flourished on the corner of Amiralsgatan. Across the street was a tall block of flats, five floors high, in a style that placed it at the end of the nineteenth century, with gables, towers and a plaster façade. According to the map, this was my destination.

At street level there were shops. I noticed an antiquarian book shop calling itself Alfa Böcker, and a little café called Clara. The storeys above appeared to be flats. There were several entrances, but by the door in one of them I saw the name I was looking for: Magnusson. The door was locked. I was not surprised.

I quickly rehearsed what I was going to say. Then I pressed the bell beside his name. I stood staring at the intercom as I waited for a reac-tion. No one answered. But he had picked up the phone when I had rung earlier in the day. I had then rung off without speaking. I hoped he wasn't far away, but if he was I had made up my mind that I would wait. There was no reason to hurry any more. Mari and Thomas were still in

Italy. Helleve and Hamre had my statement. My creditors could afford to wait a few more weeks.

I went into the book shop. At a little table by the wall sat a frail man with a luxuriant moustache and large glasses. He didn't know anyone called Magnusson. At any rate he wasn't a regular customer in the book shop. He obviously wasn't at Clara's either, if she was indeed Clara, a blonde, middle-aged woman who served me a cup of coffee and a cake in the café facing the pavement. There were two empty tables outside, but no one chose to sit there in the chilly October weather. 'No,' Clara said. 'There are so many people living in that block. Most of them in virtual seclusion. When they go out it's probably to more sophisticated establishments than mine.'

'It's sophisticated enough for me,' I said.

'Yes, but you're from Norway,' she said with a little smile.

From where I was sitting I had an uninterrupted view of the relevant door. I had to lean forward and look hard to see properly. From her place behind the counter Clara, or whatever she was called, stared at me with her inquisitive, blue eyes, but she said nothing. She knew where I was from.

At some point a taxi stopped outside. A man and a woman got out, both in their fifties, him small and delicate, her with crimson hair beneath a green beret. Fifteen minutes later a tall, broad-shouldered man in a leather jacket appeared, stopped by the door, studied his surroundings warily and pulled out a bunch of keys from a side pocket. Then a young woman came, with fair hair fluttering in the wind, pushing a buggy in which there was a small child. The tall man held the door open for her, and they exchanged a few words as she passed by. Then he followed her in. After fifteen more minutes another taxi pulled into the kerb. It waited there until an elderly, white-haired woman wearing an elegant but old-fashioned cape came out of the house. The taxi-driver got out and opened a door for her, and she took a seat in the rear. Five minutes later a well-dressed gentleman turned up, around sixty years old, a prosperous accountant type, rang one of the doorbells and waited to be buzzed in.

After that, the comings and goings tailed off. I took the last bite of the cake, drained my cup, thanked Clara and strolled over to the door again.

This time someone answered. 'Yes,' came a dark voice from the speaker.

'Stig Magnussson?'

'Who's that?'

'My name's Veum. I'm Norwegian. I have an important message for you.'

'A message for me? From Norway?' He sounded unconvinced.

'… From Mons Mæland.'

Silence. It went on for so long I felt I had to say something. 'Hello?'

'What was your name again?'

'Veum. Varg Veum. It's important we talk.'

Again silence. Even longer.

Then the door buzzed. From the speaker I heard: 'Come on up. I'm on the second floor.'

I pushed the door wide open. There was an elegant staircase, in the same style as the façade. On the stone floor there was a worn chequered pattern and light streamed in from the backyard windows. As I approached the second floor he was waiting for me in the doorway. To my surprise he turned out to be the first arrival, the frail man in his fifties. At close range I could see he had a thin moustache, so thin it was barely visible in the dim light of the stairwell. He was wearing a yellow suede waistcoat over a pink shirt, brown slacks and elegant shoes. He kept his unsmiling eyes on me.

I stopped in front of him. 'Stig Magnusson?'

'That's me.' His voice was conspicuously dark and deep. It didn't match the person at all.

I held out my hand. 'Varg Veum. Have you got a moment?'

He shrugged. After all, he had let me in, so he had agreed to talk to me. 'You'd better come in. My wife has put the kettle on. We were going to have a cup of tea and a couple of biscuits.'

In the hall he took a clothes-hanger from a wardrobe, draped my coat over it and hung it in the wardrobe. With a brief gesture he ushered me into the flat.

We entered a light, spacious lounge. The tall windows faced the street, the three middle ones were part of an oriel. The room was fitted out with heavy, old-fashioned furniture, the pictures on the walls had gold frames and in the main showed Swedish rural scenes. A bookcase revealed rows of brown, leather-bound spines while a grandfather clock of impressive vintage had a pendulum that swung from side to side as time audibly ticked by, minute by minute. The aged, floor-length curtains were of green velvet, and the walls were papered with a discreet lily pattern, also ravaged by time. There was a TV set in one corner and a newspaper lying on a small table. *Sydsvenska Dagbladet*, I saw.

Stig Magnusson motioned me to a chair by a small coffee table. I sat down. He left the room without making any comment. I heard sounds coming from the kitchen, and after a minute or two he returned carrying a tray of tea cups and dishes, which he placed on the table. He set three places, still without saying anything. Then he left the room again.

When he returned this time he had his wife with him. She was wearing a light-grey dress with a little belt tied loosely around her waist. He brought in a dish of biscuits and a bowl of jam; she carried a pot of steaming tea. She set down the teapot and said: 'It has to brew for a while.'

I nodded, got up, shook her hand and introduced myself.

She met my eyes. 'Eva Magnusson.'

Her dark-red hair framed a face with attractive, regular features, on which life had not failed to leave its traces. Her eyes were blue, and the gaze she sent me revealed a mixture of curiosity and concern, as though she was wondering who I was and what my business with them could be.

We sat down. As no one took the initiative I leaned back in my chair, looked at Stig Magnusson and said: 'So you did know Mons Mæland?'

He sighed. 'There once was a business connection, as it's called, yes.'

'A business connection?'

'Yes. In Norway.'

'What business?'

He coughed. 'Now I think we should start at the very beginning, *herr* ... Veum. Who are you?'

'I'm a private investigator.'

He had no comment to make, just gestured for me to continue.

'About a month ago I was given an assignment to track down Mons Mæland, who had disappeared. I found him after a few days, but ... He was dead.'

He raised his eyebrows. His wife gasped.

I looked at her. 'You knew Mæland, did you?'

She shook her head. 'No, I was just reacting to the terrible news.'

'The reality was indeed terrible. He had been crucified.'

She opened her eyes wide and grasped her throat. 'What did you say?'

'Crucified?' repeated Stig Magnusson. 'As in the Bible?'

'In a way, yes.'

'Hm.' He looked concerned, but made no further remark.

His wife watched me with a mixture of disbelief and abhorrence. Then she seemed to pull herself together and become the hostess again. She took the teapot. 'I'm sure it's ready now,' she said, and poured. I noticed that her hand was trembling slightly.

Magnusson pushed the dish of biscuits and the bowl of jam in my direction, but I said: 'No, thank you. I'll wait a bit.'

He shrugged, helped himself to a biscuit, spread some jam and took a bite. It crunched between his teeth. From the street came the sound of traffic. Otherwise there was silence again.

She raised the cup to her mouth, carefully tasted the tea and smiled apologetically to me. 'It's hot ...' Stig Magnusson didn't smile. He looked at me with a serious, expectant expression.

I said as gently as I could: 'So that's the end of the regular payments from Norway.'

He shifted his gaze and made a slight movement with his head, the way you do when you have a stiff neck and you want to loosen the muscles. When he looked at me again there was an expression on his face that was hard to define. All he had to say was the typically lilting Swedish 'Ja-ha'.

'It was his son, Kristoffer, who discovered these payments – just over a month ago. He'd had no idea they existed.'

'Right,' Magnusson articulated this time.

'Naturally he wondered what these payments might be. And there are a few of us wondering the same now.'

I could clearly see him weighing up the pros and the cons. In the end, he decided: 'They were payments for services rendered. That's all anyone needs to know.'

'Services rendered?'

He nodded.

'Related to his first wife's disappearance?'

He arched his eyebrows and sent me a quizzical look. 'What are you talking about?'

His wife put down her cup abruptly, as if she had scalded herself. I looked at her. 'It's not that hot now, is it … Lea?'

Stig Magnusson rose from his chair. I stayed seated. I wasn't afraid of him. Nothing could frighten me any longer. 'What the hell are you …?'

'Stig …' Her voice was resigned and clear. 'I knew this had to happen. One day someone would come.' Within two sentences she had switched from Swedish to Norwegian. She straightened her back and looked into my eyes. 'But I'd never thought it would be a total stranger.'

'Fate has its own envoys,' I said. 'More demanding guests may come later. Your children, for example.'

Her mouth twitched, and she exclaimed with vehemence: 'My children! They were … misadventures! But I've never expected anyone to understand what I was thinking, why I did what I did.'

Stig Magnusson was still standing. 'Eva …'

She smiled wryly. 'We can take off our masks now for a while, Stig. This man here is waiting for an explanation. He's been sent by fate, he says. A diplomat from hell.'

I softly shook my head. 'It's not that hot where I come from, I'm afraid.'

She riposted with a jeer: 'No, but it might be when the curtain comes down for you, too. What good will it do you, coming here and raking up the past?'

'There were a lot of people left with unanswered questions after you disappeared.'

'I've got a question too! For you. How did you find …? When did you realise that I was here?'

'A quarter of an hour ago when I met your husband here for the first time. I saw you both arrive earlier and …' I glanced at Stig Magnusson. '*Herr* Magnusson doesn't exactly look like a contract killer, and dyeing hair is pretty standard for a woman who wishes to remain under cover.'

'What!' Magnusson shouted. 'A contract killer?'

'I don't know if you have a neighbour – a tall, well-built man with a leather jacket?' Neither of them reacted. 'That was more what I had imagined.'

'So you thought that Mons had … that Stig was supposed to be …' Slowly she began to see the light. Then she stared mutely into the distance.

Magnusson coughed. 'I hope you're not planning to exploit the situation you find yourself in …'

'I haven't planned to do anything except get to the real truth in this matter.' I leaned across the table and looked at Lea Mæland again. 'What was the deal you and Mons struck when you disappeared in 1982?'

She let out a heavy sigh, raised her eyes and looked at me with a resigned air. 'I know you've … I'm going to tell you everything. But first you have to tell me something. Mons: Was he murdered?'

I nodded. 'Yes, I suppose he was.'

'By whom?'

'By an old friend of yours. Bjørn Brekkhus.'

'Bjørn!' She seemed genuinely surprised. 'But why on earth …?'

'Whether you believe it or not, Bjørn Brekkhus was besotted with you, Lea. I think you can probably say that … besotted. You must have noticed.'

She nodded, and two red patches high up on her small cheeks

appeared. 'Yes, now you say that … Of course I knew he was a bit in love with me. But …' She tossed her head coquettishly.

'There were so many of them?'

'Something like that. At any rate I can assure you there was never anything between us. I've never been unfaithful in my life … to anyone. Unlike some people.'

'Your husband, for example?' I quickly added: 'Yes, now I'm talking about Mons.'

She eyed me sharply. Then she gave a slight nod of the head. 'He … When he came to me that time and told me about Ranveig and said he wanted a divorce, that came like a bolt from the blue. I thought we had the perfect marriage. When I think about what I had sacrificed for him: the relationship with my parents, the break with my childhood environment. And that was the thanks I got. Being … stabbed in the back. It was true to say the initial passion had cooled, but that's true for most people, isn't it? We had children. We had a house, and a cabin and a secure life. What did he see in her? What did she give him that I couldn't? Everything seemed to collapse around me. The difficult pregnancies, the complicated births, the time afterwards. Everything I had fought for, only to return to the daily grind. And then this was how he rewarded me!' She tossed her head. 'What was I to do? I had no formal training. I hadn't been home since I was a girl. I would have drowned myself if I hadn't …'

'If you hadn't … ?'

'If I hadn't been so happy to be alive. But I faced up to the realities of life, and when he suggested … Together we made a plan.' She paused.

'An insurance scam.'

'Well, I had to live! Fair enough. Call it that if you like. Mons had his connections …' She glanced at Stig Magnusson. 'He made a call, fixed me up with a job in Sweden. Nothing brilliant, but something I could do: Secretary. Typing, simple bookkeeping. And so I went. Took the train the whole way. First to Oslo, later down through Sweden to Malmö. He took care of everything at home. After two years I was declared dead, the insurance company paid up and then the money started to come …'

'But not in your name?'

'No, in the meantime Stig and I ...'

Magnusson coughed yet again. 'Yes, to cut a long story short. Eva – which I will always call her – came here, found a job in my company, and after a few months we established ... an understanding. An understanding which developed, at least for me it did, into the great passion of my life, and we married on New Year's Eve 1983. We've been happy ever since, haven't we.' He looked at his spouse, and she nodded solemnly, though also pensively, as if not quite sure yet that this was the correct conclusion to draw.

'But surely you needed papers to do this, didn't you?'

His face was impassive. 'We fixed it. Everything can be arranged if there is the will. And the money ...'

I glanced from one face to the other. It sounded so reasonable when they told the story like this. In the end my eyes remained on her. 'But there's something I don't understand ... You had two small children: a boy of twelve and a girl of only four. How could you just leave them?'

With a blank expression, she replied: 'What did you say your name was again?'

'Varg Veum.'

'Varg. There's something you men will never understand, and that is what we women go through to give birth to the children you implant in us.'

'Implant? You're fairly active in the process, aren't you?'

Her eyes flashed. 'It's not you, though, who have to go through the pregnancy, is it? You don't find yourself on your back in the delivery room, with your legs wide apart, screaming with pain, being cut open sometimes – your perineum or straight to the womb. You don't have to put the wet, still bloody, creature to your breast or feel bare gums on your nipples or feel life being sucked out of you, maybe for ever, by a tiny creature – a little ape ...'

I didn't answer. Right now, she was beyond all dialogue. She was back in her own painful past.

'I still feel nauseous when I think about it. It makes my stomach churn. I'll tell you this: I never felt any love for those two children. After I had finally recovered from the first birth I promised myself never again. But seven years later I was pregnant again once more. Even though I took very great care, but he ...' She was whispering now. 'He raped me. Once he came home very drunk and we had unprotected sex, as they call it. When I found out I was ... I wished I could have it aborted. But you have to understand ... If you only knew the people I had grown up among. My parents, they were fundamentalists. They thought the world came into being four and a half thousand years ago. They thought Adam and Eve really lived, that the serpent was a dominant force in life and that Moses came down from Mount Sinai with two stone tablets given directly to him by God. They held true to the letter of their religion. The very idea of interrupting a pregnancy ... Abortion was a dirty word for them, as bad as invoking Evil itself. I couldn't have an abortion. It was impossible! So when Else was born, an equally complicated, equally painful birth as the first, I had a breakdown, a complete breakdown. I was admitted to hospital, and when I came out ... well, I functioned, more or less. But – as I said – I never felt any love for them. Leaving them was the easiest thing I've ever done.'

'But did you never think about them, about how it must have felt?'

'Yes, but that's precisely why it was easier for them to believe I was dead. Being drowned was like being cleansed. Everyone would think it was an accident. After a seemly period of mourning Ranveig and Mons could ...'

'Not long enough according to your children – today.'

She sent me a vacant look. 'Really?'

'And Mons, did he stay in contact with you in any way? Did he pass on any messages? Pictures of your grandchildren? Kristoffer has two children. I think they're ...'

'Never. All he passed onto me was money, via his old business connection. Why would he send me anything else? I was as good as dead and buried. Well, at least dead.'

'Lise Brekkhus – Bjørn's wife, that is – she called you an angel. That was what her husband considered you.'

'I did the best I could. I wished no one any harm, not even Mons and Ranveig ...'

'Mons, on the other hand, had skeletons in the cupboard. A young child on Brennøy, for example.'

She blinked in surprise. Then she shook her head. 'What are you talking about now? Surely not Ole?'

'Yes, your nephew.'

'You've heard the rumours, too, have you?'

'The rumours?'

'Yes, I don't know who spread them, but, if you ask me, there were some real busybodies on the island, both male and female. And one thing I can tell you for sure is that Mons was not Ole's father.'

'Really?'

'Kristine came to me for a private conversation when she heard that Mons and I ... that we were going to get married. She wanted me to know, as the only person in the world apart from her, that Mons certainly was not Ole's father. She and Mons had never been together – in that way – she said.'

'So it was your brother after all then? Lars?'

The surprise in her eyes was so deep I couldn't see the bottom. 'Lars? No, it wasn't Lars either. It was Bjørn.'

'Bjørn Brekkhus!'

'That's what Kristine said anyway. It all happened at a dance they'd been to at Soleibotn. Brekkhus had been on duty at the arrangement. He was a few years older than Mons and her, good-looking and elegant, and she had felt what my father would have called the devil in her blood. In the course of the evening he had got her behind some rocks, kissed and hugged her and ... seduced her.'

'Right.' I recognised Bjørn Brekkhus' own story of a few weeks ago, only with a slightly different narrative.

'Six weeks later she discovered something was wrong, but in the meantime she had got engaged to Lars. And what was more it was Lars she loved after all. Bjørn was just a passing ship in the night.'

'So he never found out?'

'Never. Kristine and I are the only two who know. Now there are two more,' she said, looking from her Swedish husband to me.

I sat watching her. She was still an attractive woman, but her crimson hair set her apart. For Stig Magnusson she was the great love of his life. For others she had been an angel. Yes. An angel of death. That was what she was. Because of the decision she and Mons had taken on that fateful August evening in 1982 two people were dead sixteen years later. Mons because of Bjørn Brekkhus' raging temper; Karin a casual bystander, a victim, in the wrong place at the wrong time. Lea herself had found a new life in one of Sweden's biggest towns, a safe distance from her origins, an island in Gulen, as far west in Norway as you can go.

We sat there for a while yet, but we didn't have much more to say. I gave Lea a slightly more detailed description of what had happened between Mons and Bjørn, and I told her about the wind-farm controversy on Brennøy.

'Wind turbines? Is that such a problem? We've got lots of them, on this side of Øresund and the Danish side,' she said.

When I left they accompanied me to the door, both of them. We said our polite goodbyes. However, she told me not to mention her existence to Kristoffer, Else or indeed anyone. I didn't think I would tell a living soul about whom I had met in Malmö and what I had discovered. Not everything has to see the light of day. We still have to carry the pain within us, each in our own way.

I hailed a taxi to the harbour and went back home the way I had come: ferry to Copenhagen and taxi to Kastrup Airport. In the tax-free shop I bought a whole bottle of aquavit. Before the plane took off I had already knocked back half of it.